LOOKS CAN BE DECEIVING

LOOKS CAN BE DECEIVING

JIM CONNERS

To order additional copies of this book, contact:
Xlibris Corporation
1-888-795-4274
www.Xlibris.com
Orders@Xlibris.com
114945

PROLOGUE

H E CLOSED THE DOOR behind him without locking it. He never locked it anyhow because no one, except the owner of the dry cleaning business below his humble studio apartment, knew anyone even lived up here. He turned and stopped in the early twilight to once again admire the picturesque vista of the Clinton River from his small balcony.

How many evenings had he stood in this same spot admiring the landscape? Actually, more of a seascape with the river's swirling currents, reminiscent of the painting which now haunted his memory—*Rowing Home*, a classic watercolor by Winslow Homer, one of his major artistic influences, aside from Andrew Wyeth.

The painting was what led him on his new adventure—reuniting him with his far-too-long-exiled daughter. The painting's name alone and the emotions the piece evoked within him led him onward to his mission's fruition, however sinister it might be.

On this chilly early December late afternoon, he had neither the time nor the enthusiasm to capture on canvas the moment in his own style. This panoramic palette of gray before him would be perfect. But the circumstances prevented it. His strategy was as good as it would ever be, he thought. It was now time to finish what he had begun.

He descended to the next landing with his target in mind, keeping focused on his plan. Maybe it could have been better conceived but as they say, from his somewhat limited knowledge of clandestine activities, even the best laid plans can go astray.

Once he was in the alley, he made his way to his destiny. Stealth was the word that kept permeating his thoughts. His objective was to get more photos of his prey committing his crime. Being that what it may, when it came to push or shove, whatever the phrase, he could corroborate his facts that this crime was more than just a single event, but an ongoing criminal exploitation. He approached the *Rear Window* as he likened the purported crime scene to be and readied his camera for one final round of photographic confirmation.

The next thing he felt was the cold barrel of a gun at the back of his head. Nothing was said, but in the next millisecond, he experienced a searing pain simultaneously along with the resounding retort of a gunshot.

Coldness and darkness swept over him faster than he would have ever imagined. And as things grew darker, his final thoughts were not of mortal things, but of Winslow Homer's *Rowing Home*. Not so bad on one hand, but unfinished with fading hopes of closure to his scheme on the other. His last conscience thought was, *thank God for my plan B.*

The lifeless body was hefted into the trunk of a BMW and driven a few blocks downriver to an access road. The body was then unceremoniously dragged out of the trunk and tossed onto the bank of the swift-moving currents of the Clinton River. The driver snorted another lid of nose candy and then doused the limp body of his nocturnal intruder with a half-gallon of cheap vodka, dumping the final third down the dead man's throat. That accomplished, he rolled the man's lifeless body into the river. He didn't even wait to see where the current took his victim.

Satisfied his problem was rectified; he climbed back into his luxury sedan, took out his vial of security, inhaled some pseudo confidence, and went back to his lair. *His* final thought for the evening as a self-satisfied smile twisted its way onto his lips was, *no mess, no foul. Done, over, and I'm back to business as usual.*

CHAPTER 1

*T*HE DARK ROOM WAS *filled with flashing red lights, the wail of sirens, the sound of sleet pummeling the windows, and the deadly knowledge that all this somehow was being replayed for the all too many times to count. The terrible feeling—that when played out in its entirety, my soul was going to be filled with so much pain and anguish that I would never recover—pounded in my head and yanked me violently from a sweat-soaked Jack Daniels—induced coma into the stark reality of consciousness.*

The room was deathly quiet again, except for my heart pounding in my chest. As I looked around in the emptiness of the semi-dark room, I realized again it was not real, but *the nightmare*. All too many times, the nightmare had overpowered the Jack to snake its way from my subconscious to the big screen of my mind, and tonight was no exception. Here I was again. Shit, so many times the same nightmare—just like a broken record.

I reached for my Luckys, and my hand was trembling so much I knocked the pack from the nightstand; this whole thing was like déjà vu all over again. I switched on the light and looked at my hands, rolling them over and back, wondering if the trembling was from the nightmare or the evening's belly full of booze.

I took the final gulp of my leftover nightcap and leaned over to pick up my cigarettes when I realized the disquieting distant sound of sirens in the cold, sleet-laden night was probably what had triggered the nightmare, again.

As I lit the Lucky, I needed another swig from the bottle I kept on my nightstand and turned off the light and propped myself against the headboard. Now I was starting to feel some calm or the effects of the Jack. I didn't know which and didn't care. The only light in the dark was the glow of my Lucky as I listened to the wail of the sirens getting closer.

After one more swig, I finished and stuffed out my butt and settled back against the damp pillow, beginning to realize that my recurrent response to the actual nightmare was in reality becoming part of the nightmare itself, shades of *The Twilight Zone*. Eerie, so I let the effects of Mr. Daniels take me once more by the quieted hand into the twilight of sleep.

CHAPTER 2

JUST LIKE IN *GROUNDHOG Day*, I begrudgingly dragged my
sluggard's ass into the newsroom on yet another dreary overcast
day in good old Western New York. It was like my body had no mind of
its own and was being guided by an Ouija-like magic, straight for the
coffeepot, not acknowledging anyone along the way. Not that anyone
paid much attention to me anyway, especially on a Monday morning. I
was not passing go nor collecting $200.

Brooding over my black brew, matching my mood, starting this
prosaic job wasn't one of my favorite things to do anyway. But it did
keep me sober, during the day at least.

I work, a phrase some would dispute as to being an accurate
description of my existence here, for the local Clinton Journal as the
social page herald, obituary columnist, and, on a rare occasion, news
writer. It's not the most prestigious occupation in this once-flourishing
but now-wilting city, but it paid for the booze and butts and got me
out of the house. Besides, it was at present the only game in the entire
town—thanks to Kristen Harden, the managing editor. Nobody wants an
undependable drunk in their employ, unless of course, she saw something
in me no one else did. Sometimes the way she acts around me, I think
maybe she and I—but that's more than likely just my besotted male
ego raising its *little* head. Who knows what her motives were; I am just
thankful to have a steady job.

As I approached my desk, Melissa—the ever-cheerful and
doughnut-bearing mail girl, a title by the way that always struck me as a
bit oxymoronic—came bounding over to me with a glazed in one hand
and a hard roll in the other, singing the praises of a good morning. She
always did this, and it always pissed me off because mornings sucked,
thanks to the previous night's overindulgence of Jack and his Lucky
friends.

"No, missy, I don't care for a fucking doughnut—not today, didn't Saturday, nor will I want one fucking tomorrow either, thank you." Every day, same dialog and same response.

"Oh, Dirk," she cooed, "you're such a kidder. You know you love my doughnuts as much as you love me."

After saying this, she struck the all-too familiar sideways pose, with her hands on her hips just like a 50's calendar pinup girl in an unsymmetrical kind of way.

I said nothing further; I just closed my puffy eyes, turned, and slouched away.

Strewn about on my corner desk in the pile of wedding announcements, obituary notices, and country club functions was a handwritten piece of mail addressed to Dirk Crandell, C/O the *Clinton Journal*. This, needless to say, caught the attention of my red-rimmed eyes. I opened it using my typical fingernail letter opener. I read the trifolded single sheet of eloquent stationary, which wafted of lilacs.

It read as follows:

Mr. Crandell,

You knew my father by the name of Rembrandt, the local eccentric folk-art artist.

I just read in your paper (which I always receive a few weeks after the fact) that it was reported that an indigent, who went by the name of Rembrandt, was found dead floating in the Clinton River. It also stated he must have been drunk when he fell in and drowned. This can't be true, not like it was reported anyway. I'm sure of it because as far as I know, he *never* touched a drop of alcohol. I suspect foul play led to his death.

I am his daughter. Yes, I know this is a surprise. I'll bet you didn't know he had a daughter nor does anyone else in Clinton. Dad, whose real name is William Edgar Mintz, sent me to live with my aunt and uncle in Los Angeles at a very early age, so I could have a better life. He also needed to care for my mother, Samantha Hobbs, who had some pretty serious mental issues.

He considered you the closest thing to a friend he had. He wrote that if anything untimely happened to him, for me to contact you and you would uncover the truth about his death.

In his last letter, he said he had caught one of the people responsible for my mother's problems with his hand virtually in the cookie jar at his prominent business. He was going to confront him with evidence proving his present crimes and also his part in a twenty-year-old rape and beating resulting in the ultimate death of my mother. By doing so, according to his plan, he was going to make right at least some of the injustice our family has suffered. He wrote, not only would the tables of that injustice be turned, but financially, he hoped it would be possible for us to be able be together again and expectantly he was also going to pay back my aunt and uncle footing the bill for my college education.

That same last correspondence explained that people there may think you are and are not a lot of things, but if he was no longer around, I should trust you. So now, you're the only one I know I can trust to find out what really happened to him. After all the community spirit and service he contributed to Clinton, he deserves a better remembrance than just the disgraceful news article he received as his only eulogy.

More than anything, I want the truth about what happened to both of my parents uncovered, and the people responsible brought to final justice. I now live with my Aunt Kathleen and Uncle Hugh in California. Unfortunately, I can't pay you anything for your help. I'm beseeching you to honor him, my mother and me, and please help me! If you decide you will to do this, call me and I'll tell you all I know and try to help you any way I can.

It was signed simply "Baby." With that, she left me her phone number.

I reread the letter and then checked the postmark on the envelope to see where it originated. Los Angeles, California, and it was postmarked December 15—over a month ago. Maybe if Melissa spent more time delivering mail than doughnuts and her frigging dimpled cheer, things would happen in a more timely fashion around here. But then again, maybe it's been here for a while, and I just didn't see it through my drunken haze.

I vividly remember Rembrandt; hell, everyone in the whole city over the age of drool and diapers knew of him. He was a fixture in this city ever since I was a young kid many years ago. He never aged, smoked like a chimney, and was *the* most talented artist this city—hell, even this whole part of the country—to those who ever had the fortune to witness in his artistic schemes.

He painted for his dinner, literally. It was said he never took money in payment. I remember when I was a kid, Clinton had a hometown city USA downtown like all the downtowns across the country, almost a metropolitan Mayberry. Rembrandt used to paint or whitewash the storefront windows with his own flourish of creativity for merchandise most of that being food, clothes, or his painting supplies. His mercantile canvases appeared in places like the local meat market "Sirloin Steak $1.29 a Pound," and he'd embellish it with a hammer or something unique to add flair to his work. His resulting gratuity would be of a pound of baloney or something somewhat similar. The local bakery, the same thing; ads for their fresh bakery items would earn him perhaps a loaf of bread.

His art even went to the city's clothing shops. This would keep him in his unvarying wardrobe which was, regardless of the season, a flannel shirt with the sleeves rolled to the elbows and dungarees.

Several shoe stores were in his barter stable along with Clinton Paint and Crafts, which supplied him with his artistic supplies. Just about every business in Clinton used his talents at one time or another always different, always unique.

Word of mouth exalting Rembrandt's true creative talent and use of tempera paint as his only medium actually brought people here just to see his folk artwork, especially during any kind of holiday. Some art aficionados in fact truly believed that Rembrandt had been a student of Andrew Wyeth, arguably one of the best-known American realist painters of the twentieth century. I read somewhere that Wyeth was a man of extraordinary perception, and that perception was found in his thousands of images—many of them iconic.

Even the local major manufacturing plants utilized his art. Not that long ago when most products were manufactured in this country and the owners of the companies lived in and were morally committed to those communities, the two largest plants in Clinton were a family-owned steel plant called Wittenberg Steel, and another large manufacturing company called American Clockworks. They used to get together twice a year—during the summer for a family picnic and again at Christmas for a kids' Christmas party. Several local businesses would contribute to make these events a total community event.

Rembrandt's services would be enlisted to spice up the information boards throughout the plants to instill interest for attendance. In gratitude, his medical checkups, dental work, and usually free bus passes for the year were taken care of.

As time went by, the down-home atmosphere changed. This was mostly due to the downhill slide in economic conditions resulting from the big companies selling out to even bigger companies. The local plants were forced into massive layoffs or *right-sized*, as the parent companies referred to the loss of jobs, for better profits. Of course, this meant a lot of local businesses went under and as another almost unnoticed consequence, so did Rembrandt's source of livelihood.

For years, he could still be seen at the parks, little league fields and high school sporting events, just sitting there, smoking and yelling words of encouragement to the youth of the city.

He started selling his paintings at the local arts and craft shows or anywhere he could to merely exist in his ambit, the shrinking downtown district. Yet he still found time, and I always thought of it as community pride, to paint murals about the community's history or other intuitive concepts generally, beautifying in content, on unsightly places throughout the city making them more—well—sightly.

But as I look back on it now, it seems like almost overnight, Rembrandt, once a unique fixture of the city's culture, went to near obscurity. When my own life went in the toilet, I am sorry to admit, I lost track of him too. Rumor had it he was homeless living under the Main Street Bridge spanning the Clinton River which flowed through the center of city.

For several years, as the rumors went, he was seen nearly every day walking down the delivery alley behind the Center Street business district, or what was left of it, with a paper bag containing for those who noticed what was thought to be booze, Prior to her untimely death, my wife Marie, her sister Karen, and I were included in this observation.

Funny, but after reading Baby's letter, it's sad but true; I can't remember ever having heard anyone ever refer to him as anything other than Rembrandt.

Well, this was sure something out of the ordinary to start the week off with. I definitely needed another cup of coffee though. One thing I had to give Melissa credit for, she made some of the best coffee you'd ever want to burn your lips on.

On my way over to the gossip or bullshit area—depending on your outlook on life—I headed over to the bullshit pit. I spotted Kristen Harden jiggling her way toward me with a huge smile on her face. I say jiggling her way because she had this way that some well-endowed woman have of walking in that special way with that little bounce they get going which makes their breasts bounce to their own silent rhythm; amazing to watch, almost hypnotic.

Anyway, the huge smile usually meant that she had some piece of shit story she wanted me to write because no one else wanted it.

I was greeted with one of those near-miss kisses on both cheeks and a subtle breast brush on my arm. She was easy on the eyes; not exactly drop-dead gorgeous, but her business acumen and self-confidence as a woman in a man's profession at age thirty-two made her extremely attractive. Oh, and she also has a great body.

Most of the testosterone raging studs in this building did everything you could imagine to try to get her naked and bed her. For whatever her reason, she didn't date much, mostly business lunches or charity events. And for some unknown reason, she seems to have become infatuated with me. Maybe it's just the challenge because I'm unavailable.

I'm usually attracted to women with Harden's qualities, but ever since my wife Marie died on that nightmarish, sleet-laden night five years ago, I haven't had much interest in getting into another relationship. God, has it really been that long? It's hard to remember when you've been drunk for almost the entire time.

Besides that, Harden at times, with her total lack of subtlety, can be a royal pain in the ass, to put it mildly. I suppose one of these days I ought to call her on her flirtatious ways. Listen to me. Now I sound like all the other assholes I was just ragging about.

Once all of her stopped moving, she handed me an assignment memo and said, "Dirk, honey, I would be so ever in your gratitude if you would cover this country club gala for me."

With that, she spun around and left in the same special bouncy manner with which she arrived.

Getting a Saturday night Club gig wasn't all that bad; free food, and more importantly, free booze. Added to those perks, the Clinton Hills Country Club was within crawling distance of my house.

I usually kind of looked forward to these galas because most of these third generation, good ol' boys who were now the pillars of Clinton and club members, and I went back a long way. Back to the summer nights of drinking beer down by the river or playing pranks like lighting up bags of dog shit on our most pricky teachers' porches, ringing the door bell, and then running like hell. Then we watched from a discreet distance as they'd stomp out the fires, spreading the shit all over the place. Which, when I think about it, the boys were still doing—spreading shit all over the place, only now while doing it they wear Armani suits.

Yep, almost all these *clubbers*, as they referred to themselves, along with their wives and I go back to the good ol' days when they were only pre-pricks and pre-Junior Civic League brats. All of us guys having dreams of getting laid before our senior year in high school. As for the league of virgins, a marginal term at best, they were already putting their name tags on the young *clubber* turks, who would eventually go to college and get their wild oats out of their systems. Then they would come back to Clinton to take over Daddy's and Grandpappy's business or practice.

Those of us referred to callously by the clubbers as the *clubbies* when on their home turf who had remained home city bound, and whose hard-earned, blue-collar business dollars then provided those elite with lifestyles consistent with the generations of the pricks from whose loins spewed them. It just works that way. Every Clinton across the country has the *clubbers* and the *clubbies*.

If I seem perhaps a little bitter, not at all, I'm a lot bitter, because us *clubbies* had to work long and hard, sweat, eat bag lunches, and in a lot of cases, go off to Vietnam. Meanwhile, the *clubbers* played at working, ate at *The Club*, and if they went into service at all, and not many did, it was in some wimpy ass circumstance. The chances of them seeing any combat action was about the same as *the club*, and it's thirty six-hole, five-star rated golf course being donated to the local homeless shelter and raising crops and livestock to feed the poor.

In fairness, I guess not all those members of the Clinton Hills Country Club were of this lineage. Some actually made it to the club membership on their own resources literally, after approval by the board of course. The board consisted of the charter members and/or their heirs.

For those outsiders, if you were a CEO, doctor or surgeon of some notoriety or fame, transferring to Clinton and its surrounding areas, you could apply for membership. Once the board went over your application and financial records, actually one in the same, you would be permitted to join—after a substantial initiation fee, of course.

So going to cover and photograph the one of several annual galas would give me a chance to rub elbows with some of my old chums. Harden would probably attend and wear one of her seductive gowns, and I could watch the boys maneuver away from their wives and try to discreetly seduce one of Clinton's most unattainable women. Just for the bragging rights of *doing* Kristen Harden to the other good ol' boys in the locker room after a Wednesday afternoon's round of golf. So far, none had, or they all wouldn't still be trying.

I swear to God, all I have to do is think her name, and like magic, Harden appears.

As she came up to me again, she seemed even a little more bouncy than usual.

"Dirk, honey, I'm afraid I've got some good news and some bad."

"Shit, what now?" I asked myself.

As if she read my mind, she said, "First, the bad news. When I called Bridget Pennyhurst in public relations at the club to confirm we would send a reporter to cover their event, she said great, as long as it wasn't Dirk Crandell. She went on and on about how the last time you were there you got so drunk and obnoxious, not to mention the disgusting way you watered their artificial palm trees at their annual Hawaiian Luau, they have barred you from the premises."

"If it's the one I remember," I said, "And it's hard to keep track because they have more annual events that you can shake a stick at. Anyway, I tried to explain to them that I got confused from drinking too much of their spiked Hawaiian punch, I told them that "journal" and "urinal" sounded an awful lot alike, but as usual, they didn't find much humor. So I told them I really didn't care for the punch anyway and was inconspicuously trying to return it without offending the caterer. They just didn't care for my night deposit system. When called upon to handle the embarrassing situation, for them, the security guard got a little gruff when he pulled me off to the side by my free arm by the way, and said he'd seen and heard enough from my wise ass and told me to, get this Kristen, piss off. To which, I reminded him as I zipped back up, that's pretty much what I was doing when you snuck up behind me and scared the shit outta me. You don't have to ask me twice to leave somewhere I'm not appreciated."

She just stood there and did that slow, rhythmic scolding-type head shake that only a woman can do. Especially those who don't understand about the macho significance of men pissing on things or places they don't like and muttered, "Dirk, Dirk, Dirk."

Then, without even batting one of her long eyelashes, she continued like this last indiscretion on my part made no difference to her whatsoever and added, "Now for the good news," she beamed, "I lied a little and told them you were sober now, and after much pleading and promising, they have agreed to let you cover the event, on one condition."

"What's that?" I asked, not really wanting to hear the answer. "That I don't touch a drop the whole evening? No can do."

"No," she said. "It's actually hardly any kind of condition at all. I just had to agree that I would escort you and keep you under wraps all night," adding with her renowned subtlety, "Mine, of course, I mean, I hope."

I think she gave me the bad news and then gave me worse news; although I have to give her a ten for persistence.

"So let me see if I've got this straight," I said. "I get to go to an assignment; no one here, including me, really wants to go to. I'm a drunk, and everyone in this godforsaken little burg knows it, and you promise I won't touch a drop of booze while I'm there. I have to actually talk to these pompous assholes for an entire Saturday evening sober when the local bars are open until 3:00 a.m. where sometimes reasonable and every now and then intelligent conversation can be had at least after a few brewskis anyway. Then to sweeten the pot even more, I get to have you and yours on my arm for the entire night."

"That's about it," she smiled. "Did I mention it's a $1,000 a plate, and the *Journal* it picking up the tab."

"What if I have to take a leak?" I mocked. "Do you, uh, go with me there too?"

"Well," she crooned, "I'll be there, anytime you want me, Dirky."

God, I hate it when she calls me that.

"So," I inquired without really caring, "what's this one for? The midwinter's night toboggan wonderland?"

"No, silly, it's their annual ACRE."

"Oh shit," I really didn't want to, but I knew I had to ask. "The what?"

"The ACRE."

"And just what the fuck, pardon my French, is an ACRE? I know going to one of these things is a real pain in the ass, I know it, you know it, and most of the dorks who attend them know it, but did someone out there finally realize it and name one for what it really is?"

"No," she said, moving closer into my space so that now her more than ample breasts were once more actually gently caressing my chest. "It's an acronym for Annual Club Renovation Extravaganza. See, ACRE, isn't that clever?"

"I like my characterization better," I added.

Now don't misunderstand me, as she slinked in closer, her looks, her perfume were very inviting, and I like to cop a feel as much as anyone, but this is exactly what inspires me to keep my distance from Harden. She really can crowd your space. And crowding my space makes my chest tight and turns me off.

"Well, Dirk," she said as she toyed with the top button of her already low-cut blouse. "What's it gonna be? Another drunken night alone in some dive that smells like urine, or a night of free, fit-for-a—king, $1,000-a-plate food. All the Jack you can sneak and, of course, the grand prize. If you behave, might be mine," she said invitingly.

"Grammatically speaking, don't you mean me?" I asked so foolishly.

"No," she said, "mine."

At that, she nonchalantly undid the next two buttons of her blouse without taking her green eyes off mine, and with no concern for anything or anybody, flashed me a glimpse of probably the most perfect, unencumbered glorious cleavage I've seen in the flesh, so to speak.

Just as fast, she coyly redid the buttons, and most of the remarkable grand canyon was gone, but not in my mind though; never, ever, no sir, not even Jack will erase it's memory.

"Well, sneaking Jack from those dorks out there, including all the city's finest, comprising of the chief of police, Mr. Mayor, and especially my old buddies in the Clinton Hills Country Club click, is pretty inviting, so I suppose, if I really have to."

"Great," she said, "It's a week from, well actually, it's this Saturday. By the way, Dirk, it's black tie, for a while anyway," and she winked, turned and wiggled away.

I'm not sure what just happened, but this I do know—I can breathe again, and she wiggles just as good going away as she jiggles coming at you. Could be worse things, I guess. But honestly, I'm really not all that interested. Besides, by the time things could get that far, I plan to be wasted, and maybe looking for an artificial tree or two of some kind, they always had some kind of decorative trees around at these galas, and I would take it as my civic duty to see if they might need watering.

I perused the remaining notices, invitations and announcements of births, deaths, and retirements heaped upon my desk. Well not exactly heaped there, after all this is January in a very small city with not much going on this time of year. Finishing that I decided since it was 10:30 a.m., it was time for my daily eye opener.

I headed to the Crypt, which many of us used as our very own and personal lunch room, happy hour spa, and late night workers' bistro. It is located in the bowels of our illustrious fifteen-story, former bank-turned-media center/ boutique mall. Bloody Mary was the eye opener of choice. Even though officially the Crypt didn't open until noon, I had an in. My sister-in-law Karen was the day time waitress and bar keep. Unbeknownst to the executive staff or at least avoided by them, Karen and I usually tipped one or two before the official noontime opening and the onslaught of our coworkers.

CHAPTER 3

KAREN AND I HAVE remained close over the years. We share a lot of grief and guilt surrounding the death of my wife, Marie. As I said, Karen was my late wife's much younger sister. Actually, she was twenty years younger. Their relationship was special as Karen grew up. Marie became both a surrogate mother and an icon for big sisters. They became and remained very close. When I met Marie, I also met Karen, and we became instant friends.

Karen was a surprise addition to the O'Donahue family. A special addition, thought Marie and her mother Catherine, at first at least. However, Catherine's husband Patrick, or Patty to his buddies at the mill, was devastated. Being a black Catholic and true to the form of their generation, there was no option for the unwanted pregnancy but to have the baby. Patty blamed his wife for not taking *proper care* of things to prevent this catastrophe, whatever the hell that meant, and made Catherine's life from then on, a living hell. The only resolution of the mistake would be if she were to bear him a son, which she should have done for him in the first place. When Karen was born, Patty berated Catherine for wrecking his life by adding another mouth to feed and just packed his bags and left, never to be heard from again.

It was several years after her husband's departure that Catherine, trying to make ends meet working two low-paying jobs, started having health and personality issues. As things degenerated, and with Marie not living at home any longer having married me, her mother Catherine began blaming Karen for her troubles and also for Patty having left her.

"If it hadn't been for you, my Patty would still be here and I wouldn't have to work these two stinking jobs," she would harangue Karen with more and more frequency as her physical and mental conditions deteriorated. "I'd have my fingernails all manicured and pretty, like they used to be."

This went on for years.

The day after high school graduation, Karen moved out to be on her own.

With Karen not being around to bitch to and at, she turned to Marie to vent her frustrations. One thing led to another, and Catherine became more and more difficult for me to be around. I kept alienating Marie because I called her mom, *the hag*. Catherine's issues started coming between us, as these kind of things do in families. Karen, a frequent visitor to our home, was not immune to the friction. Consequently, this was now beginning to seriously affect Marie's and my relationship, and even threatened our plans for the future.

I started to drink and continued to drink. I began staying out more and longer to avoid the constant confrontations. Sometimes the benders were with Karen, who drank for her own but related reasons. Seems like every conversation my wife and I had wound up in an argument, and somehow, *the hag* was in the beginning, middle, or end of it.

At any rate, at about 4:00 p.m. on our twentieth anniversary, Marie called me and reminded me that she had a doctor's appointment for her six-month checkup at her breast surgeon in Buffalo, about seventy five miles away. I said I'd rather not go with her. After a moment of controlled silence on her end, she recovered quickly and said she had made dinner reservations at Susan's Steak House for 10:00 p.m.

I said, "Great, meet you there."

She said, "love you." I didn't say I love you back. I don't know why, because it was usually automatic; we always did, and to this day, it eats my heart out why I didn't. Have another Jack, Dirk Boy.

That night, Marie died.

Karen had called me right after Marie hung up wanting to come over because she needed a shoulder to cry on. She'd just broken up for good with her boyfriend and live-in companion of two years. It was only about five o'clock so I said, "Sure, if you don't mind talking around me getting ready to meet your sister for dinner, our anniversary dinner by the way, which I'd totally forgotten. But not to worry, I don't have to meet her until ten."

I figured she would only stay a few minutes, and I'd have a drink with her to make sure she was going to be okay and still have time to shower, change and since by now all the florists would have closed for the day, I'd stop by Wal-Mart to buy some flowers, and still make it to Susan's on time. Maybe I could still salvage some of our anniversary celebration.

Karen arrived at our house sobbing with two water glasses in hand and a very large bottle of Jack Daniels. So we sat there at the kitchen table with absolutely no will power over the booze and its anesthetizing effect. Our conversation ranged from lost love and infidelity, to what an asshole Jason, her former boyfriend, was. We talked a lot and drank more.

I don't remember much if anything of what happened that fateful night, like how Karen and I wound up in my bed together, although most of it comes in hazy flashes late at night, after the *Jack* o' lantern goes out. All I know for sure is Marie is dead, killed in a car crash hurrying to the anniversary dinner I was too drunk to remember or to be at. And I never got to say good-bye or that I loved her that morning or even again later when she called about the dinner reservations. There's no doubt in my sorry ass of a heart that I died that night too. And of course, the nightmares are always there to remind me.

Since then, I've lost everything—my job in public relations at the Clockworks, and all my friends. I've also pissed away the respect of both my and Marie's families, except Karen, who for some reason, probably mutual guilt and lost love, still remain close. Add to my losses my self-respect and every other fucking meaningful thing in my life and it pretty much sums up my present existence. The only redeeming thing to happen out of this whole nightmare is that *the hag*, who totally blamed me for Marie's death, has since gone to live with her niece in Topeka or some other goddamned place, and I haven't heard from her since.

Karen doesn't blame me because I didn't go with Marie. If I had driven with her to the doctor's, she wouldn't have been rushing back to make it to dinner on time. It wouldn't have mattered if we were late. Karen doesn't condemn me probably because of shared guilt; it was just as much her fault as well. She hasn't really been able to totally cope with her sister's death—not only about her unplanned indiscretion of sleeping with me, but it's really more about never giving her big sister a big hug, along with the anniversary card she had bought and planned on giving her. More than anything, it's about never getting the chance to say I love you or getting the chance to say good-bye.

So as I plopped myself down on the first overturned barstool of the day, she already had two really good-looking Bloody Marys up. We looked each other in the eye briefly, smiled almost in perceptively and downed them babies like a contest. As was the daily ritual, we wiped our lips on our sleeves winked to each other and said, "Now let them assholes in the door."

She went about her business of getting ready for the lunch crowd, and I ordered another Bloody Mary. Karen used to say, "Are you sure." Now it was automatic. She would have just the one at lunch because she was working. After hours though, it was a different story.

I couldn't seem to get the letter from Baby out of my mind. I'd have to visit the archives to catch up on the obituary if there was one, and any news related items surrounding Rembrandt's death.

As I downed my second daily rousing antidepressant and was about to leave, Karen came over and raised her eyebrows in a questioning fashion shrugging her shoulders as if asking "one more?"

"No," I said. "Believe it or not I'm intrigued by a letter I received from a woman named Baby from Los Angeles regarding one of Clinton's old folk denizens, I guess you could call him, named Rembrandt.

She said, kind of startled, "Did she give you her last name?"

I said, "No, but I assume it's Mintz, because she wrote that she was his daughter and that was his real name, although no one in Clinton knew it. She felt pretty adamant about the events concerning his cause of death."

Karen said, "It may be just a coincidence, but when I was, oh I guess about fifteen, I used to go fishing down by the Clinton Bridge. Marie used to go there to do her sketching. It used to relax her. "Better than a doobie," she used to kid.

"She'd sketch away, and I'd fish, and we'd talk. We'd talk about everything, and I mean *everything*.

"Every once in a while I used to see this little urchin of a girl, maybe four or five, hard to tell exactly because she was always, I don't know, not grubby but more like unkempt and very allusive. When she would see me catch a fish, she would ask surprising politely if she could have it. I never knew where exactly she came from or where she lived, but I always suspected, I don't know why, it was under the bridge. Funny that should come back to me."

Then she must have remembered why it did I thought, because she was gazing over my shoulder and a dark shadow, the kind nightmares are made of passed over her like maybe her own demons about her sister's death had been awakened, and she said, "Sorry, I hope you find what you're looking for. I gotta go. See ya tomorrow, Dirk."

I don't know why, but I turned around as I got up to leave to see if something else had triggered Karen's sudden mood swing, and the only thing I saw was Carl Southerland looking over our way smiling; he must have just come in. I said to myself, smile at this, you ass, as I adjusted my zipper and walked out the door.

So I had some time to spare in between reading wedding announcements; actually, there aren't that many in January. And as far as the obituaries go, they were pretty much a standard form—born, lived, died, yada, yada, yada. Besides, my curiosity about the letter I'd received was getting to me, so I thought I'd go down to the archives to see what I could find on Rembrandt and his demise.

As I got into the elevator, who should I bump into but Ms. Kristen Harden. God, but she never gives up.

"Hey, Dirk going down," she grinned.

"With you? Sure I'd love to." I said as invitingly as I could to her, "But only as far as archives and dead files."

I don't know why I encourage that woman. I mean it's really flattering to be the obvious object of her what, affections or hots, or whatever, but as said, I'm not ready for any woman in my life right now. She's such a tease, but maybe somewhere in my subconscious, I want to tip her upside down every way from Sunday and screw her brains out. But then I suspect the games would be over. So I guess I keep it alive if for nothing more than my own personal amusement.

Harden got off one floor above me, and as she exited, she looked back over her shoulder to me, gave her little girl's pout, then smiled and made sure I got a good look at her ass wiggling away before the elevator doors closed.

Once I reached the archive file room, I immediately saw Kelly the *mortuary queen*, as she had come to be known. Just like a computer search engine, one or two words, and she could pull up just about anything you wanted to know newsworthy about Clinton, past or present.

I asked Kelly if she remember anything about a death about six months ago concerning a guy known as Rembrandt. I didn't know much more about him other than I think his given name was Mintz, William Edgar. It was probably listed as the death of a transient found floating in the river.

She thought for a second and then her perky young face lit up and said sure.

"I think I remember the story."

What an amazing memory this young woman had. Sometimes I can't remember what happened yesterday let alone six months ago, but then again she probably doesn't drink a fifth or so of booze every day.

She had her own access to the microfilm on articles regarding Journal archives. Our reporters could tap Kelly for reference material without going through the effort of looking the stuff up on their own.

After a few clicks on her computer, she went onto read:

"According to the police report, 'A local transient known only as Rembrandt was found floating in the Clinton River. My brother, Clinton County Coroner, Oliver Harrison's report states the deceased was discovered near the shore under the Main Street Bridge. Due to the bloated condition of the body it appears the decedent had been in the water for several days. Several empty liquor bottles were found nearby. From the evidence at the scene, it was concluded that he had gotten liquored up again and this time, fell in the river and drowned,' declared local chief of police, Stanley Harrison, in his official statement.'"

She said the article was date December 2.

She hit the print button and handed me a copy of the article.

So I took the printout of the news article and gave Kelly a kiss on the cheek, which always made her blush, and I said, "thanks, doll," and headed back up to my desk.

Something's weird here. In Baby's letter, she said that her dad never touched a drop of booze to her knowledge, and yet that conflicted with the police report in two aspects. First, he was often seen walking down to the river's edge carrying a bag of booze, and second, neither Oliver, the coroner nor Stanley, the police chief, said anything about an autopsy. I thought that was standard operating procedure, especially under the circumstances surrounding a case like this, not even a hint of foul play.

Could be that Oliver and Stanley, boy, I bet they took a lot of crap in school about those comedic names, just assumed Rembrandt was drunk when he went in the river. Or maybe Baby didn't know her father as well as she thought she did.

CHAPTER 4

WELL, MONDAY LED TO Tuesday, and Tuesday led to, well . . . sooner than I'd hoped, Saturday, the night of the big Clinton Hills Country Club gala. Nothing of any real significance happened in Clinton during the week, with the exception of Mrs. Green's toy poodle getting loose and doing her business, as they politely say, on Mr. Wiley's welcome mat.

Apparently, as the investigation revealed, when there is no snow on the ground, Fifi or Fufu whatever the little pissant dog's name is, selects Mr. Wiley's prized garden to do her business. But I guess when there's no garden to be found because of the snow, a welcome mat, Mr. Wiley's of course, has new meaning and would just have to do. I expect one of these days the headline of the *Clinton Journal* will read "Mr. Wiley, How does your garden grow? With silver bells and cockle shells and one goddamn dead poodle."

So that news item along with its photos of the seemingly smiling little poodle and the angry Mr. Wiley pointing to his violated welcome mat, along with my night sweats and frequent trips to the corner liquor store, made it a pretty much status quo snowy gray January week for me in Clinton.

That's about how exciting this place is since the "right sizing" of the big businesses siphoned off the jobs and as a result a lot of the population. Even the druggies are going elsewhere to do business. No money, no drugs, no whores to take the money to do the drugs to pay the pimps and keep the ugly circle going. One way to clean up the city's act although a pretty costly one.

So Saturday night arrived, and I was dressed to the nines in my rented tux, and I made sure I had a fresh pack of Luckys in my breast pocket and my trusty notepad along with my good old number two pencil, well sharpened in my side pocket. I sometimes wondered why the number two pencil, being the most popular pencil, was still number two; you'd think it would make it to the number one ranking. Who knows how these things work?

As I waited for Harden to pick me up, I decided to relax a little with a small glass of Jack to calm my nerves. Right at 8:00 p.m. sharp, as agreed, Kristen Harden pulled in my drive and then, battling the snow flurries, made a gallant effort to make it to my front door reasonably intact without falling on her sweet little ass because I'm too damn lazy to shovel out the fifteen-foot drive.

I opened the door for her before she had a chance to ring the doorbell and she entered with a rush, shaking off the snowflakes from her hair and then removing her coat, seemingly all in the same fluid motion.

One look and all I could muster was, "Oh sweet Jesus!" If she had visions of this being the night of the great seduction, she had a great head start. As she removed her coat and exposed a very clingy red sequined lace gown that well, just that! With her auburn slightly windblown hair and jade green eyes, she was both the picture of elegance and pure sex. Son of a bitch! I had promised myself never, never, never would I ever sleep with, or fondle this woman. But even though she could be a total ass once in a while, she was standing before me as this vision of pure sensuality and lust provoking womanliness. Against all my instincts and drunken promises to myself, seeing her all cleaned up and dressed like Aphrodite, she was radiating both the slight tangible scent of expensive perfume and the intangible aura of "Come hither and ravage me." This roused me to say to myself, Dirk Boy, this might be the night you might just have a change of heart about your self-proclaimed, booze-induced, guilt-ridden celibacy.

I asked her if she wanted something to drink, and she said she was in the mood for champagne, and I said, "I don't think Jack Daniels makes bubbly."

She said, "Well then, maybe one small shot one to take the chill off."

I poured one short one for her, and of course, one slightly longer one for me. She slugged it down, and never batted an eye which kind of surprised me.

I said, "Shall we?" Then I grabbed my coat, helped her back on with hers, pausing ever so slightly to observe the swell of her generous breasts which were barely, no pun intended, covered. I gently helped her free her shoulder length auburn hair from her coat. She turned around and gave me a slightly lingering kiss on the lips, not too friendly, not too romantic just, well, just very interesting.

Nothing more said, I picked up my camera and off we went.

Once we reached the club, we kind of hung out arm in arm as promised for a while. During which time, I played sommelier and fetched her two glasses of champagne as we kind of checked out the gathering. Harden, always being the managing editor, kept whispering in my ear about the notes I should be taking so that when Monday's society page was published, it would be filled with the legend of yet another bullshit fairy tale gala at the club so that egos and the narcissism of Clinton's elite would be sated for another few months anyway.

Before long, Harden got caught up in the persona of the event and its attendees. The club manager, Bob McNeil, was making the rounds, shaking hands, kissing the cheeks of the women and generally just plain sucking up so he could keep his six-figure job for another season. Oh, and over at the bar was my favorite group of local providence purveyors. With my present, slightly cynical life's frame of mind, I reasoned that they were probably plotting their next dastardly deed to somehow extort more money from this dying little burg from the remaining trusting souls whose dependence was still entrusted blindly unto them and/or their professional wisdom.

Dr. Bernard Johnson Jr., OB-GYN, or Junior as known to friends, was there. His entire family: mother, father and three sisters were in medicine in one form or another. I always found it quite ironic that Junior being in that particular field of medicine; never had any little Johnson's on his own, of course other than his obvious male part of the same name.

Then there was David Weatherford IV, a fourth-generation jeweler whose jewelry store was *the* store to buy anything from soup to nuts as long as it was at least 14 karat gold or contained a *carat* cake of diamonds. I don't think there was one woman in Clinton in the last one hundred years whose beau, who could afford a diamond engagement or wedding ring, did not buy it from one of the Weatherford clan.

Leaning on the bar, one of my personal favorite positions by the way, was TR Foster. No one ever called him anything, but TR for as long as I could remember. Even when we were in high school back thirty-plus years ago, the teachers even called him TR. He is the local entrepreneur.

And that title puts it mildly. He either owns everything in Clinton or will eventually. He started at his father's local Ford dealership, and his business just kept growing and growing. No one could believe where the financial evolution came from, especially since there were several big GM plants in the county, but the big wheels keep turning, big wheels, big money, and big business.

There has been much over the bar speculation that the financial backing came from and with the help of a recently missing local job site catering entrepreneur who was rumored to be making several trips to South America monthly for the purchase of uncut cocaine. This would explain a lot. The local catering mogul, Dick Highland, was not here tonight, nor would he be, only in the wallets of most of the *clubbers* who financed his sabbaticals to the land of milk and money. This had been working out fine for everyone involved, until that is said caterer, alias pharmaceutical entrepreneur, got shot down by a rival drug-running cartel. His Lear jet, with its suspicious cargo—suspicious my ass, everyone knows it was a half a ton of coke—was blasted out of the sky somewhere over the Gulf of Mexico. This left a very rich ex-wife Darlene and two kids set for life, and gee, wouldn't you know it, a lifetime membership to the Clinton Hills Country Club. She was supposed to be here tonight, but I hadn't seen her yet. Darlene and I had a history from back before I met Marie. Nice girl, but money does strange things to people. We've always remained friendly even through all the shit on both sides.

Also in the elite group were two attorneys, Allen Truehardt, which for an attorney's name was a bit satirical, and Carl Southerland. Truehardt was an excellent criminal lawyer who often won cases by just his reputation alone. I've heard that once, a new assistant DA, during his first prosecution, actually wet his pants from just a very stern stare from Mr. Truehardt. His legal résumé, win-loss record, and billing rates say he's good—very, very good.

Southerland, on the other hand, was an ass. He was born into an asshole family of money; he grew up an ass; and was sent to a private asshole academy where they gave lessons on how to be a bigger asshole and smile while you are being one so no one thinks you really are one. He graduated with flying colors from the private school, but failed miserably the part about learning how to cover up the fact that you are an ass. Truehardt, being a lifelong friend, took him in as an associate in his prestigious firm—Truehardt, Graham, Dexler, and Assoc.

Because of their relationship, the boys let him hang around because he was too stupid to know they were all using him for their gofer and taking care of business for them, which was of no significance but had to be done nonetheless.

So the boys mingled with their arm holding Stepford-like token wives, who by the way, had their own little social club which included—tennis pros, pool boys, caddies, waiters, bartenders and lifeguards. I've been told by Darlene they actually kept scorecards on who did who.

The call to dinner had Kristen and I at a table with a Pakistani doctor and his wife, who were new to Clinton, and to our surprise spoke, very little intelligible English. The dinner consisted of barbequed squab with apple juice and fennel marinade. It was accompanied with lightly roasted garlic asparagus spears, poached apricots, and roasted baby red potatoes. A cup of fresh tropical fruits finished off the menu. It was an excellent meal, not worth $1,000, but I wasn't paying which made it taste all the better.

A short while after dinner and the pitch for contributions to the ACRE fund, and having performed their obligatory niceties, the boys headed down to the cigar room for their weekly high-stakes poker game.

So I just kind of wandered around the Victorian clubhouse. I was taking in its historic splendor with the paintings of all its benefactors and their sons and their sons. Even some women benefactors, whose husband's estates had left them the legacy of being a trustee, were mounted, for lack of a better term, here. This meant they could still wield some clout financial or otherwise around the inner circle of Clinton.

Taking in the majestic atmosphere along with a few—well maybe more than a few—JDs on the rocks, I kept catching peeks of Harden as she made the social rounds, ever laughing at the witless witticisms spewing from the men whose eyes never quite made it above Harden's ample breasts and whose wives tolerated the usual flirtations all the while plotting how to get even by visiting David Weatherford IV's jewelry store.

Every once and a while, I caught a glimpse of Harden catching a glimpse of me, and she would smile. *Looking better all the time.* Who knows, maybe there could be a fling in the air after all.

Well after about an hour, a half a roll of film and several pages of superfluous notes just to make it look like I was earning my keep, nature was calling and I needed a place to take a leak. Harden was nowhere to be found at present, so I guess I couldn't take her up on her lyrical offer and not seeing any artificial trees on the main concourse, I was on my own. I remembered their johns were down in the locker room so I maneuvered my way down the stairs to the mahogany-paneled Gents room as it was labeled. I have to admit these johns were decorated a lot nicer than the ones I was used to. These even had doors on the stalls and actually had real linen towels to dry your hands.

On my way through the maze of towel rooms, locker rooms, shoe-cleaning rooms, and massage tables, I finally found the john. On my way out, I made a wrong turn and accidentally started to walk by the cigar room which was where the boys were playing poker. I saw a cute little waitress come out of the room with a tray of empty glasses. These guys must have their own special staff.

I was about to go back up the stairs when I overheard Carl Southerland say, "Did you see the body on that waitress? When she comes back, we ought to bend her over the table and show her what serving board members really means."

Weatherford was in an ugly mood, and I understand as of late, that temperament was pretty usual. Maybe he'd lost a bundle again to Foster, or he just needed some more blow. In the club circle, he was known to be a pretty heavy user, and his demeanor would certainly justify that assumption.

He ripped into Southerland by saying, "Fuck you, Carl. Every time you're away from your little prissy missus, you want to fuck anything with tits and a skirt. Your wife, Sandra, told my wife you couldn't get it up if your life depended on it. So why don't you just drink up, play cards or play with yourself, and shut the fuck up!"

With that, David Weatherford got up and went over to the small bar on the other side of the cigar room and took out his vial of coke and proceeded to do his hourly "get normal" routine.

Southerland, meanwhile, was really taken back by Weatherford's remarks, especially that his wife would have told anyone about his problem in the sack. Getting more angry and embarrassed by the second, he snapped back to the mellowing fourth-generation jeweler.

"Well, I certainly didn't have any trouble getting it up for that waitress last year down here at the Christmas party did I?"

Now he was beginning to get really red-faced and angry and continued his retort.

"What about when we all banged the shit out of that cute little waitress slut Sammy or Samantha, or whatever her name was a few years ago. Three times I slipped it to her. As I remember, you were the one with the limp dick that night."

At this point, Allen Truehardt who had been just sitting back enjoying his Cuban, rocked his chair forward and glared at Southerland.

"You know Carl, not only are you an asshole, but you are a loudmouthed, stupid asshole. First of all, that was a long, long time ago, and it's been all but forgotten except obviously by you, you shit. Is your sex life that pathetic that to cite your sexual conquests, you have to go back, twenty years ago, give or take to a night when we were all young, stoned, drunk, and very stupid? We're all guilty, even for those of us who were only a witness to what has to be classified as *the* giant cluster fuck of our lives when you, Junior, and David had your way with a young girl tied to a massage table.

"We all agreed after that unfortunate incident with that young woman we would never speak of it again. Should any word leak out that we were responsible for that, it would put us all in the precarious position of an investigation I'm sure none of us would want to endure. Do you understand me, you little dickless weasel?"

Weatherford, still skiing on light powder, tried to placate the situation and hopefully bring to an end to it once and for all.

"Carl and I took care of that little bitch when it was over. Just like I said we would. We took what was left of her after Southerland finally had finished with her. I still don't know why he had to beat her like that, she was tied down for Christ's sake and half conscious, maybe that's what it takes for you to get it up. Anyway, no sweat, we took her out the servant's entrance, put her in my trunk and took her down by the bridge and tossed her in the river. They never did find the body, and since she apparently had no family, no one ever reported her missing. So it's cool, you guys. I totally agree with Allen. Let's not forget who and we what we are." After which, he went back to powder his nose again before joining the weekly Clinton fraternal high-stakes poker game.

TR Foster finally spoke up. And when TR spoke everyone listened, just like the old EF Hutton commercials. "All right boys enough! We are a fraternity, *the* Clinton fraternity and that means we are brothers. What's done is done, and it was a long time ago. We all have a lot at stake here—our reputations, our homes, our businesses, and our families. For Christ's sake, we've got Clinton County by the balls. Why jeopardize any of it over a petty little piece of ass so many years ago? Forget it, I had until you, Carl, you dickhead, brought it up just now. Forget it and I *mean* forget it!

"Carl, get some Viagra or something to help you get your sex life up and going again, preferably with your wife. She's running out of young men here at the club to humor her. And Carl, if I ever hear you utter one more word about that young waitress, I will personally cut your useless dick off and shove it up your ass. And David, I strongly suggest you seriously curtail your drug use. It's turning you into a surly bastard and if you continue, it will eventually ruin your life. Here in Clinton, for us in the fraternity, life is great. Let's not screw it up shall we, boys? None of us need to have this regrettable incident ever brought up again. Now my friends, shut up, have a cognac and a cigar on me, and relax; let's play cards."

I could not believe what I just overheard. The pillars of our community rapists! Inconceivable; I knew they were shits but this, holy shit!

Now I had to get by the room without them knowing I was within earshot of their unsolicited admission of evil doing. I was in luck. The young waitress was just bringing the boys back fresh cognacs and a cigar tray; so while their attention was diverted to her, I slipped past the doorway and back up the stairs to the main ballroom.

I had a wad of incriminating information; no proof, just my hearsay, and without hard, cold facts, who would believe me anyway? What was I supposed to do with it? Well, for starters, I'd start by doing my usual method of checking out the facts. Fact one, I needed a drink, pronto. So I headed to the bar and ordered a double Jack straight up with another as a chaser.

Standing there while I let my favorite amber elixir do its thing, I had this uncanny feeling in my gut that somehow this unsolicited incriminating information was connected to the letter I had received earlier in the week. As the Jack worked its way to my brain, its racing thought process was slowing considerably.

"Hey barkeep, one more time."

I got a slight negative shake of the head which wasn't a good sign. I wasn't anywhere near as drunk as I'd wanted to be. But alas, Harden to the rescue. I actually smelled that incredible fragrance she was wearing this evening a split second before I felt her breasts rubbing against my arm.

"Hey, handsome, buy a girl a drink."

"Sure, but my warden here thinks I've had enough."

Harden batted her eyelashes at him and leaned over the bar giving him a breathtaking view of cleavage that could hurt you and said, "Please."

"Okay," said Warden Homer, according to his name tag. "One more, but that's it, Mr. Crandell, bosses orders."

"He's my responsibility, and I'm driving so it will be fine."

She winked to Homer as she said, "I plan to be on top of him for the rest of the evening."

"Well, if I can only have one more, make it a triple, no ice."

Homer rolled his eyes and said, "If he gets in trouble, he's your responsibility, not mine."

"I accept," smiled Harden. Maybe she's not such an ass after all. As I drained my last freebee of the evening, I thought to myself, what the hell kind of name is Homer for a bartender?

True to her word, she kept me on her arm for the rest of the evening. It was tough being cut off from my buddy Jack, but Harden did like her champagne so every time a waiter walked by with a fresh tray of flutes, being as chivalrous as I am, I naturally plucked one for her and of course, one for me also.

I took a few more pictures of the misters and missus, daddies and daughters, and the couples dancing around the ballroom watching who was watching them and trying to remain non-perspiring and unwrinkled all the while.

I really needed to get out of this place. All this social crap was starting to take the Jack buzz off. How can people call it an evening's entertainment when all they do is kiss ass, check out what the other women of the night—probably not the best choice of words but so what at this point—are wearing, try to figure who has had work done and how the Joneses manage to afford to keep up and remain members of the club.

Besides it was still very unsettling overhearing the locker room conversation about what's been going on during the fraternity's poker games to the poor unsuspecting waitress's serving them. Probably most of them knew what they were getting into when they took the job, as do most waitresses in high-class establishments. But how many didn't? Was Samantha one of those innocents?

Even though my mind was slightly blurred by booze, somewhere I knew there was a connection between Samantha, or Sammy, Baby, and the little homeless girl Karen was telling me about. I was determined to find out about it. After what I overheard, there would be a lot of personal satisfaction in bringing to light that the good, old boys of the Clinton Country Club were not all they were presumed to be. Also, if there was any truth to Baby's letter, I wanted to set the record straight about Rembrandt. He was after all, one of the only real things Clinton had ever produced that was not prostituted by position and money.

Having had more than enough of this whole frigging night, I was about to leave and take a nice, thought-provoking walk in the cold and snow home, but should Harden appear at my side and then on my arm. All things considered after the events of this night, being in her presence, this close wasn't a bad way to end it. Not a bad way at all; she was a beauty to behold. I had the feeling she was going to ask me to spend the night with her just from her body language, and the fact she'd been making some sort of physical contact with me every chance she got the entire evening, starting from when she picked me up at my house to even now. Plus she'd had several glasses of champagne to loosen what resolve she might have had.

I was right, damn.

"Dirk," she said, "Will you sleep with me tonight?"

I knew I would probably regret this the rest of my life, but I really didn't want to.

"Harden, you flatter me, and I know I'll hate myself in the morning, but I've had too much to drink, as usual. I've heard too much bullshit and I really need to just take a nice quiet walk home in the snow alone to sort some things out. And when I do, I'll want to talk to you about it. It's some pretty serious stuff, so thanks, but no thanks. I don't suppose you would consider taking a rain check on that offer?"

She didn't say yes or no, but on the positive side, she didn't look put off or hurt, so I took that as a maybe.

Then she smiled impishly and asked, "Are you going to make it home all right, or am I going to read about them finding you frozen like a popsicle in a snow drift tomorrow?"

I said, "Yes, I'm okay to walk, and no, they won't find me frozen tomorrow because I've still got enough antifreeze in me to stay thawed until spring."

With that, I left, a slow walk the mile or so from the club to my house was refreshing, to say the least. I couldn't get the feeling out of my head that what I'd overheard tonight and the letter I'd received were connected, but how? My gut was telling me that something was very wrong here in Clinton. I didn't much like the fraternity anyway for reasons stemming from way back when. What's weird is, a long time ago we were all friends, I thought. Over the years, it became apparent we were living on different sides of the tracks. People change.

I mostly harbored resentment because none of these friends came to Marie's funeral, or even sent a card. I took it very personal and felt that it was because I wasn't one of them. It was okay to hang out growing up and getting stoned together during the college years, but once they became club members on their own, they were too good to associate with a factory worker and his factory working wife. It wasn't just my wife and I. Clinton itself became *club members only* and then there was everyone else, no *tweeners*.

Maybe it's jealousy on my part but damn, they sealed the deal for me of being the ultimate snobs when they snubbed me and my dead wife. Fuck 'em. If they were involved in something criminal, and after what I heard tonight, that was a distinct possibility. And if there was any truth or connection to Baby's letter, I was determined to find out and let them know that even they were not above the law.

I finally arrived home, not any to soon because it was frigging cold outside and maybe I didn't have as much antifreeze in me as I thought. But there I was on my docrstep, cold, weary and alone. Not an entirely unfamiliar set of circumstances for me.

I let myself in, lit a fire to take the chill off, and poured myself a JD on the rocks. As I sat and watched the dancing flames, I was intoxicated by their movement and warmth. Slowly, I began to drift into the land of who gives a rat's ass and started to feel the familiar warm glow Jack gives me when I heard the doorbell ring.

Who the hell would be coming here at one in the morning on a night like this?

As I opened the door, there stood Harden with the snow still swirling gently around her looking just like she did when she picked me up earlier this evening. "What's a girl got to do to get a drink in this place?"

"Hey, look, Krissy, I'm really not in the mood for conversation right now."

She stepped into the small foyer and with a slight bit of intoxication showing and leaned in close and whispered in my ear, "Who said anything about conversation?"

She let her outer coat slide off her with the same fluid motion it did earlier in the evening. When it finally came to rest on the floor, she took one leggy step forward and then she slipped out of her lacey red dress, one spaghetti strap at a time and stood before me completely naked with the flames of the fireplace behind her, licking up and down the curves of her body; not a bad sight or thought for that matter if I don't mind saying so myself.

Meanwhile, with the seductively dancing flames as a background, all I could focus on was the silhouette of those curves with my imagination um, imagining.

"Well," I said, "still want that drink?"

"No," she said, "I want you."

Not wanting to put her off again, I said, "Since, you put it that way."

"Shall we go upstairs?" I said, feeling like a dumb-ass schoolboy.

"No," she said huskily "Here, in front of the fire will be nice."

CHAPTER 5

I WOKE UP SOME time later alone. I was covered with a throw from my couch which we had lain on earlier. All that remained of Harden was her scent. The fire was all but out, and the room was blanketed in darkness, not something I relished at all. There was however a small light on my desk in the adjoining dining room I used as my office-slash-bar. The light peeked into the near darkness of the living room.

I got up and found it quite drafty with no fire or clothes. I shuffled to the desk with the throw around me, not so much for modesty but for her lingering bouquet, a gentle mixture of her woman's scent and her perfume. It's been a very long time since these post-coital bouquets had played knock-knock on the door of my senses.

There, perched on top of my unfinished glass of JD, was a folded note.

It read:

> Hey, Dirk Boy. Glad I came, and boy, did I! But gotta go.
> Have to sing in the church choir in the morning. I was going to
> wake you, but you looked so peaceful, and besides I thought if
> I did, I'd never have left. Never did get that drink, but we can
> trade rain checks if you like.
> Soon, I hope, Krissy.

It was sealed with a lipstick kiss.

That's right, tomorrow, or actually today is Sunday. I had nothing planned for the day, and it was still dark so I thought I'd top off my drink and head up to bed. I'm getting too old to be sleeping on the floor, conscious that is.

Once again, I woke in a sweat with a pounding filling my chest.

Harden's earlier erotic presence had not even made a difference. Here I was again. Shit, so many times the same *nightmare*, just like a broken record.

I sat up on the side of the bed trying to calm myself, and I took the final gulp of my leftover nightcap and leaned over to pick up my cigarettes and as usual, my trembling hands nearly betrayed me. Firing up a morning after Lucky and a slug of Jack finally did their job.

By the time I finally dragged myself out of bed, it was four in the afternoon. I was hungry as hell, but I knew the cupboard was bare, so I decided to shower, shave and go down to one of my favorite pubs for a bite to eat and a couple of beers.

The snow had stopped for now anyway, so I brushed off my car just enough so that I could see out of the windows and headed downtown to the Bridge Tender.

Over the years, the place had several name changes but always retained the same cook, Carla. She had been there for at least twenty years that I knew of and she had mastered and preserved the magic touch of the short-order cook, a lost art now a days. She was also the best damn bartender the Tender's regular, seasonal, or even the occasional patrons ever had the privilege of having serve them. She used to be a cute little thing, and she still had a great smile and a pretty nice figure going for her. She had always been a sucker for hooking up with sweet-talking bad boys and so as they say, she kind of looked like she was rode hard and put away wet.

But, man, she could stand her own against any of the chefs in any of the finer restaurants around. Every day, but especially Sunday's, she always had a special going, and today, it was meatloaf, baked sweet potatoes with her own receipt for cinnamon butter and green peas. If you really wanted to delight your palette, she had handcrafted a pot of white bean soup—which in itself is to die for.

During the boating season, the Bridge Tender is known more as a fine restaurant for lunch and dinner rather than a local pub, and it caters to a lot of tourists. Clinton's full facility marina is within walking distance of the restaurant, and its open upper deck and first floor veranda which actually blends as one with the two-mile wooden river walk. The River Walk is dotted with a few quaint seasonal boutiques along the picturesque river's edge. So the location, along with Carla's great culinary reputation, has made it one of the best restaurants on the entire three hundred-mile stretch of the scenic, winding Clinton River.

During the off-season, the Tender became the locals' pub of choice, and Sunday normally was the only time Carla worked days as a cook. Lately, she'd been working every day; she must be between beaus and needed the money.

I hung up my coat on one of the coat hooks fashioned as boat anchors, and walked over and leaned on the bar and said, "Hey, Carla, what's good today?"

Her stark answer to me was, "Me, of course, and I'm even better when I'm marinated, but you're too late. That special was last night.

"Today, most of the guys here are having meatloaf," she said with a wry smile.

"Bummer about missing your special last night, but today's sounds great, and give me a Labatt Ice along with that, will ya?"

"You're just in time, my shift changes at six. Ten more minutes and you would have had to settle for little stale gold fish and broken pretzels in a paper bowl."

Once football season started in late August or early September, the local clientele started to patronize the Bridge Tender on Sundays once again. Buffalo Bills games were shown on a big screen TV in the old bar area in the backroom. By the time football was into the regular season, the tourist season had pretty much wound down so there was no conflict between the diners and the fans. It worked out well and everybody was happy, except when the Bills lost.

But being late in January, the Bills were out of the playoffs, so the jukebox was playing nonstop. The doors to the backroom were open to allow for those who wanted to dance or shoot pool. Most times, the Sunday tradition began around noon and ended by eleven because tomorrow it was back to the monotonous life a small manufacturing city has to offer.

With the Clinton Mall all but empty and the nearest cinemas being seventy-five miles or so away in Buffalo, the Tender, along with the other local gin mills, got their share of business on Sunday. There wasn't a whole lot else to do in the form of entertainment on the last day of the weekend in late January for those people like me—the bored, the alone, and the restless. So usually I come here where there is booze and kindred spirits. Being sober and alone is probably not healthy for me at this particular stage in my life.

Weekends in Clinton began, of course, with Friday. Friday was payday, and a lot of the family folks and those with significant others went out for the fish fry at the VFW.

Saturday mornings and afternoons, bowling in the leagues at Ten Pin Alley was a popular activity. Again, the single bored and lonely usually carried it over, if they could still see straight and prolonged the partying at one of the neighborhood gin mills, where everyone seems to know your name.

If renting a movie, downing a six-pack, and munching a bowl of popcorn wasn't your idea of Saturday Night Live, then there was for those looking for a little more action—Saturday night at the Dungeon in the Holiday Inn. The Dungeon could be cool, except for the first two or three hours Stan and his Karaoke Free for All, or whatever he called his entertainment claim to fame took center stage. I mean after two or three years of hearing the same drunken wannabes sing "Strangers in the Night," or some regrettable Stevie Wonder rendition, you had to be pretty well on your way to shit faced to even recognize the songs.

For the players if you got lucky, during the live music that followed, you might spot one of the amateur singers who would hopefully—in return for your enthusiastic support and appreciation of her performance should the routine go really bad, which most do—get a chance to console her. Either way, the strategy was that she would get to see if you wore boxers, briefs, or went commando, which was the general plan anyway. Personally, I'm not a Dungeon kind of guy.

Wednesday, as was everywhere in the working-class USA, was hump day, and in several bars, it was ladies' night, which meant another reason to go out and party, anyplace where there was music, and shots of whatever the drink specials were.

Not exactly the city that never sleeps, but to be honest, for those of us who live and work here day by day in Clinton, things could be worse. There was very little crime, except maybe an altercation or two when someone's wife couldn't remember who she came with or who she was leaving with, or maybe a little poodle getting roughed up for taking a crap on someone else's front porch, but nothing serious.

Carla brought my order over to my table, which was near the corner window overlooking the river; a really peaceful view. Sometimes it looked as though the river was flowing in conflicting directions at the same time. It was mesmerizing if you watched it long enough. I could see the bridge from where I was.

The Clinton Bridge—what a clever name for a bridge that spans the Clinton River—is a beautiful piece of construction mastery and architecture. Its length, of course, traverses from one side to the other, but the unique part is that its width is several blocks long with the historic Clinton River Mall at its center point. In the summer, the local thespian society, the Clinton Players—no one ever said the people who name these things here were clever—produced and presented one—and two-act plays at the beautiful gazebo. People also enjoyed our local string quartet playing classical music at sunset and into the early evening.

I was almost finished with my meal when the staff shift change happened. Normally not a big deal, but my sweet Carla was replaced by Clyde. Now Clyde is not to be confused with Homer from the club last night. Clyde was six feet nine, very big with lots of muscle, bald, and had more tattoos and body piercings than any other person I have ever seen. Almost instantly, the crowd started to change and most certainly did the music.

During football season, some of this new age and sometimes gothic crowd usually joined the Bills fans in the back. In Clinton, as well as most of Western New York, everyone loved their Bills. Once the season ended and the jukebox ruled, when the shift changed and Clyde became the bartender, so did the nature of the customers. No more Journey, Rod Stewart, Phil Collins, or Sheryl Crow tunes. Assaulting my eardrums and sanity now was the nasty shit they call rap or crap, hippity hop, or whatever. I don't understand if they're singing, talking, or chanting. I can't tell one song—if that's what they are—from another. I'm thoroughly convinced this type of music has something to do with the hole in the ozone layer or, at the very least, global warming. Oh well, live and let live, but this shit was killing me.

So I grabbed my coat and took my beer outside. It was not quite dark; my favorite part of the day. I took out a Lucky and lit it. I inhaled deeply the first drag, which was always the best; it went right to your central nervous system. I think more probably it goes to the slow-growing malignant tumor that all of us smokers have lurking inside and preparing us for our final passage to that great R. J. Reynolds nicotine cloud in the sky. But it sure tasted and felt good.

My wife wouldn't have waited for cancer to kill me from smoking; she'd have choked me after the first puff when I promised to quit right after we met twenty-five years ago. None of that means shit now. She never smoked a day in her life, and now she's dead and me, well let's just say, I'm doing everything damaging to my body that she tried to get me not to do to stay healthy. Live long and prosper, I said to myself sarcastically.

As I was leaning on the railing and looking out in to the depths of the river with the sun setting behind the towering twin steeples of Christ the Savior Episcopal Church, its spires caught the fading glint of light just so and made them look like sparkling gold. If I were a religious man, I might have been feeling some kind of spiritual revelation as a sign to mend my ways. I mean, I was seeing the light, the temples of gold, and I was looking out over troubled waters. Weird, but no revelations here.

After Marie's death, I ceased being a believer, except for the concept that one is responsible for one's own actions and all the praying, begging, and wishing to change places or to even go back in time to say I love you one more time is bullshit—plain and simple bullshit.

As the darkness snuck in, I thought I saw a smallish man hunched over carrying, what looked to be a small travel or doctor's bag, shuffling with purpose toward the bridge along the maintenance path of the river. What would someone, especially an old someone, be doing walking under the Main Street Bridge at dark? That could be dangerous shit. There were homeless people living under there.

I'm not a very brave or really concerned citizen, but after getting the letter from Baby and finding out Rembrandt had been found floating in the river, I thought maybe I ought to check this out. Besides, I am sort of an investigative reporter in my own mind. Although not everyone at the *Journal* would agree to that.

I left my empty bottle on the railing. I couldn't face going back into the Tender and that crap music. Or could I face looking at body piercings in places they shouldn't be. Nor did I want to see more tattoos than naked skin on people with multicolored colored hair; not tonight anyway.

So I made my way over the bridge and down the maintenance steps to the underbelly of the bridge. It was almost completely dark and being as how wide the bridge was I couldn't see much. Naturally, like all half-assed investigative reporters, I had no flashlight. I did however have my lighter. I lit it and what do you know? I still couldn't see shit.

Well, if the little old man was going to get mugged and tossed in the river, he must have known what he was headed for because he was sure headed under here with a definite idea in mind. Not like me, who had no clue what I was doing here, couldn't see shit and decided tomorrow I would come back, only this time with a flashlight. I made my way back over to the Tender and fought the very strong urge to say fuck it and just get in my car and go home but my curiosity was aroused. Who was this little old man that had ventured into the village of vagrants after dark and why?

So resisting the urge of peace and solitude in front of my crackling fireplace and a nightcap with my buddy Jack, I opted to fight the rap, crap, tattoos and neon hair and reentered the Tender. It was now about 7:00, and the place was surprisingly not as rowdy as I thought it would be. I suspected the really strong aroma of pot had a lot to do with the mellow mood of the place.

I didn't want to spend any more time than I had to here, so I went right up to Clyde. I asked him if he had ever seen the little old guy with the bag go under the bridge.

"What guy, bub?"

"The little old guy I just saw go under the bridge."

"I said what guy, bub?"

Finally, it was dawning on me. So I said, "While you're here, I'll have a Jack Daniels up."

He reached behind him, flipped the bottle up like Tom Cruise in *Cocktail*, poured the shot, and said, "That's $20."

"$20, do I drink it or put it in my safety deposit box?"

"You want to know about the Doc or not—$20. The Jack is free."

I slid a couple of tens across the bar, and he picked them up and shoved them down the front of his leather pants. I was glad I didn't need change.

"Well, what about the doc?"

"Yeah, okay, bub, Doc Bernard Johnson."

"It's Dirk, by the way, but Doc Bernard Johnson, the old retired pediatrician?"

"Yeah, bub, that's the doc. Maybe you even know his son, Junior, I think they call him. He's one of them stuck up assholes that hangs around the holier than thou country club."

Since he was refusing to call me by my given name, I thought of reciprocating and call him some clever variation of Clyde, but at 6'9" and about three hundred pounds, with biceps bigger than my thighs, I thought better of it.

"So, Clyde," I relented, "how often does the old doc make his little jaunt?"

"Just about every Sunday as far as I know, since I worked here anyway."

"How long might that be?" I asked.

"Another Jack, bub?"

"Sure, Clyde."

This time I slid a $20 over the bar—same results. He "cocktailed" me another Jack and said, "Can't say for sure exactly but off and on, I'd reckon been about fifteen years."

I told him thanks, left another $10 on the bar, and left.

As I drove home, I realized I had even more questions floating around in my head than I did before. When I got there I poured myself a Jack straight up and went to my desk and took out a tablet and pencil. I started to write down in no particular order some notes while I could still remember them.

Who was Baby really?

Why the letter to me?

Was this guy going under the bridge really old Dr. Johnson?

Why was he doing it?

How long had he been doing it?

What connection, if any, was there to Rembrandt?

What was the significance of the conversation I'd overheard at the club?

Did it tie in at all to the letter, since they both mentioned Slammin' Sammy, and/or Samantha?

Why no autopsy on Rembrandt?

What ever happened to Samantha the young girl that was raped and left to die under the bridge?

Why did Baby call Rembrandt and Samantha, Mom and Dad?

Why did Rembrandt write he was on to something that would provide Baby with college expenses and what was it?

Finally, my brain taxed enough for one night, I added as a sidebar;

Just what the hell does all this mean and why me. Why should I give a shit about what's going on in Clinton unless it affects my deteriorating liver?

So I finished my drink and went to bed. I don't know why, but I went right to sleep for a change. No night demons, and I actually woke up before the alarm and was looking forward to going to work.

CHAPTER 6

A S ON ANY OTHER Monday morning, I headed straight for the coffeepot. At my desk the ritual continued. Melissa came over, as I said, ever so cheerful and asked like time was stuck in a time warp or loop or whatever the sci-fi term was and inquired, "Good morning, Mr. Crandell, glazed or a hard roll?"

I think I nearly gave the poor young thing a coronary when instead of my usual ungrateful response I said, "I'll take a hard roll please. With some butter, if you have it."

She automatically turned to walk away before she realized I had actually said something other than my usual "fuck off" to her. She turned around to stare at me, as did everyone else in the newsroom within earshot with their mouths agape while she said. "Excuse me?"

I said, "Yeah, I'd like a hard roll with some butter, thanks. But if you don't have butter, that's okay."

She said, "I'll have to go get you one because you see, since you always say to me—pardon me—basically "fuck off" every morning, I really just go through the motions, and I don't actually have a doughnut or a hard roll with me. If you're serious, I'd be happy to go get you one."

I said, "Yes, I'm serious, and if it isn't too much bother, I really would like a hard roll this morning."

It wasn't ten minutes later that Harden came bouncing up to me inquiring as to my mental state. Was I okay, was I sick or as an alternative explanation to my sudden Monday morning personality change, did she just screw my brains out Saturday night?

I answered back, "What are you talking about? I feel fine, even a little inspired this morning, and my dear lovely Kristen, even though you are one fine example of what you see is what you get in bed, I assure you my brains are indeed still intact. Maybe slightly pickled, but still intact. I have not though, by the way, been able to find my boxers from the other night, but that's no biggie, I have another pair."

"No, silly," she said. "Word has it you've accepted a hard roll from Melissa this morning without your customary vulgar rendition of no, thank you."

"Wow, this really is a newsroom isn't it, and a pretty efficient one at that. Yes, I did take a hard roll from dear sweet Melissa, and I didn't mean to cause such excitement. What, all of ten minutes for word of the roll, the hard roll that is, on the third floor to get all the way up to the tenth floor, amazing."

"Speaking of rolls," she said, "I really enjoyed Saturday night and wouldn't mind doing it again sometime."

"Sounds like a plan. And by the way, I've come," and paused for effect, "To understand your subtle innuendos and your plays on words, especially when it, again pardon one of my own, comes to sex."

She tipped her head back and laughed and started to wiggle away.

"Kristen," I called after her. "Gotta minute, there's something I'd like to run by you, seriously."

"Sure," she answered and came back over to sit on the corner of my desk. She was all business now, which was what I really found intriguing about her.

"Shoot," she said.

"Okay, it may be something, and then again, it might just be my imagination running amok with a Jack Daniels in its shaky little hand, but I think I may have stumbled onto a story, a really big story that could implicate some of Clinton's most prestigious citizens and then again maybe it's nothing. But I'd like to pursue it, if it's all right with you."

She said, "Let's hear what you've got or what you think you've got and I'll decide if it's worth taking you off the society page gig and make you a genuine *Clinton Journal* investigative reporter."

"Fair enough, here's what I've got, it's nothing but circumstantial and hearsay, but I can't help but think it's all connected somehow and I suspect there could be a lot more to this than what I'm speculating on at the present."

So she said again, "Shoot, and I'll help you decide."

So I began with the letter I got from Baby and showed it to her. She read it and said what else. So I told her about the trip to archives and the lack of an autopsy and the half-assed police report by Laurel and Hardy, the police chief and coroner brothers.

Then I tossed in the overheard conversation by the boys in the cigar room at the club the other night, which definitely pointed to some kind of evil doings and a typical money backed cover-up.

I also mentioned about David Weatherford IV's admittance of dumping the poor assaulted waitress's battered body down by the bridge thinking probably she was dead or if not, she soon would be. That act completed would insure all the blame would be put somewhere else.

Then I mentioned that last night while at the Bridge Tender I saw old Dr. Johnson shuffle under the massive bridge span with his doctor's bag and then found out he'd been doing it every week for the last fifteen years or so.

"I think something's fishy here in Clinton, and according to this letter from Baby, somehow Rembrandt, aka William Mintz found out about it and was about to shake someone down for it to help Baby with her schooling. That part's purely speculation by me. But Kristen, I feel it in my bones, something is fucked up here, and I'd like to try to get to the bottom of it."

"Are you sure this is not just a personal vendetta that you have for the boys, as you call them? Everyone in this city knows what a hard-on you have for these people, and I'm afraid it might just look that way if you start anything to blow out their party candles."

"I realize that probably more than anyone," I said. "But I can't remember ever or for a long time at least having this feeling that these guys stepped over the line with this waitress years ago, and I'd really like to just check it out. Regardless of the outcome, at least I can in clear conscience, tell Baby I did what I could and did not betray whatever trust Rembrandt had in me telling her I was the go to guy. It would mean a lot to me, Kristen. I know you've gone out on a limb for me already, giving me this job and all, but I need this. Who knows, if there's a major crime story cover-up in the making, you might even get a raise or something, and somehow I might redeem myself in this community and in my own mind."

"Dirk," she beamed, "Other than the other night at your place, I haven't seen you this enthused about anything in a long time. Since this is a slow news time, I'll assign Melissa to do your obits and social stuff temporarily. This city hasn't had a good scandal since I've been here. But as much as I like you and appreciate your talents, both on and off the job, I have to warn you that if you put your personal grudge with the members of the country club ahead of good, honest news reporting, I'll have your balls in a hand basket. Not exactly the way I'd prefer them, but okay, Mr. Studly, I'll trust you to check it out. But keep me posted."

I went back to my desk and sat down. I felt, I don't know what did Harden say; enthused, yeah maybe; excited, yeah maybe that too. I couldn't really put my finger on the emotion, but it was like when Marie and I would find a baby bird in our yard that had fallen out of the big old pine tree. We both knew we had to try to give the poor little bugger a chance in life so we would try and put him back into his nest. Unfortunately it was always me who had to climb up the brambles of the pine tree, experiencing scratches, thwaps in the face, and enough pine sap stuck to my hands and arms to warrant a lengthy de-sapping with lighter fluid.

After the hapless little chick was secured back in the nest, you just felt damn good. I always knew on the way up I was doing the right thing, despite what scrapes I would endure; it was the right thing to do.

This was kind of the same thing, only on a much larger scale. If I could prove what I overheard was true, and some poor teenage waitress had been beaten, raped, and left for dead and the good ol' boys had covered it up because it would tarnish their standing in the community, it was more than wrong it was criminal, and no amount of money or lineage should keep their pompous asses away from justice.

So I picked up my notes and scanned them over again.

Who was Baby really?

Why the letter to me?

Was this guy going under the bridge really old Dr. Johnson?

Why was he doing it?

How long had he been doing it?

What connection, if any was there to Rembrandt?

What was the significance of the conversation I'd overheard at the club?

Did it tie in at all to the letter, since they both mentioned Slammin Sammy and/or Samantha?

Why no autopsy on Rembrandt?

What ever happened to Samantha the young girl that was raped and left to die under the bridge?

Why did Baby call Rembrandt and Samantha, Mom and Dad?

Why did Rembrandt write he was on to something that would provide Baby with college expenses and what was it.

With the sidebar, just what the hell does all this mean and why me. Why should I give a shit about what's going on in Clinton unless it affects my deteriorating liver?

Okay, so Sherlock, just where the hell do you start?

I know I'm not much of a detective, but I watch a lot of TV that is before I fall asleep. I used to read a lot of crime novels by the likes of James Patterson, Robert Parker, and Jeffery Deaver. Where would they start?

Well, if all else fails, why not start at the top?

Okay. Who was Baby? According to her letter, she was the daughter of Rembrandt and Samantha. If that's true, then it should be a matter of public record I would think. I thought if anyone could find that out it would be Kelly in archives, so I gave her a call.

"Kelly," I said when she answered on the first ring. "Hey, doll, I'm kind of following up on the Rembrandt thing from the other day. How would I go about finding out if there is a birth certificate on record somewhere by only knowing the names of the parents, especially if they weren't married? Or if a birth certificate was ever even issued?"

Kelly said, "Dirk, I know that birth certificates are a matter of public record. Let me see what I can find. She did a quick search on her computer and couldn't find any record of a birth certificate ever having been issued for Baby Hobbs or Mintz.

"So," she said, "that's a dead end. I'm sorry I can't help you on this."

"That's okay, doll, I didn't figure this would be that easy. Thanks anyway."

I picked up the letter from Baby and reread it and at the bottom was a number I could reach her at. So let's see, 10:00 a.m. Eastern time would be, I don't know but pretty early on the west coast. I thought I should wait a while before I called out there for a couple a reasons. First I didn't want to get her out of bed with an off-the-wall call and second, I didn't have a clue what I was going to ask her.

Since it was close to the time for my daily trip to the Crypt anyway, and I needed to pass some time, I thought a good stiff Bloody Mary made by my favorite bartender might help my thought process. By the way, I seem to recall some important literary genius once said "I never met a bartender I didn't like." I think it might have been Hemingway.

In this case, I much preferred Karen to Clyde or whatever his name was at the club, Chad or Brad or wait—Homer, that was it. Homer, bite me, not literally, but Homer for Christ's sake, give me a break, get a friggin' nickname like, Butch, Sam, even Mr. T—that'd be cool but again, I digress.

As I entered the Crypt, I didn't see Karen, which was unusual. So this young skinny kid with a severe case of acne comes over to me and tells me he's sorry but "We're not open yet sir, it's only 10:15 in the morning and we don't open until noon."

So I say, "And who might you be?"

"I'm Bruce, the new assistant manager."

Bruce? Where by Jesus are these people coming up with these names. If you want success for your kid, name him something authoritative like George, David, or Rutherford, for Christ's sake, but Bruce. Bruce, Homer, Chad, give me a break.

"Where's Karen," I asked the new assistant manager.

"She called in sick," he said, slightly put out. "That means we have to double up our waitresses and bartenders to cover for her."

"So what's the problem?" I asked. "Let the waitresses keep doing what they always do, and you tend bar for a couple of hours, and life goes on."

Bruce snapped back at me, "I didn't go to the Bridgeport Community College for two years and study food service to wind up tending bar."

I said, "Food service, huh? Then why don't you, waitress or waiter or whatever and serve food for a couple of hours then and let someone else tend bar. It should be problem solved, should be easy actually since it will be the lunch hour and most of the customers will want food not booze, with the exception of me of course, so you can go ahead and do what food service taught you to do, serve food. Problem solved. Mr. Assistant Manager Bruce."

He just gave me an exasperated exhale, put his hands on his hips and turned to strut away.

"Bruce," I called after him, "did Karen say what was wrong with her? It's not like her to miss a day's work."

"I really can't say," he replied. "Just said she was sick and wouldn't be in. It just totally spoils my first day as manager here."

"Assistant," I corrected.

"Assistant?" he mimicked.

"Yeah," I said, "Assistant, you said you were the assistant manager, Brucey, so I would guess that would only half-ass spoil your day, never mind any concern for the well-being of one of your most loyal and best employees."

With that exchange, I lost my appetite for my Bloody Mary, if you can believe that and I went back up to my desk. I made a mental note to check on Karen after my call to Baby in California.

Back in my cube and looking at the clock, I figured it was as good as a time as any to try and call Baby. As far as what I was going to ask her, well I would just have to wing it. So I picked up the letter, asked for an outside line, and dialed the number. On the third ring a female voice husky with sleep picked up and said, "Mr. Crandell, I thought you'd never call."

Caller ID never ceases to amaze me. It's like how the hell do they know who's calling them. Is there a little video camera videoing me, or whatever it is that video cameras do? I'm just used to saying when the other party answers the phone, "Hey, this is Dirk Crandell calling and blah, blah, blah."

I personally don't have caller ID. I still like the little surprise at the other end finding out who's calling. But then, almost everyone has the ID thing now, so they expect you to know who's calling, and it surprises them that you don't already know who's calling you. Weird, go figure.

I said, "Is this Baby?"

"Yes, is this Mr. Dirk Crandell?" she replied with the slight hint of a chuckle. Can the knowledge of my lack of technical expertise with all this new electronic programmable crap have preceded me all the way to California?

"Yes," I said with authority.

"Then, yes, too," she said, with a mischievous laugh.

"Do you have some time to talk to me Baby or should I call back when it's more convenient for you. I'm good anytime," I added.

Her husky voice continued to smile and said, "No, this is good for me, I'm off today and I would rather talk to you sooner than later."

"Great," I said, "I don't know exactly where to begin but first, is your name really Baby?"

"Yes."

"Baby Mintz?"

"Yes."

"In your letter, which I just received a couple a days ago by the way, you said Rembrandt or more precisely, William Mintz, was your father and Samantha Hobbs was your mother."

"Yes."

There was a pause as she seemed to be waiting for my next question. "Baby?"

"Yes."

If I was going to get anything from this conversation she was going to need to be a tad more talkative, in fact a hell of a lot more talkative, smiling husky voice or not.

"Okay, Baby. First of all, if this conversation is going to go anywhere, you are going to have to give me more information than one word answers," I said.

"Okay, Mr. Crandell," she almost whispered.

"Three words, it's a start," I responded, "Let's try for whole sentence, or even a paragraph or two, okay?"

"Okay, Mr. Crandell."

This was going to be a very long conversation at this pace. Or maybe a very short one, if I didn't start getting some information I could use to satisfy her letter. "Baby, and please don't say yes just yet. You say that Samantha Hobbs and Rembrandt excuse me, William Mintz were your parents, how come the different last names?"

"They were never married. After I was born, Mr. Mintz took care of me and my mother. He was the only father I ever knew, so I always called him Dad."

"So who was your paternal father, if I might ask?"

"I don't know for sure," she said flatly. She never told me, she said she really didn't know and really didn't care. Rembrandt was a good man, and he was all the father I ever needed."

"Excuse me for this, and I don't mean to sound crude, and you can stop me anytime you want, but as I seem to remember in your letter, you said your mother's reputation hinted at," as I fumbled for an easy way to ask this, "I don't know, promiscuity maybe. It's says she was referred to as Slammin Sammy. Is that the reason she didn't know who your father was?"

"No!" she snapped into the phone, and was then silent for what seemed to be a long time.

Then she said calmly. "That was after I was born. That's part of the reason I want you make things right for her, and for him—to expose the people responsible for this whole tragedy. It's all wrong, I mean, most of it anyway."

"Baby," I said as genuinely soothingly as I could, "Why don't you tell me what is wrong with this whole picture, and then I'll have something to work with besides bits and pieces. Talk to me, Baby, tell me what happened to your mom and dad here in Clinton, and why I got a letter from you, someone I don't know, never heard of, and who wants me to clear the reputations of two people no one seemed to really have cared about much, except you."

"Dirk, may I call you Dirk?"

"Yes," oh, shit, now she has me doing the one-word thing.

"I'd rather do it in person. My aunt has a job consultation in Buffalo this Friday, and she asked me if I'd like to go with her and maybe we could get in some skiing while we were there. At first I wasn't going to go with her, but now it will give me a chance to sit with you face-to-face and tell you the whole story. I don't want to do it on the phone. Okay with you?"

"Sure," I said, somewhat disappointed at having to wait. But maybe it was better this way, eye-to-eye. Besides it would give me a couple a days to nose around to see if I could find out anything on my own.

"We'll be staying at the Marriot. I'll call you when we get in. It'll have to be Friday night because that's the only time I'll have free. Is that okay with you? Maybe we could have dinner or a drink or something."

"Now you're talking, about the drink I mean. You have my number here at work?"

"Yes, I do, and I look forward to meeting you and get this thing going after all these years. My father never wanted to say anything until about three months before his death because he didn't want to bring up bad memories. He said he wanted to protect me from what destroyed my mother. Then he changed his mind. Anyway, we'll talk Friday. Thanks for calling me Dirk, I was beginning to think you were like the rest of them."

"Baby, one last thing. Why should I believe you?"

I could almost hear the smile come back into her voice. "Oh, you'll believe me all right."

I checked in with Harden on my way out to keep her posted concerning my conversation with Baby, and my unexpected plans to meet with her

Friday night to get her story. "Do I get overtime for this, being on my own time and all?" I asked.

"No," she said and then added, "Make sure her story is all you get from her, stud."

"You flatter me. Kristen, she's only nineteen, I think. What could she possibly want with an old lush like me?"

"Same as me," she grinned that lusty way she does. Then she turned all business again. "Seriously, Dirk, remember what I said about your hard-on for some members of this community. I'll support you on this all the way if you can convince me there's a real story in it, understood?"

"Gotcha boss," and I left.

I stopped by the Crypt just to peek in and see if Karen had showed for work yet. I didn't see her; all I saw was Brucey, in even more of a tizzy then earlier, which must mean she hadn't made it in at all today. I didn't want to go in without some cheese to go along with the whine from the "I'm meant for better things" assistant manager. So I decided to go home and call Karen from there.

After I got home and checked my messages, none as usual which is fine by me, I tried Karen's phone and got her machine. I didn't want to leave a message so I just hung up. Wouldn't be the first time she just got drunk or stoned or both for a couple a days, especially after a weekend of serving drinks and taking orders from others. I could tell from the other day she was about ready for a "trip to normalcy" as she called her binges. I saw the demons just below the surface then, which was a sure sign of things to come. Oh well, I'll try her again tomorrow.

My cupboard and fridge were bare except for beer and Jack. So I fixed myself a Jack on the rocks and glanced at the TV section of the publication which keeps me gainfully employed and discovered there was a Sabres game on tonight. They were playing Toronto which was always a pretty heated rivalry. Sounded like a plan to me so I called Umberto's Pizza and ordered a medium thin crust, double cheese, double pep, green pepper pizza with anchovies on the side, my usual. Umberto's makes the best friggin' pizza anywhere, anytime, says me anyway.

The pizza arrived just about the same time as the first period face off. So I popped a Labatt Ice and settled down with my made-to-order gourmet Italian dinner and watched the Sabres kick some froggy butt, eh.

I actually woke up Tuesday morning before the alarm went off, which was a rarity for me. I slept good in fact and what's even more amazing is, that I remember finishing about half the pizza, having a couple of Labatt's in the process and watching the entire Sabres game, which they won 4 to 1.

I had also stowed the remaining pizza, box and all, in the naked fridge and then went to bed. No nightmares, no night sweats, no waking up in the middle of the night to use my Jack Daniels pacifier to numb me into slumber. But then again, I don't remember hearing any wailing of ambulance sirens last night either.

So experiencing an unaccustomed refreshed morning feeling, I got the coffee going. An ironic twist is I use a Jack Daniels gourmet blend of coffee for which I have to drive all the way to Buffalo to get and pay probably twice the price of regular, but Karen, my sister-in-law, turned me on to it. And it's actually very good. The brand Jack Daniels has no significance to the fact that I drink mass quantities of the bottled stuff; it just has some good, hearty, kick-ass jump start morning flavor and also acts as my surrogate breakfast.

So I showered and shaved, scanned the morning Journal, mostly for typos, and in actuality, enjoyed my cup of coffee.

So this is what most people feel like in the morning, holy shit, it's been a long, long time. Maybe I've been really unfair to Melissa for her morning for her cheeriness. But then again as the old adage goes: "I feel sorry for those who don't drink because that's as good as they're going to feel all day."

I, in fact, don't expect this morning euphoria to last all day without an alcohol supplement of some kind, but this was a unique start for me today anyway.

As I finished my second cup of coffee, I made some notes for the day in my planner. Planner, not exactly your executive everyday planner. I used to keep a Franklin Planner, and I kept track of everything in my life, even bowel movements I think. Since I got canned from the Clockworks, my planner was now a 3' x 6' pocket calendar mailed to me every year for my donation to the local Save-a-Pet organization. It works great, considering my business and social calendar at present. I make my important notes on Post-it notes of which I have cut the pads in half, both for space and economic reasons and stick them on the appropriate pages. Not really professional, but functional.

I started my car from the front doorway with one of those automatic remote starter thingies that Marie had insisted on. She said, "You can freeze *your* ass off waiting for that son of a bitch to warm up waiting inside the car or inside the house. Me, I'll take the house."

Then she would add, "God, I can't wait to retire and move someplace where is doesn't snow."

We'd gotten another three or four inches of light snow overnight. I didn't brush it off, "That's what windshield wipers were for."

Marie used to also say, "If they can't take a lousy six inches of snow off the windows what good were they, buy a vehicle that will."

I always liked that philosophy. The same with the driveway, "What's the sense in shoveling or snow blowing your driveway when you can buy a four-wheel-drive vehicle, God will take it all away in the spring anyway, so why waste the time and energy."

It was at times like this that, Christ, I really missed her.

I arrived at the *Clinton Journal* on time for a change. Melissa spotted me and as usual came bounding with her usual enthusiasm over to me with a tray in her hand. "Good Morning, Dirky, how about a bagel this morning, something different for a change?"

Dirky made me cringe, but the bagel and the enthusiasm kept me on my roll—again, sorry for the pun.

"Do you, my sweet little Mel, have any cream cheese to go with the bagels?"

"Sure do," she beamed, "Regular, poppy seed, or a blueberry bagel?"

"Poppy seed, toots, with cream cheese will be excellent."

I couldn't believe how this day had started; maybe there was something about sobriety after all. I'd tried it once or twice before, but the shakes and headaches far dissuaded any serious attempt for the sober thing to have any kind of chance for success. Weakness, yeah pure weakness is a good phrase to describe my fall from the graces of the clear headed.

I wandered over to grab a coffee and saw Melissa head back to her desk with purpose. So I stopped by and inquired, "Harden said anything to you about taking over my society and obit stuff for a while."

"Yes, she did, but I'm not sure I can handle it. What if I make a mistake on somebody's wedding or even God forbid an obituary?"

"Don't sweat it, toots," I soothed.

"Weddings are a piece of cake." God, I amuse myself with these puns. "And the obits are a standard form unless the deceased's family wants to write their own. Then you just retype it, spell-check it and make sure you have the right schmuck dead that's dead. Seriously, feel free to run anything by me you're not sure of. Just go back over some of the recent stuff and change the names and dates. No one'll know the difference. Oh, and one other thing, nobody gets married in Clinton this time of year that wants any publicity on it anyway. Don't sweat it, Melissa, it's a no brainer. Why else do you think they have me doing it?"

So here I am, sitting at my desk about to play sleuth. I had no clue how to do it, but I've read enough mystery novels to fake it. Besides, all my instincts were yelling at me to find out what was going on here in Clinton and in sunny Los Angeles. I know pretty much for a fact if the conversation I overheard at the club was indeed true, our illustrious community leaders were covering up a pretty dastardly thing that happened a long time ago and did such a good job of it, it appears no one even knew about it. And then, what's the deal with Baby. I get the feeling she suspects foul play in the death of her father, Rembrandt. I'll get the scoop on that Friday. *Scoop*, now I'm even starting to sound sleuthy.

I thought to help pass the time until Friday and go through the archives back from, what did lawyer Truehardt say? Eighteen or twenty years ago, to see if there was any news item of a body found floating in the river, or any reports of a missing seventeen—or eighteen-year-old girl.

I took the elevator down to archives and approached Kelly. She must have heard me coming because she said without even a glance up from her screen, "You know, Dirk, we really have to stop meeting like this. You know how office gossip can be, and besides, I don't want Ms. Harden to think I'm trying to cut in on her squeeze."

She must have heard my mouth drop open because she looked up.

I finally gathered my slightly shaken composure and said. "Talk about office gossip, what'd you hear about me and Harden, whatever it is it's not true. Well, maybe some of it, actually probably most of it, but what'd you hear?"

"You slept together, and she can't get enough of you and so now you're the teacher's pet."

"Nothing like beating around the bush," I said

"Exactly," she smiled, "Heard you did that too."

"Okay, okay," I said as I put my hands up in mock surrender. "But it was only a onetime thing, we were drunk."

"Riiiight, uh-huh, sure, Dirk, one time, huh, this sounds like an old Lay's Potato Chip commercial, 'Bet you can't eat just one.'"

"All right," and this time my surrender was genuine. "Whatever you say. Look Kelly, I want to nose around in some journals from eighteen or twenty years ago. Do our archives go back that far?"

"Yep, their all on microfilm. Anything in particular that I can help you with?"

"Not really," I said. "I'm not really sure I even know what I'm looking for."

After hearing how fast the gossip goes through this building's goose, I didn't want to say anything to anyone that could somehow come back to bite me in the ass before I had something to back it up. Telling a woman who works down here in the basement by herself all day, my half-baked suspicions would be just loading the gossip gun for sure.

"If you go down the hall to the last door on the right, you'll find the microfilm room. It's all organized by date. It's really pretty easy."

Once a local college student, who was looking up some Clinton history for a paper he was doing, showed me how to get started it was pretty easy. After I got to the right time span, I spent the remainder of Tuesday, all of Wednesday, Thursday, and finally finished Friday about noon going through several years of *Clinton Journals*. Time really passes fast when you're having fun. After a while, everything becomes a blur except what you're focused on.

I had narrowed my search plan to just something simple, or so I thought. I tried to focus on just the Clinton Crime Scene column, which had been a front-page stalwart for over twenty years. It gave names and a brief synopsis of any crime reported the previous day, except weekends, which were included in Monday's column.

Nothing seemed to jump out at me regarding unsolved disappearances, rapes, floating bodies, or any suspicious unresolved events of a similar nature.

So then I concentrated on any newsworthy items involving the *clubbers,* other than on the society pages. This too proved to be a mistake. It seems that every friggin' copy of the *Journal* contained a story of some nature concerning the pillars of our community. But as far as crimes and/or unsavory behavior—nope, not even a DUI. That doesn't surprise me one iota; they were getting away with it in high school—why would it change now?

One thing I learned though was that if I was going to get a crime story on these shitheads—whoops, I better stop calling them that until I can squeeze them and make that title a reality—I was going to have to really dig for it. Tonight should be a step in the right direction.

I checked my messages at my desk before I headed home about 2:00 p.m., and there was one from my nineteen-year-old date for tonight, informing me she had arrived and was going to take a nap and if could I meet her in the bar at the Marriot by the Buffalo Airport at 6:00 p.m. She had taken the liberty to make reservations for dinner at seven. If there was a problem with her plans, she was staying in room number 3311 and to please call her and not worry about waking her up.

I went home to shower before I met Baby, and I can't friggin' believe it, but I did not have a drink. My reasoning was that I wanted to have a clear head when I talked with her, and depending on how things went, I'd always have the option to slug down a few later. Besides, I never met a bar I didn't like and that didn't have my drink of choice.

I got dressed in some casual clothes rather than my usual coat and tie. Even though the *Clinton Journal* was a small-time newspaper, Harden required a dress code—sort of—meaning men wore coats and the women wore dresses, except in winter or when it was cold. Then they could wear pantsuits. This being Western New York meant they could wear pantsuits about ten months out of the year.

Being not the most domestic-minded bachelor, I had to sort through my closet and try to locate the least-wrinkled slacks I could find. Then to my sweater drawer. After doing the guy thing—the smell test—I selected a coordinating sweater.

I scanned my note cards before I left. At the last minute, I grabbed my trusty notebook and number two pencil, and I was off.

It's about a two-hour drive from my house to the Marriot, but on a Friday night at 4:00 p.m. with traffic, I thought I'd rather leave early. Besides, I wanted to be there before Baby so that I could check her out before she spotted me. When I thought about it, she probably didn't know what I looked like either.

The drive was uneventful; the roads were clear which believe it or not they almost always were in Western New York, where the roads crews stayed on top of things in the winter. I suspect a lot of overtime influenced the crews to stay on the job eighteen hours a day to make travel easier. Now if only they took care of pot holes as well . . . but yeah, I stray again.

I put on a tape of Burton Cummings who had been one of Marie's favorites along with Elvis Presley. Cummings was cool, but Presley; well, he sucked.

I arrived at the Marriott about 5:30 or so, and the parking lot was already starting to fill up; popular place on weekends in Buffalo. There's a lot to do in the surrounding area, if you're into winter things, which I am definitely not—unless, of course, planting my ever fattening ass on a bar stool for peace, solitude, and escape counted.

I decided on valet parking so that I wouldn't have to brave the elements and went into the hotel, checked my coat, and went into the bar. I was lucky to find a stool facing the guest entrance. This would give me a chance to scope out the single women entering. I had this silly notion that perhaps if in the genesis of my assumption that Baby might be the resulting child of a pregnancy conceived during the rape of Samantha, I might recognize her from her resemblance to any of the good old boys since I've known all of them for most of my life. That is assuming of course and a very large assumption this is, is that:

A: Samantha was indeed the Sammy they were quarrelling about, and

B: Baby is Samantha's a.k.a. Sammy's kid, the product of the rape.

Of course, this would make it all too easy if she looked exactly like David Weatherford IV or Carl Southerland, for example.

I ordered a glass of house red wine while I was waiting for Baby. House red for the king of JD, ye ask? I don't know; I figured that's what the young lady would order so what the hell. I didn't care much for wine, but it was easy to sip while waiting.

Several young women of varying descriptions came through the lobby entrance, mostly in pairs. The same went for the guest entry. So far, none gave the impression of being here to meet someone. That's wrong; they all looked like they were here to meet someone, just not *meet up* with someone.

At six on the button, a very striking, statuesque blond with amazing violet eyes appeared in the guest entryway. Several of the men at the bar turned and checked her out. I watched her look around, subtly surveying the crowd, obviously looking for someone in particular. Could this be her? The timing was right, but as I looked at her, I could not discern any resemblance to any of the *clubbers*.

We finally made eye contact. A very charming smile appeared on her face, and she waved at me and glided over to me the way models glide down the runway. It was amazing how on her approach the crowd at the bar seemed to part to let her through. Kind of like the story of Noah or Moses or whoever; I never was a big fan of the Bible. Anyway, when she arrived, and that's exactly what she did, she arrived at my stool, and said, "Dirk, Dirk Crandell?"

I was caught a tad off guard. First, by her striking beauty, and second, by the fact, that she knew who I was.

"Y-Y-Yes," I stumbled.

"Baby?" I queried a little louder than I needed to, and with that the older woman sitting next to me looked over her shoulder with disgust.

"Oh really, Baby, . . . you chauvinist!" she spat.

Then, Baby leaned in and kissed me on the cheek.

Upon seeing this display, the woman hissed at Baby, "Have some respect for yourself, girly."

Very matter-of-factly, Baby leaned over to her, close enough so people around wouldn't hear above the crowd noise, but not so close that I couldn't hear, and said, "Fuck off, bitch."

With this, the newly anointed bitch—although I seriously doubt it was the first or last time she was dubbed that title—picked up her white wine and left, giving up her seat next to mine.

"Cool," I said as Baby settled in on the empty stool. "You look absolutely stunning."

"And you, Mr. Crandell, look exactly like your picture."

"What picture?"

"The one in the *Journal* next to the column you used to do called Around the Town with Dirk Crandell."

"That was a while ago, living in California. How did you ever see it?"

"In case you don't know, Mr. Crandell, I get all of the *Clinton Journals* mailed to me in LA."

"So you actually waste your meant-for-college money on a subscription to this rag?"

"No, Mr. Crandell, it is mailed to me out of friendship from Dr. Bernie."

"Okay," I said. "Let's get two things straight. First, it's Dirk, not Mr. Crandell, makes me feel too old, even if I am, humor me will ya please? Second, who is Dr. Bernie?" I swiveled my stool around ninety degrees to face her and my curiosity about this whole Rembrandt-Baby scenario was rapidly reaching a state of erection.

Before she could answer me, the bartender came over to us and said as she placed fresh coasters down in front of us without really looking up, "What'll it be, you two?"

I was still waiting for an answer and realizing it was not imminent, I turned back to the bartender and who should it be, but Karen, my MIA sister-in-law. I nearly had a coronary on the spot.

"Dirk," she smiled awkwardly, "I never expected to see you here. I didn't recognize you without your suit on."

That brought a surprised smile to Baby's lips.

I was really dumbfounded and my mouth must have been agape with surprise because Baby leaned over and said, "Dirk, you should really close your mouth before people start putting quarters in it and expecting tunes to come from it and what's the deal about not recognizing you with clothes on? Perhaps I should let you two get a room." She laughed.

"No, no," I managed to mumble, "It's—it's m-m-my sister-in-law. What in Christ are you doing here and why haven't you answered my calls? I've been worried sick that maybe something dastardly happened to you."

"Dastardly," they both guffawed which seemed to mellow the tone of my inquisition.

"Dirk," Karen said, "I desperately needed a change in my life and this was it. Now's not the time or place, but I'm fine, great, in fact. I'll call you soon and explain everything to you. Who's your lady friend," she asked and then added, "I think we've met before, you look kind of familiar to me, have we met?"

Baby answered, "Funny you should say that because I saw you earlier and I thought the exact same thing."

With that, she reached out her hand and said, "I'm Baby, Baby Mintz, formerly of Clinton a long time ago, I might add, and now I live in LA."

"I'm Karen O'Donahue, Dirk's sister-in-law."

"Hey barkeep," came a bellow from somewhere down the bar, "Are you going to serve drinks or spew bullshit all night? I need a drink."

Karen waved and said, "I gotta go. I'm off at seven I can talk more then if you're still here."

"That's great," said Baby. "We're having dinner in the Runway Room at seven, please join us, I insist."

Karen said, "Okay, that will be nice, but now I have to work. What's your pleasure?"

Baby never even hesitated, "Two Jacks straight up, Karen."

Karen lifted an inquisitive eyebrow and said, "I should've guessed," and with that, she went to the bellow fellow. Funny thing about guys like him, you can put him in class, but you'll still have an ass.

It was nearly seven when our drinks arrived. They were not served by Karen, but by a very muscle bound, Adonis-looking guy, who said as he set down our drinks, "Hi, my name is Jeremy, and Ms. Mintz and Mr. Crandell, your table on the Runway is ready at your convenience, and Karen says she'll meet you there in about ten minutes."

I didn't say anything about Jeremy's name but, again, give me a friggin' break, moms and pops, whatever happened to Dick and Jane? Anyway, I left a $20 bill on the bar and picked up our drinks and followed Baby to the dining room.

We were instantly met by the maître d', who wished us a good evening and escorted us to our table.

What a view! We were seated overlooking the runway of the airport so that while we were dining, we could watch the planes take off carrying travelers to adventures and destinations unknown.

Marie and I used to come here and sit in the upper lounge on Sunday afternoons, drinking Bloody Mary's as we'd watch the planes take off and land, all the while making up little stories about these travelers. That seemed like an eternity ago.

We both just watched in silence as a 747 took off into the dark snowflake mosaic sky—an awesome sight that never ceases to enthrall me, and judging by the look on Baby's face, ditto.

Our waiter came over and said, "My name is Chuck and I'll be your server this evening. Are your drinks okay, or would you like to order from our wine list?"

I looked at Baby and she nodded demurely, and so I said to Chuck, "We're fine for now."

Chuck—now we're talking about a name—then proceeded to recite the menu from memory, and we placed our orders.

I couldn't help but admire the beautiful young woman sitting across from me in the candlelight. Once more, stunning was the adjective that was foremost in my mind.

Chuck brought our salads, and while we played around with them, I asked Baby who Dr. Bernie was.

"Dr. Bernie is what I call him, and he's my oldest and dearest friend. His name is Dr. Bernard Johnson. I've known him and loved him my entire life.

"I know why we are both here tonight Dirk, and I have quite the story to tell you so I should start from the beginning. I see Karen looking for us over there, and I think she might want to hear this also. She might even be able to verify some of what I tell you as the truth." With that she waved to Karen, and smiled.

CHAPTER 7

NO SOONER HAD KAREN sat down than, like magic, Chuck appeared with a salad for her.

"I hope you don't mind, Miss but I took the liberty to bring you a salad with a few choices of dressing so that you may all dine on your entrees together."

"This will be fine, and I'll just have water with lime please."

Chuck took her order and then left.

"Karen, do you remember when I told you about a letter I received from a woman in California telling me about a gross miscarriage of justice done to the memories of her mother and father here in Clinton? Well, this is the woman. She thought it might be beneficial if you were to sit in while she tells me her story, and I agree because I seem to remember you saying you remembered some stuff from when you used to go with Marie down to the river while she sketched.

"I'm beginning to get a gut feeling that all is not kosher in Clinton and hasn't been for a long time, especially with the *clubbers.*"

"Anything I can do to help. I've got an ax to grind or better yet, whack em' with myself, at least one of them anyway," said Karen.

I glanced quizzically over at Karen with her last statement, but Baby spoke before I could say anything.

"Who's Marie?"

"My deceased wife and Karen's big sister," I lamented as my glance went back to Baby and then down to my hands on the table. "It's a long painful and depressing story, but suffice to say, she was a wonderful, talented woman."

I was struggling to keep my anguish under control, and I know my voice was probably barely audible but she had asked, and for some reason, I continued. "I wasn't there for her when she died or probably for the last few years of our marriage even. I was and am a drunk, hiding my guilt in booze. The worst part is I was too self-absorbed to even tell her I loved her the night she died in a car crash hurrying to a dinner I was too drunk to be at. End of story."

I looked at Karen, praying she would not add to this, but it didn't matter; it just didn't fucking matter anymore. She just sat there toying with her food and did not look up until Baby spoke again.

"Dirk and Karen, I'm so sorry about your loss. I didn't mean to bring up bad memories, but grief is why we're here tonight. I can empathize with you because the story I'm going to tell you is about not only the loss of both my parents but, and this I believe with all my heart, but their murder and the subsequent cover-up behind it."

This got my attention despite the roiling in my soul from opening the portal of my curse.

For the next hour or so, Baby unraveled a web of history, suspicions, and intrigue that supplanted our dinners, our splendid view and even cocktails, if you can believe that.

She began with her earliest memories which included her own experiences and the details of her family as explained to her by her father, William Edgar Mintz, or Rembrandt, as everyone knew him.

"My name *is* actually Baby, Baby Hobbs-Mintz. I'm the daughter of the late Samantha Hobbs who mercifully committed suicide at thirty five. My mom started working as a waitress at the Clinton Country Club from the time she was sixteen. She was able to work there so young because she was very beautiful and mature beyond her years, so she passed easily for eighteen, so my dad told me. She had run away from home just a few weeks before getting the job there. She had told my dad that her father had sexually abused her, and her sister before her, for several years and her mother became a drunk to escape the truth about what was going on in their home.

"My mother had taken a bus from Utica, New York, to Clinton because that's all she had money for. She answered an ad for a waitress job at the country club, and Dr. Bernie was the person who interviewed her. Suspecting she was without enough money to support herself he offered his small furnished efficiency apartment above the garage at his home office free until she got on her feet. Her life was starting to turn around, or so she thought. Her looks and aptitude for the job made her an instant favorite for the special dinners and closed parties.

"One night, at one of their big events, she was raped repeatedly and beaten by some of the members and later left to die by being tossed in the river. Somehow she did not die, and managed to make it to the shore where my father found her unconscious. My father took her to Dr. Bernie's house because it was close. He recognized her and together with my father, got her up to her apartment, and treated her. Dr. Bernie told my father it was best for all concerned she not be taken to the hospital and that he could take care of her there.

"My father told me he, at the time, didn't quite understand why, but as long as she was getting care that was all that mattered. During the next three or four months, my mother really never progressed to more than a semiconscious state. She was able to eat and take care of herself, but she remained 'out of it,' as my father said.

"My father stayed with her as much as he could, especially at night because she had horrific nightmares and would wake up in mortal fear. Sometimes while holding her to calm her down he would get bits and pieces of the events contributing to her present state. Dr. Bernie would give her sedatives to calm her, and at first, they helped, but after a while, he needed to increase the potency.

"My father, never having been around women much, didn't notice she was not having her periods. When the morning sickness started, Doc, being an OB-GYN, had his suspicions. So he tested her and revealed she was pregnant, with me. My dad, who as you by now know, is not my biological father. He loved me and raised me and he was the best father anyone could ask for. So as far as I'm concerned, he *is* my father.

"He continued to care for my mother almost day and night. He hardly ever went back to his own place across the river above the One Hour Dry Cleaners on Center Street. When I was born, Dr. Bernie, by law, had to issue a birth certificate and listed Samantha Hobbs and William Mintz as parents, but since the birth did not take place in a hospital, the certificate did not have to be of public record, which again he said was best for all concerned.

"Although Doc contributed financially some to our new family, his wife, also a doctor, kept a tight rein on their finances. He had somehow managed to keep this whole thing from her. The time he spent away from her and with us was of no consequence to her, but any unaccounted expenses would be. In order to provide the necessities for his newly inherited family, Dad tried to get more work but it was scarce. Over the years. he'd had many offers from area art aficionados to sell his works for him at a wide variety of venues. Being a time for revenue—not pride—he relented and began selling some of his own stash, as he called them, piece by piece.

"My mother, in the meantime, became addicted to the drugs given her to calm her and when it didn't kill the demons, she added booze to escape. When she couldn't satisfy her needs at home, she took to the streets and prostituted herself for money or drugs, leaving me alone. I was maybe two or three at the time. My dad, learning of about this, decided he just couldn't care for me, work, and keep my mother off the streets. He talked to Doc, and they made arrangements for my mom to be admitted to the River View Sanitarium for treatment. Fast forward ten years, during which time I was home-schooled by my dad and Dr. Bernie. I spent my free time playing down by the bridge with some homeless friends of mine, while my dad painted and did odd jobs to enable us to survive."

Karen interrupted at this point and said, "That's where I remember you from. When I used to go down to the river with my sister, I used to see you there!"

"You're right, because I'm pretty sure I remember you and your sister, although I thought she was your mother at the time. The reason I remember is because no one else from your side of the river ever paid any of us any mind, except to try to get us to move on down the river so we wouldn't tarnish their precious tourist season."

"Sorry for the interruption," said Karen. "But I just knew I'd seen you somewhere"

"Well, to sum up this woeful saga, my mom was released from River View after ten years when I was fourteen, and she was okay for about three or four months. One day, she ran into one of her attackers, although she wouldn't say who, while walking home from buying some groceries and it rekindled all her suppressed memories, not only from her rape, but also from the sexual abuse she faced at an early age.

"We were living at my dad's place on Center Street. I remember she told us, 'I can't live here and subject Baby to the same degrading rape and theft of innocence I have gone through. I have to protect her from that.' Then she left. I never saw her again.

"My dad said she'd be okay, she was strong now. I never really knew her, only the last few months and besides I was now in Junior High School, thanks to some strings pulled by Doc and I was doing well, especially in art class.

"Several months went by and things were pretty much the way they were before my mom came home, except my dad seemed a little more worried. One day, he came up to me and told me he'd just located my mother's sister in California, and he was sending me to live there with her and her husband until I finished high school. It would be a really better life for me, and it wasn't up for discussion. He said he had found my mother, and this is what she wanted for me too—actually it was her decision.

"We argued and cried for days, and finally, I told him okay if you don't want me, I'll go! Dad was crying when he said it wasn't that he didn't want me, it was he wanted what was best for me. He told me my mother had gone back to her old habits. He was buying her booze every day to keep her off the streets. He even had Doc going to see her trying to convince her to go back to River View for treatment. He convinced me that when he had things in order here he would come out to Los Angeles and we could be together again. Besides he said, my aunt promised him she would put me through college if I came to live with her because it was the least she could do for us after all we had been through. So I got on a plane and off I went to my Aunt Kathleen and Uncle Hugh's house in sunny California.

"My father wrote me every week, asking me how I was doing and telling me about his new paintings. After a few months, he skipped a couple of weeks, and I began to worry. When I finally received his next to last letter, he told me my mother had committed suicide. He and Doc had found her with her wrists slashed under the Main Street Bridge, a refuge for the city's homeless, where she had been living for the last few months. It appears that besides my dad taking her booze every day, Doc had been going down there once a week to check on her, along with the other homeless people living there.

"My father wrote that her brutal rape sixteen years ago had actually killed her. Her suicide was merely the end of the sentence to a lifetime of fear and mental anguish imposed by those who took her innocence. Even though he couldn't prove who committed her rape, he was pretty sure he knew who at least one or two of them were, and he was going to try to make them pay one way or another. He added that it's about time these animals stopped holding this community hostage for their own profit and amusement. His last letter followed two weeks later, and that's the one Dirk I wrote you about."

We were all quiet for a moment while we let this all sink in. I finally told Baby and Karen about the conversation I overheard at the cub the other night.

I said, "It had to have been those bastards. They, for all intents and purposes, admitted it. We got those smug pricks. Excuse me, ladies. but I've waited a long time for those guys to get their collective asses kicked, and I'm really sorry for you, Baby, that it took your mother's death to bring these scum to the surface, but she may not have been the first one or the last one that this kind of terrible thing has happened to."

Then she dropped the bomb. "Dirk, I don't want to get involved in this personally any more than this conversation. Sure I want to see my father's murderer or murderers brought to justice, but I don't want to drag this whole sordid saga through the media frenzy it will generate if these good ol' boys are guilty of what we suspect. I don't want my aunt and uncle brought in to it. They don't deserve it, any of it. My mother is dead and now, so is my father. I only wanted to vindicate their names and reputations. I know you'll be hard pressed to accept this, but what's in the past is in the past. My mother did what she did because of something evil that happened to her many years ago. It went unsolved, even unreported then. What makes you think that it will be any different now? These men have an even tighter choke hold on this community now than they did twenty years ago. Besides, I know who my father was, and I don't want one of them thinking anything else.

"What I do want is for you to find out what my father found that he was ultimately killed for and who did it. Will you try and do that for me and for my father?"

"But it's all got to be connected somehow," I said excitedly. "Don't you see? If these guys were indeed responsible for what happened to your mother, they should be strung up by the balls for the whole world to see. Everyone should know; it doesn't matter what your position in society is. If you do the crime, you do the time."

Baby and Karen both snorted again and then once again in unison said, "Get real, Dirk."

Karen volunteered, "That's not going to happen, Dirk, not here not anywhere. I'm sorry to say but maybe if it happened yesterday and Jesus Christ himself was a witness maybe, just maybe you'd have a chance, a slim one at best, but a chance."

"What about Doc Johnson? He knows what happened. We'll get him to come forward."

Karen came back with, "If my memory serves me, isn't his son one of the good ol' boys? Wasn't he involved in the clubbers' confessional conversation you overheard the other night? What makes you think he'd rat out his own son? Like I said, Dirk, get real."

Baby looked at her watch, not a good sign that I was going to win her over on this. So I thought, oh, well I'll just pursue this on my own.

As if reading my thoughts, Baby said, "Dirk, my father said you were the only one in Clinton that whatever you might appear to be, you were the only one he felt he could trust to help me if something ever happened to him. Was he right or was he wrong?" Her violet eyes pierced me clear to my soul.

"I'll never really understand why he thought that of me, but okay. One thing though, if in the course of my investigation—"

"No buts, I mean it, Dirk. My father was a good-hearted, compassionate, and extremely talented man. No one here, except Doc and my mother, even knew his name. That didn't bother him. Notoriety meant squat to him. He deserves better than what he got. I don't want him remembered as a drunk who fell in the Clinton River and drowned. I want it known he was murdered and why, period"

"You know what Baby. So do I—so do I."

With that, Baby said she had to go—that she had an early morning ski date with Aunt Kathleen and then they were flying home early Sunday. She said she'd like to keep abreast with my investigation and she'd stay in touch.

Karen said she was bushed, and she was going to bed which also happened to be at the hotel. She knew I was about to ask a bunch of questions, but she silenced me by saying, "Dirk, here's my phone and room number. I will call you in a day or so and explain everything. Just know I'm great, best I've been in a while. Good night, Bro."

And with that she gave me a peck on the cheek and turned and headed toward the elevators.

So there I was. One minute sitting with two beautiful women, and now I was left alone to try and absorb all that was said tonight. What did she call it—my investigation?

Well, at least whatever it was, I was supposed to do now to keep everyone happy—had an official title. One which I was not sure I was up to, but I was beginning to feel some responsibility here, a feeling which had not been in my cupboard since Jack Daniels took up residence there. I kind of liked the feeling.

Since the weather out on the runway was getting worse, I decided against having an intimate conversation with Mr. Daniels, so I got up and left the dining room. I retrieved my coat and called the valet to bring my car around and went home.

CHAPTER 8

I WOKE UP UGLY. *The nightmare* again. I probably shouldn't have had that last dose of JD before I went to bed. When I got home last night, instead of going over Baby's story, I started thinking about Marie again, probably the Burton Cummings tape set it off, plus the snowy night. I don't know, but if these friggin' nightmares keep demonizing my sleep, I'll be at the River View Sanitarium myself making little arts and crafts, or I'm going to wake up dead one morning.

I decided I should share this new information with Kristen Harden on Monday, off the record. I'd promised to keep her posted on the progress of my story. Story, what story? All I had so far was an overheard conversation; the tale of a family shattered by an unreported, unsubstantiated rape that allegedly took place over eighteen years ago. This, from a young woman in Los Angeles with no record on file of a birth certificate or any other kind of proof what she said was true. Great, just friggin' great; Harden ought to love this.

I just kind of vegged the rest of the weekend. I watched some basketball and caught some old movies on TV. I ate whatever I could scavenge from the freezer and drank some Labatt Ice. Well, maybe more than some.

On Monday morning, after I showered and shaved, I headed to the *Journal*. It was about 9:00 a.m. when I got to my desk. I called Harden and caught her in. I asked if I could talk to her about my story, and she said she only had a few minutes, but to come on up.

When I got to her office, the door was open and she told me to come in and close the door. She had arranged two leather-bound office chairs facing each other and told me to have a seat. I did, and she took the one facing me. She crossed her legs, giving me a pretty good view of her shapely thighs. She noticed that I noticed and we both smiled, mine sheepish and hers playfully seductive.

"Okay, Dirk Crandell, what's up?"

"Kristen, you said to keep you posted on how things were going on my story. So that's what I'm doing. But this has to be completely off the record for now until I can sort through what I have and can prove any of it, okay?"

There it was, that switch from a seductress to an all business managing editor. I don't know how she does it, but her hemline even seemed to come down to cover more. "All right, let's hear what you have."

She already knew about the letter from Baby because that's what got this whole thing going. So I proceeded to tell everything the best I could as to what was said Friday night. I left out nothing, not even my outburst of excitement about finally nailing these pompous assholes once and for all.

And I also told her of Baby's request that she just wanted her father's recent "murder" resolved and the subsequent defiling of his reputation undone. I was to leave the rape part alone because of the "media frenzy," as she put it that would surround a case of this magnitude in this rinky dink community. Not her words exactly, I said, I may have embellished some of it, but that was the gist of it. Baby had demanded that her and her aunt's and uncle's lives be left out of it.

Harden seemed to mull this entire story over for a mere few seconds and then she rendered this directive to me. The manner in which she did this left no doubt as to its meaning.

"Dirk, I totally agree with Baby's decision to skip the part about the rape. Here's the way it would go down. First, it happened what, eighteen years ago, no report, no witness, nothing. If you were to bring this up now everyone in Clinton is aware of the hard-on you have for these guys at the club. You have the reputation of being a drunk, and even if this story is real, of which I have some doubt, who would touch it? You need to walk very softly and respect her wishes on this. Besides the *Clinton Journal* is owned by none other than TR Foster, one of the as you call them, the good ol' boys who coincidently was there, according to you. Finally Dirk, what lawyer or public defender would want to commit political suicide and try this case. So as of now, purely from a politically logical point of view, Dirk, as far as nailing these guys for their alleged rape of Baby's mother, I'd say you've reached a stone wall."

"This is not just fucking right, Kristen!" I said heatedly. "These guys went overboard with this and then they just go merrily on their way as though nothing happened. It's just not right, damn it!"

"No, it's not right, Dirk, but that's life in the little city. But hold on, before you go stomping out of here to the Crypt and get shit faced. What if in your investigation of Rembrandt's murder it turns out that somehow one of these guys is involved. It seems kind of obvious to me that in a small town like Clinton when a man known for his art work and benevolence in the community and was never concerned about money, dies suspiciously after writing his daughter that he couldn't prove the rape, but he had something else on one or more of the suspected criminals. And, that it was going to earn him some money to help the child of the crime. Think about it, Dirk. If you solve Rembrandt's murder, you may kill two birds with one stone."

I sat there for a moment, letting what she said sink in. She could be right.

"I'll have to think about this. I want to talk to Dr. Johnson about it to see if he'll verify any of Baby's story."

Harden said softly, "Dirk, I'm afraid that is impossible. You see Dr. Johnson had a massive heart attack last night, and he died in the hospital this morning. I'm sorry."

"Shit, I'm never gonna catch a friggin' break on this, am I?"

I went back down to my desk, and just as I got there Melissa was dropping off a package at my desk. I said thanks and then opened it. There were two keys on a key ring in it with a note that said:

> Dirk I forgot to give you these Friday night. They are the keys to my dad's apartment over the dry cleaners and the other is for the garage apartment at Doc's home office. As far as I know, they are unrented because of my father's paintings and things. You may want to check things out. I don't think they can do anything with them until the court is sure there is no family to take possession. Don't wait too long, and you'll be lucky if anything is even still in either of them.
>
> Take care,
> Baby

Too bad about old Doc Johnson. As it turns out he was a pretty compassionate old guy, checking on the well-being of the homeless and taking Samantha under his wing and all, especially after her assault. Maybe it was just protective guilt for his son Junior, who happened to be one of the good ol' boys. Maybe good ol' boy Junior was in on the assault, and his dad knew or at least suspected he was involved. Regardless, a good man had passed.

Well, I needed some place to start, so I took the keys and since I figured it would be insensitive even for me to intrude on the Johnsons so soon after old Doc's passing, I thought I'd check out Rembrandt's digs. Given that it was only about a four-block walk to the One Hour Dry Cleaners, and it was a balmy above freezing Western New York day, I decided to walk there.

After checking with the oriental proprietor Hung Lo or Wang Hie or Hu Flung Poo whatever, I learned that the entrance to Rembrandt's apartment was in the rear of the building—in the alley running along the Clinton River. I said I was a friend and asked if it would be okay to see it.

He told me it was okey dokey for now, but soon he was going to let his cousin from Hong Kong live there when he arrived next month to help with his business. At least that's what I think he said.

So around back I went. The alley was actually just a service road for deliveries and garbage pickups for the businesses on Center Street.

I had no trouble finding which set of stairs led to Rembrandt's loft because the steam coming from the vents at the rear of the building left no doubt it was the dry cleaners. The apartment was up two flights of stairs which ended with a small balcony of sorts which had a spectacular view of the river and the marina. With the air clear and crisp and the sky as near to Carolina blue as Western New York would ever see, the vista was an artist's canvas just waiting to be personalized. No wonder Rembrandt lived here.

I tried one of the keys, it wouldn't work. Voila, the old 50-50-90 rule. If there's a fifty-fifty chance of making the right choice, there's a 90 percent probability one will make the wrong one. So I tried the second key and enter I did.

It was dark and musty, but I found the light switch and switched it on. I couldn't believe my eyes. Sweet Jesus! The place was completely trashed, and I mean trashed. I opened what was left of the window blinds and turned around to survey the damage.

The loft was comprised of three rooms—a living room-slash-bedroom that measured maybe 12' by 15' which, from my best guess, served as his studio and sleeping area. Then there was a galley-type kitchen, with barely enough room for a small table, and a 3S bathroom—a room you could shit, shower and shave by just doing a pirouette. But none of that mattered now. He must have had fifteen paintings either completed or in the process. All were cut to shreds and cast around like Christmas morning gift wraps. His dresser was empty of drawers which were also thrown about. The kitchen cupboards and contents were also a part of the rampage as well as his 3S room. Even the toilet tank cover was not spared.

Was this part of his final inebriated rage which led to his drunken swan song dive into the chilly dark waters of the Clinton River?

I flashed back to what Baby had said that Rembrandt never touched booze. I surveyed the tornado like demolition and started my search anew. Nothing, not a trace of any kind of booze at all was apparent in what was left of his stuff. So if it was true what Baby was trying to convince me of, and it wasn't a drunken tirade, what motive could someone have had to do this?

Not money that's for sure. Everyone in town knew him. No, this was more than a robbery. This was either revenge or someone was looking for something specific. Judging by the degree of the destruction, my money was on the latter. I'd guess whoever it was didn't find what they were searching for. This young lady's suppositions were becoming more and more credible by the minute.

What a waste. Not only was a great artist dead, but the few remaining treasures of his talent were destroyed also. Now I was more than curious, I was fucking pissed.

I turned off the light and locked the door, although I'm not sure what for. What was left other than notifying the police? If the way they handled his death was any indication of how they would handle a B&E, why even bother. So I didn't.

I surveyed the panoramic view of the river one more time from Rembrandt's small balcony, and it dawned on me that unless I was mistaken Rembrandt's body was found floating under the bridge. That's upstream from here. If indeed he was that drunk, how did he make it up the alley, down the three blocks to the bridge, cross it and fall in the river? Unless of course, he took the booze with him and drank it there. That would also explain why there was no booze in the loft. But wouldn't you think if someone was as much of a drunk as he was supposed to be, there would be some remnants of it somewhere in his stuff? Even an empty bottle or beer can in the trash?

I wanted to ask the owner of the dry cleaners if he had heard any unusual noises coming from the loft over the last couple of months and tell him I was finished looking in there when on my way out of the alley, but who should I spy but David Weatherford IV slinking out of the backdoor of his jewelry business and locking it.

I said, "I'll be damned if it isn't David Weatherford. My, my, what a large red nose you have."

I think I must have surprised him, because he turned to face me so fast I think he may have gotten whiplash.

"Crandell, how long have you been here?" he asked almost too nervously.

"Calling it quits so early in the day?"

"I asked you how long have you been here?" he asked belligerently.

"Don't get your shorts in a knot," I said. "And what difference does it make anyway even if I had slept here in the alley all night. You got something illegal goin' on, Davey do?"

"What do you mean by that?" he snapped.

"Whoa, relax," I said, a little surprised by his terse response. "I meant nothing, unless of course you do. I was merely inquiring because most businesses don't close up shop at two in the afternoon on a Monday."

"Well, if it's any of your business, which it's not by the way, I'm going over to Clinton Windows and Doors to see about getting a new backdoor and have them take out my window."

"Why? The door looks fine to me, or is it that your wife is finally dumping your sorry ass and you're getting your locks changed here, as well as your mansion up on the hill?" I teased.

"Fuck you, Crandell! You're always such a wise ass. Why don't you just move away from here and do everyone in this town a favor?"

"Well well now, aren't we cranky today? Not enough powder to ski on you, coke head? And besides, if I left, who'd be here to keep adding some wang to your goofy-ass galas at the club?"

"Why don't you go drink yourself into a stupor and go swimming in the river like your souse of a friend did a while ago."

"Whoa, wait a minute here, you pompous fucker," I said, fielding that crack from *way* out in left field. "First, if you're talking about Rembrandt, he wasn't a souse, you doped-up shit, and how do you know he was my friend? How do you know anything about me?"

"You forget, asshole, TR owns the paper you work for, and he knows all that goes on there."

"Well, you shits have even more in common than I thought. TR knows all, and you're all nose," I retorted with barely controlled anger.

"Drop dead, Crandell, and go join your wife."

My controlled anger evaporated, and I grabbed him by the front of his coat and lifted his sorry ass right off the ground and got right in his face so that when I hissed at him, my spittle sprayed him. "Don't *you ever* even think of my wife's name again, or I swear by all that's good in this world, I'll kill you dead, and then I'll pick you up and kill you again!"

With that, I put him down. I surprised myself with my restraint. If Mr. Daniels had been with me, I probably would have beat the shit outta him and then lived to regret it—him being who he is with his friends, and me being who I am with no friends. I'll probably wind up in the clink for assault anyway.

As he stood there looking at me, I think he was as surprised as I was that his lights were still on and not punched out. Just before he turned to cower away, I noticed a spreading wet spot on the front of his pants, and I'm sure he knew that I knew. By God, there is some kind of justice in this town after all, although mine—as far as the *clubbers* go—somehow always revolves around urine.

I went back around to Ho Chi Min's Dry Cleaner's, and rather than explain anything to him, I lied and told him the key I had didn't fit, so no sweat. He said, "Okey dokey," and I left.

I headed back to the *Journal* to see if there was any more news on Dr. Johnson's passing and to make sure that Melissa was okay with his obit. After all that I had learned recently about Dr. Bernie, the least I could or the *Journal* could do was to make sure the one he received from us was worthy.

I found Melissa and began to tell her how Dr. Johnson's obit should mention some of the compassion in his life not commonly known should be included, but she cut me off in midsentence.

"Mr. Crandell, I've already received his obituary or as it's officially entitled, 'Dr. Bernard Johnson; A tribute to life.' from Ms. Johnson. It was personally handed to me only a few minutes ago by none other than TR Foster himself stating that, and I quote. 'This is what we'll print, period.'"

"Okay, no sense in arguing with God. Besides, I'm sure all what old Doc would have wanted said about him is included, makes your job easier. By the way how's it going?"

"Good, as you said, this job's a piece of pie, especially if Mr. Foster and Ms. Harden keep telling me exactly what to do."

"Cake."

"What?"

"Cake," I said, "piece of cake, not pie."

"Oh yeah, cake"

I'll reserve my immediate thoughts on her wisdom for another time.

I did learn there was going to be a celebration of life service at St. Paul's Church tomorrow morning at 10:00 a.m. That would give me a chance to zip over to Samantha's apartment without interfering with the mourning ritual. Besides I wanted to call Baby and break the news to her personally about Dr. Bernie's passing, and I also wanted to talk to Karen to find out what was up with her.

I placed the call to Baby in Los Angeles and as gently as I could, told her about her friend. Silence ensued for what seemed to be a very long time. I was just about to ask her if she was still there when she said very quietly.

"Thanks for letting me know personally, Dirk. I have to go and cry now. Good-bye."

And with that she hung up.

I bet she will, I thought. I bet her beautiful violet eyes will cry until there are no tears left and then I'll bet she'll weep more, not only for Dr. Bernie but for her dad, her mom, and for all of the shit that her young life has endured because of a few fuckers, literally, here in Clinton. At least, she has her aunt and uncle to help console her. Poor, Baby.

Not much going on a Monday afternoon in a snow-choked Clinton. The sunlight and Carolina Blue were rapidly being replaced by the lake-effect storm which began to arrive while we were at the Marriot on

Friday. Having given the area a short respite it was once again beginning to dump, it's glistening treasure and made the view from the my fifth story office windows look like a Currier and Ives winter wonderland. It was still relatively early in the day, so I thought now might be a good time to call Karen. I really should make the call from home and besides, judging from the increasing intensity of this squall I was observing, home was beginning to look like a very cozy place to be.

By the time I'd arrived home, the plows were out in full force. As I turned onto my street, I could see the snow and slush laden plow heading toward my house. The race was on! The only question now was could I make my driveway before the evil sultan of city streets in his monster truck buried the access to my drive. Slip sliddin' away, I skidded into the approach just in time. Rumble, rumble, whoosh, and my car was buried in. Better buried in than buried out on the street.

I trudged my way into my humble abode, shook off the accumulation of white confetti on my person, went straight to the fireplace and lit a fire. Then I poured myself a large drink and found Karen's new number and called her.

She picked up on the second ring. "Karen, it's Dirk, do you have some time?"

"Dirk, it's good to hear from you, and yes, I do. This storm has closed the airport, and it's my day off anyway, but I'm on call should the stranded passengers decide to pull a Dirk Crandell and spend the wait on a bar stool."

"Could be worse ways to spend a long delay."

"You're right."

"Hey what's up, sis. I stopped by the Crypt a few times, and you were a no show. Now I see you working at the Marriot."

"I've been going to call you, but I wanted to get settled first. Anyway, about two months ago, I was sitting at the bar here, and I ran into a guy named Tom Gardinier. I've known since just after high school, and he's the manager here at the Marriot now. We got talking and one thing led to another and we've started dating. Dirk, he's a really nice guy. I haven't met too many of them in my life as you know. Well, anyway, the day you last saw me at the Crypt, dickhead Carl Southerland, who owns the place and who's always making lewd remarks to women especially employees, grabbed my ass for the last time, so I quit.

"Besides that, Dirk, and you have to promise me you won't be mad at me for what I'm about to tell you."

"What is it, Karen?"

"Promise, or I won't tell you."

I thought it over for a long minute and said, "Okay, I promise."

"Well, about a year ago, I was really down and stoned when I went into work. Southerland was really mad at me because he was short-handed. He was going to fire me.

"I really needed the job and well, one thing led to another and he . . . well, he . . . took advantage of me in the storage room."

"Son of a bitch!" I yelled. "I'm going to kill him."

"Dirk, you promised, and besides, I was so stoned, he lost interest after a few minutes and just told me to go back to work and don't ever say anything about this or I *would* be fired. And he added by the way, I owed him one."

Again, I was silent, and I was sure she could hear the steam coming out of my nostrils like a raging bull.

"Karen," I said. "Do realize what this guy is doing to women? Didn't you hear what Baby said he did to her mother? Jesus, sis, we can't just let this continue to happen."

"I want you to let it go. You promised. I'm happy now, and I have a good job, and I don't want Southerland and his cronies causing me any more trouble. He's not worth it. Believe me, Let it go for me. He will get his one day, Dirk. Remember, time wounds all heels."

"Does Tom know?"

"I called Tom and told him what had happened. He was furious and was going to come down and beat him to a bloody pulp. I talked him out of it and told him, trust me, he wasn't worth it."

"I really don't like this, but I promised you, and if Tom can live with it well . . ."

"Please, Dirk."

"Okay," I relented and then as an afterthought added, "Hey, didn't you say Southerland owns the Crypt?"

"Yeah, sort of a silent partner kind of thing.

"Well, I'll be damned. I thought I knew everything about the bars in Clinton but this is news to me. I wonder if there is anything in Clinton the good ol' boys don't own."

"Well, anyway, Tom invited me for dinner to talk about my future, now that I was unemployed, and I said, yes. I feel so happy, and I don't know, secure maybe, when I'm with him. Dirk, we really hit it off. I really like the guy; we have a lot in common. Seems we can talk for hours about everything and nothing. When we're together, it's like we're alone, even in a crowded restaurant. So anyway, he offered me a job and a place to stay at the Marriot for as long as I want it. No strings attached."

"Well, sis, I'm happy for you. I know you looked the happiest I've seen you in years the other night."

"Oh, Dirk, I am, and I wanted to tell you Friday, but I didn't want to interfere with your meeting."

"I'm glad you joined us though. I can't tell you enough how relaxed you looked, and besides, my opinion versus yours and Baby's as to how this investigation should proceed has been acquiesced by my mentor, Ms. Harden, so the ladies have it. Me, personally, well, you are probably right. My vengeance would undoubtedly get in the way of facts. So when do I get to meet this Prince Charming?"

"We're having dinner at Salvatore's tonight as you know my favorite place. Tom says he has a surprise for me. Oh, Dirk, I feel like a schoolgirl again," she actually giggled, no kidding, she giggled.

"Well now, my little sister, be careful and take it slow. Have fun and call me when you get a chance."

CHAPTER 9

T HE STORM MUST HAVE ended early in the evening because in the morning when I opened my door to get the *Journal*, there really wasn't much snow at all, only three or four inches of the light stuff. I hadn't really looked out at it last night because I heard the plows go by a couple of times, and I just figured we got really dumped on. I'd watched the Sabres get their butts kicked by Ottawa until the fire got low and then went to bed.

So when I retrieved the paper, I was surprised. I was even more surprised even that my driveway had been plowed. Must be the kid next door finally got his plow hooked up to his truck. It's only January, and it started snowing this year right after Halloween. What can I say, the kid has a few of the pages of his book of life stuck together, but I get my drive plowed for free, so no complaints here.

Given that it was Tuesday, and all the memorials for Doc Johnson were over, I didn't think my going over to Sam's apartment located over the Johnsons' garage would be an intrusion. I called into Harden's office letting her know I was still working on this story, and I'd talk to her as soon as there were any solid developments. Damn, I was beginning to even sound like a detective.

The Johnsons have this magnificent manor overlooking the picturesque bend in the Clinton River. It's still in the heart of the city, but strategically located so as to capture all the rural majesty of a country estate and still have their practices easily accessible from the front street-side.

I pulled into the drive and headed around to the side where the garages were, suspecting that was probably where the access to Sam's apartment was located. I passed several visitor's cars in the drive meaning I should not have to explain my presence to anyone, although I'm pretty sure no one even knew about Sam's living here—especially since it was such a long time ago.

I was also hoping old Dr. Johnson had just left things as they were and not re-rented the studio or turned it into storage or something.

I entered the lower door and went up the long back stairway to the studio. I'm guessing that many, many years ago this probably served as servants' quarters for the previous owners. There were two doors at the top of the stairs. One had a padlock and the other had a new door with a key set. My guess is this would be Sam's. I tried the key Baby had given me, and I was afforded entry into the small studio apartment. Except for the layers of accumulated dust from numerous months of inactivity, the place was intact.

I don't know what I was expecting, but everything seemed to be cool. I thought there was a good chance this would be my only opportunity to check the place out and I did so, thoroughly.

I took my time and looked in every nook and cranny of which there were few. Not much here; nothing that would give any kind of indication as to the type of person who had lived here. No books or magazines. Not much in the way of toiletries or perfumes. Not much of anything really. The second to last place I had to look was a small dresser by the sofa bed. The first drawer revealed nothing really. Some nondescript women's underwear and socks. The second drawer had a couple of sweaters and blouses neatly folded. The third drawer contained a frameless painting of what I assumed to be Sam holding a baby. Even at this young age, it held a remarkable resemblance to Baby. Having seen enough of Rembrandt's work over the years, I knew this was his genius. If he was indeed a student of Wyeth, he'd been a very extraordinary learner. I also read somewhere that Wyeth had chafed under criticism from some experts who regarded him as a facile artist, not an artist but merely an illustrator. This painting by Rembrandt, or W.E. Mintz as it was signed, was anything but an illustration. It was, I don't know a word for it—maybe mesmerizing, yeah, mesmerizing.

The most awe-inspiring part of this work was the absolute love and serenity captured on the face of the woman in the painting. Talk about artistry; this was unbelievable. This was going with me and straight to Baby.

There was a small closet on the other side of the sofa bed. Again, nothing much here either, a coat and a couple of waitress uniforms, already yellowing from age. On the floor in the back there was a shoe box. There were three pairs of shoes, but only one box. Now I don't know a lot about women, but one thing I learned from Marie was that women for some reason never get rid of their shoeboxes. So I decided to have a look.

When I picked it up, it felt empty. It was, except for the tissue paper. However under the tissue paper I could see a business-size envelope. I opened it, and its contents revealed a handwritten letter addressed to me and a bunch of film negatives. Holy shit, I got goose bumps the size of marbles. I unfolded and read the letter. It was from Rembrandt.

Dirk,

I hope if anyone finds this, it's you. I told Baby she could trust you to do the right thing to end this entire Clinton charade. It's gone on entirely too long. I know you're the right person to follow up on this because it is common knowledge there is no love lost between you and who I believe you used to call them the good old boys.

By accident, I happened to discover a criminal activity playing upon the citizens of my beloved Clinton by at least one of these pseudo stalwarts, David Weatherford IV. He's been switching the diamonds in the rings he's been selling when they come back into his store for whatever reason and replacing them with other stones of some sort. I suspect this is the case because the stones he removes are put in the safe and the ones he replaces them with come from a drawer in his bench. All of this is done after hours. I witnessed this from his rear window on more than one occasion unbeknownst to the ever high and unsuspecting thief. He obviously made little attempt to cover his felonious activities and was never aware that I was watching him and eventually photographing him.

The pictures contained within the negatives were taken on a lovely Indian Summer's eve when he actually had left his back door open. The pictures I took will reveal of what I suspect and write. Enclosed are the negatives of the photos I took of him in the act of his felony.

I should have gone to the police with my suspicions, but we both know how that would have turned out. Then I thought of you, because I knew you would chomp at the bit to slay one of the evil dragons of Clinton. But alas, I knew in the end that I could never make them pay for what they did to poor Samantha. So in my own selfish greed, I contrived a plan which I related to my daughter where I had discovered something that was going to enable us to be together at last.

I felt in my heart if I succeeded I could make at least one of them, pay for his rape of innocent citizens from his jewelry store business.

If indeed it is you reading this, then I have met my early demise at their hands undoubtedly. I hid these negatives here because Weatherford had knowledge of their existence, but not of their whereabouts. I'm also convinced he had no knowledge of this apartment or safe house as we referred to it. The reason he was aware of these negatives I'm ashamed to say, was my bungled attempt to blackmail him with them. I fear I wasn't the villain it takes to successfully accomplish that on someone of his standing.

So I have enlisted you, through my daughter, to continue my quest to bring some justice to this whole sordid conspiracy. Please, do what you can for my family, for you and for the hard working people of Clinton.

With gratitude eternal,
William E. Mintz.

PS: If indeed it is you reading this, you can most likely add murder to their list of evil doings.

I reread the letter, and for the second time in two weeks, I was absolutely slam dunked by the sinister details of what seems to be a long and sordid conspiracy to cover up a good ol' boys' night out really gone bad.

First, the overheard conversation at the country club, and now this letter. Not yet time to call in the cavalry, because I didn't think I had enough proof to nail their sorry asses to the wall. I needed something more, a lot more.

I folded the letter and put it back in the envelope put it in my breast pocket. I picked up the painting and surveyed the studio one last time. Convinced there was nothing else to gain, from being here other than getting caught trespassing and trying to explain my way out of it, I closed and locked the door and left.

CHAPTER 10

I DECIDED TO GO to the Bridge Tender for lunch and see what Carla had on special. Besides, I did some of my best thinking overlooking a Labatt Ice and the swirling Clinton River, in this case not in any particular order.

The lunch crowd was thinning and so I was in luck to get a table by the window overlooking the river. I spied Carla at the bar, and she gave me one of those nods like. "Hey, I see you, and I'll be over in a minute."

While I was waiting, I lit up a Lucky and took out my notepad to make some additions to my notes, which maybe now should be called my crime list.

Rembrandt was dead, and it looked like it was not the way it had or hadn't been reported.

Scratch Doc Johnson for any help, because he was also now dead. I had in my possession some negatives that were supposed to have caught Weatherford committing a crime. What crime?

Switching diamonds from unsuspecting customers? Maybe that's why Weatherford was replacing his backdoor and window, and was so spooked when I approached him because if he knew Rembrandt had witnessed him, someone else could too. Maybe whatever Weatherford was doing that he shouldn't have been doing was photographed through that window, and he wanted to make sure no one else saw it by chance. This would mean if it were a crime, it was probably an ongoing one. Maybe it all had to do with the photos Rembrandt had tried to blackmail him with.

I felt, rather than saw Carla's presence at my table and she said, "Besides a Labatt Ice, what can I do you for? The special today is lentil soup with Andouille sausage, and spinach with an egg salad, and alfalfa sprout sandwich on whole wheat."

"Sounds perfect."

After Carla's excellent lunch, I strolled across the street to Bellamy's camera shop to see if they could develop pictures from the negatives I had in my possession, and I was about to enter when a thought struck me. If TR owns the *Journal* and the building it's in, and Southerland owns the Crypt, what else do they own, and if there was incriminating stuff in the photos who would learn about it first, me or the sinister six? Hey, I like that. Instead of the good ol' boys, I would now refer to them as the sinister six. Let's see—TR Foster, Carl Southerland, David Weatherford IV, Allen Truehardt, Dr. Bernard Johnson Jr. Only five, but I'm sure there's more involved like McNeil, the club manager, and maybe even the Harrison brothers Oliver and Stanley, Clinton's chief of police and county coroner. God knows how deep this thing goes. But anyway, I like the sound of the sinister six. Sinister is more appropriate than good as far as these pricks are concerned. There I go again; letting my abhorrence for these guys get the best of me.

I turned around at the door and headed for my car. I would go to Eastport, a little burg about fifteen miles downriver from Clinton. Nope, too close. I'd be better off going to Buffalo. Lots of photo places there and the likelihood of any recognition of the subjects in the photos would be probably nonexistent.

The roads were clear, and about an hour into the drive, I spotted a Rite Aid Pharmacy in some little town which advertised one-hour picture development and to make things even better, there was the Dew Drop Inn right across the street. I dropped the negatives off, and the clerk said it shouldn't be a problem to get double prints, and it would be ready in an hour.

I went across the street and sat down at the bar. Other than the barmaid, I was the only patron. She was engrossed in *The Price Is Right* and talking to the TV with such enthusiasm, you'd think she was actually a contestant. I tried feigning a cough to get her attention which didn't work, and finally I called to her, "Hey, bar keep."

"Wait for a commercial," she said without turning around.

Okay, I thought, it can't be that long, so I lit up a Lucky and glanced around the place. Just like every other tavern in the world. A couple of tables along one wall, a bowling machine, just inside the front door and a jukebox near the back. I eyed the idle music vendor and heard a growl from the bar keep who never even turned around, "Don't even think about it, buddy, because I'll pull the plug and you'll never get a drink."

Okay, well, I'll just count the cars going by until somebody wins or loses or Bob Barker says, "We'll be back in two and two." Maybe that is some other afternoon game show delight. Whatever, I hoped it was soon.

No sooner did that thought pass through some of my dead brain cells than did little Miss Congeniality come over to me and utter the classic, "What'll it be, bub?"

"What's on tap?"

"You're sitting right in front of them, Einstein, you tell me."

"Genny Cream Ale, the Green Death, in that case," I sheepishly responded.

She drew me a half pitcher, and I told her I only wanted a glass.

She said, "Are you going to be here a while?"

"Yeah, about an hour."

"*The Young and the Restless* comes on in ten, so if you're going to want any more than one glass, you're going to be SOL."

"SOL?"

"Shit outta luck."

"Okey dokey, Rose."

"Rose," she said with her eyebrows raised, "how'd you know my name? You don't look familiar, and I never forget a face."

"It's tattooed on your forearm so I just took a stab at it."

"Very clever, so now we're even, Einstein. Anything else, nuts, pretzels, chips?"

"No, thanks, I wouldn't want my crunching to bother your programs."

"That's okay, I'd just turn up the volume so that you'd leave anyway."

So I sat and drank my Cream Ale and smoked more than I should have, and when I checked the Shultz and Dooley clock above the TV, it was time to go and pick up my photos. I tossed a fin on the bar said, "Keep it, keep," and left.

My pictures were ready when I got there, and the clerk didn't say anything so I asked if he'd looked at them to see if they came out all right.

He said it's all automated, and he doesn't even see them. He told me to look at them, and I quickly scanned them. They appeared to be good pictures. I really didn't look that close at their content; I would do that when I got back to my car. I paid the cashier and then left.

I felt like a little boy at Christmas and couldn't wait to see what Santa Mintz had left under my tree. I opened the cardboard photo envelope and noticed the negatives tucked neatly in the back. Good, I'd forgotten to ask for them back. I had asked for duplicates in case something happened to one set I'd have a spare, which I would keep in a safe place. Consequently, I now had an even better back up.

I carefully looked at each photo. Disappointment reigned supreme as I looked at one after another. They were pictures of the Clinton River from what looked like Rembrandts balcony. I don't know what I'd expected. Maybe Weatherford doing something dastardly but not landscapes. These were not worth dying for or committing a murder for.

When I got through with the first set, I just quickly filed through the second. Holy shit; there on the bottom of the pile were some pictures I hadn't seen in the first set. When I scanned through them in the store, I must have not put them back in the right order.

I was holding in my trembling hands several photos which were remarkably clear. They were of the unmistakable—Mr. Weatherford obviously working over a jeweler's bench either putting stones in a ring or removing the same. Aha, the plot thickens. I needed to talk to a real jeweler about fake diamonds and then I needed to set a trap for Mr. Weatherford.

As long as I was headed toward Buffalo anyway, I remembered where I had bought Marie's engagement and wedding ring set. A small family run business called Steinbeck's Fine Jewelry in Clarence Center which was on the way to Buffalo, only closer. Since it was already getting dark at 4:30 in the afternoon, I thought I could make it there before they closed.

The store being just off Main Street, I happened to find a place to park right out in front. I walked in and they still had the little tinkle bell announcing someone entering the premises. Old Mr. Steinbeck was behind his jeweler's bench and glanced up at me with a half of a binocular attached to his eye. From behind the curtain in back appeared a young man who appeared to be about twenty five or so. I assumed him to be Mr. Steinbeck's grandson.

"Can I help you, sir? We were just about to close, but we are always willing to accommodate our customers, aren't we, gramps?"

"I hope so," I said. "I bought my wife's wedding ring set here a several years ago and I'd like some information."

"If there's anything wrong with them, have her bring them in and we'll correct any problems she might have. We stand by our jewelry with a lifetime guaranty," said the young man.

"Well, my wife is deceased, and nothing is wrong with them, at least I don't think there is," I replied. "I really just have a couple of questions."

"We'd be glad to help you, Mr . . . . ?"

"Crandell, Dirk Crandell, and you may drop the Mr. Just call me, Dirk, my friend calls me that."

A puzzled look appeared on his face at the omission of the s from friends but me having no friends was not really pertinent to the circumstances as to why I was here.

"And your name is?" I asked.

"James Steinbeck III."

"I guess the first is sitting over there looking for the other half of his binoculars," I quipped.

He didn't see the humor, but he said, "Yes, that's my grandfather, and it's called a loupe"

"A what?"

"A loupe. The half of the binocular thing, as you called it, is a loupe."

"Okay, James, that wasn't really one of my questions, but it's interesting to know. So anyway here's my question. Would it be possible to switch a diamond out of a ring or other piece of fine jewelry without the owner's knowledge?"

This got the elder James's attention.

He looked over to me and said, "Yes, in fact it would, because the high price of gem-grade diamonds has created a large demand for stones with similar characteristics known as a diamond simularts or imitations. Diamond simulants may be artificial, natural, or in some cases, a combination thereof. While their material properties depart markedly from those of diamonds, simulants have certain desired characteristics—such as dispersion and hardness which lend themselves to imitation. Trained gemologists such as I, with appropriate equipment, are able to distinguish natural and synthetic diamonds from all diamond simulants, primarily by visual inspection. However to the average person, they wouldn't have a clue as to the difference, especially Moissanite. Although more expensive than cubic zirconia for example, Moissanite will even pass a Ceres CZeckpoint Tester. When pressing the point of the instrument to a diamond, it turns green. Moissanite does the same."

He went on to explain that, "it's becoming more and more popular for women travelers to come in and duplicate their settings and use cubics to travel with in case of loss or theft and leave the real jewelry at home."

So I asked, "Would it be worthwhile for some unsavory jeweler, not that there are any of course, to replace a real diamond with a high-quality cubic zirconia?"

"Most definitely. A three-quarter carat diamond with good color and good clarity costs about $3,600—a one carat of equal quality about $5,200. The price of a good quality cubic the same size is about $150."

"Holy shit! I'm in the wrong business."

Gramps continued, "and to your other statement, yes, there are unfortunately unsavory business people. I refrain from calling them jewelers, who would and do stoop to ruining people's keepsakes and heirlooms for their own ill begotten profit with no conscience whatsoever."

"Okay, one last thing. If I brought my wife's wedding set in to you, could you tell me if the diamonds are genuine?"

"If you purchased them here, I guarantee they are genuine and GIA certified," he said, somewhat unnerved.

"No, no what I'm getting at is—that although I bought them here, Marie took them to a local jeweler to be resized and personally, I don't trust the son of a bitch as far as I can throw him. She just assumed I bought them locally, and he never told her otherwise."

"Certainly, by all means, bring them in. It only takes a few moments to check them out. I can probably do it by eye. Unless of course if they are Moissante, then I'll need to test them further, which would involve removing them from their setting. But I can definitely tell you if they are indeed the gems you purchased here. You see, every diamond we sell here is GIA certified. The GIA, being the Gemological Institute of America. It is probably the foremost internationally recognized nonprofit authority of diamond grading and documentation."

He went on, and I could tell the information I was about to hear was critical to my plan. "Just as houses have deeds, vehicles have titles and registrations, pure bred pets have pedigree papers and an education is validated by a diploma, the GIA documentation verifies independent positive identification of diamonds. This is done with a GIS Diamond Grading Report or a GIA Diamond Dossier. The long and short of it is that this report contains the diamonds unique analysis of its four C's—color, cut, clarity, and carat weight. So aside from this report is a micro laser inscription on the diamonds girdle, the thin outer edge if you will, for an extra fee which I include in my cost. You can see by the decal in my window that I sell only GIA-certified diamonds. If you show me the rings you purchased here, I will unequivocally tell you if they're the same gems. I also keep duplicates of the certifications on file here."

"Do you advertise this GIA thing in your Yellow Page ad?"

"Certainly, jewelers of any repute would be foolish not to."

"Can I see your phone book for a minute please?"

I looked up Weatherford's in the Yellow pages, and sure enough there was the little logo saying all diamonds sold there were GIA certified.

"Mr. Steinbeck, I can't thank you enough for your time and information, and I'll see you tomorrow."

I stopped by the *Journal* to let Kristen know about my progress, and she was on her way out the door to some kind of fund raiser later that evening, but asked if I wanted to grab a quick drink and we could talk a little there.

Me want a drink? Is the Pope Catholic?

"Sure," I said.

We walked down into the Crypt, and we sat at a table on the far side of the room, away from the jukebox. The place was already filling up because it was happy hour and two for one drinks.

I flagged down the ever harried Bruce and ordered a Jack on the rocks for me and a Chardonnay for my impromptu date.

Placing our coats on the backs of our chairs, Harden wiggled and squirmed into her seat. Kind of reminded me of a dog getting ready to lie down, but that's where the dog resemblance ended. Maybe I'm getting horny again but damn, she was looking fine today.

The drinks arrived, and she and I both halved them in one swallow and after wiping her pouty lips on her napkin, she said. "Okay, Dirk, let me have it." Always with the double entendre.

"If you mean what I'd like you to mean, later after your meeting or whatever."

"No, silly. I mean what have you got for me, oh, shit," she said, "I already know that," as her eyes smiled playfully.

"Let me try this again, Hmmn . . . What have you found out about the thing you're working on. But I have to tell you, I only have a few minutes."

"Okay," I said, "In a nutshell, here's what I've got and let's not go there again. Remember, you're the one in a hurry.

"I am reasonably certain that Rembrandt did not get drunk and fall in the river and drowned. I'm also pretty sure that he was murdered for something he saw and took photos of. Then he tried to blackmail that person for enough money to go to Los Angeles to be with his daughter and help repay her aunt and uncle with her college expenses. Now hear me out before you lecture me about my hard on for the sinister six, as I now and forever will refer to them. I'm in the process of trying to set up a sting, if you will, to prove the information Rembrandt gave me implicating at least one of these assholes to be true. I am going to try to get Rembrandt's body exhumed to prove my theories of conspiracy to commit at least one murder and grand larceny. I'm hoping first of all that you, my boss, friend and lover will sit on all of this until I can get the toxicology report on Rembrandt. Then together with what evidence I already have in my possession, get charges brought against these criminals once and for all. That's about it, in a nutshell as I said."

"Lover?"

"Okay, maybe not lover for a one night stand, but you did want a rain check if I recall."

"It's fine by me. How about tonight after my Clinton Historic Restoration Committee's meeting? Say ten o'clock? Oh, and yes, to the other thing too."

"Other thing?"

"Yeah, the thing about sitting tight. I think from the sounds of it, you may be really on to something and I knew given the right set of circumstances your talents would rise from the ashes you created for yourself. Little did I suspect that I would enjoy the rise as much as I have and obviously will again."

"Kristen Harden, you're really something else, and thanks by the way. I'm looking forward to later, and I really think I'm on to something, and oh Jesus, just let it go at that."

After she left I grabbed a Beef on Weck and some fries and another drink. I then went home to wait for Kristen. At exactly nine the doorbell rang. I opened it and there she was with a bottle of Chardonnay in her hand. "I couldn't wait for the meeting to end thinking about happy hour."

"Happy hour ended at seven," I said

"Oh no, it didn't, Dirky, it's just starting and I'm hoping it's still twofers."

"So do I."

And it was.

CHAPTER 11

*T*HE DARK ROOM WAS *filled with flashing red lights, the wail of sirens and the sound of sleet pummeling the windows and the deadly knowledge that all of this somehow was being replayed for the all too many times to count. The terrible feeling—that when played out in its entirety, the terror that my soul was going to be filled with so much pain and anguish from which I would never recover—pounded in my head and yanked me violently . . .*

"Dirk, Dirk what's wrong?" I awoke to an image silhouetted in my bedroom doorframe.

"Marie, is that you?" I said, still groggy and lost in my nightmare.

"No, Dirk, it's me, Kristen."

By now I was fully awake and said, "Sorry, it's just that it seems anytime I have some kind of experience that involves anything concerning my wife. I have this friggin' recurring nightmare."

Kristen came to the edge of the bed as I turned on the bedside table lamp. She was sitting on the edge of the bed in all her glory and if I wasn't awake before, I was now. She gently stroked my cheek with the back of her hand, and I could actually feel my pounding heart slow down.

"I was taking a shower when I heard you yelling in your sleep, and I came to see what was wrong."

So I began the guilt laden trip through memory lane trying to explain that fateful night when Marie died and I slept through the sirens rushing past my house; then picturing the EMTs frantically trying to save her life while I slept, or thought so anyway, and just rolled over in my drunken stupor and slept while she died, alone.

"Dirk," she said softly, "it's over, and she's gone. Nothing you can do now can change that. I can't even begin to imagine how you feel, but it's been what, five years? Time to get back on the horse and ride. There's no double meanings here, friend, just some heartfelt advice. We've all had regrets in our lives, some more difficult to move on from than others, but we have to move on, or we die inside.

"I see in you a man who has qualities that a lot of other men can't even begin to wish for. Honesty, real honesty, maybe even too much so, and compassion. You are trustworthy or Rembrandt would not have entrusted this entire dilemma to you and without trying to diminish any of the love you have for Marie—you have a lot of love to give—especially to a woman."

She continued, "So in a nutshell, as you said earlier, it's time to give it up and move on, or frankly as I said, you're going to die—inside at the very least. I truly believe and I think in your heart you do too, that's not what you really want to do."

Then she kissed me gently on the lips.

She made sense. I'd not felt this much alive in a long time since I'd started this investigation. Kristen had definitely relit a fire in me that I never thought I'd feel again.

Sitting there with no modesty, I reached out to hold her and tell her thanks for understanding.

The hug slowly turned to an embrace; and before I knew it, we were lying next to each other, looking deeply and intoxicatingly into each other's eyes and ever so gently caressing each other. We made slow, very slow, and passionate love while never losing that eye contact. It seemed to last forever—maybe it did.

Later, Kristen turned to me and said, "Now maybe I can finish my shower without another startling interruption, and I think to make sure of that you better join me."

I did. This time, all lathered in soap, our lovemaking was much more hot and frenzied and left us both spent.

"Dirk," she said as we toweled off, "it's late or actually early tomorrow, and I really have to leave, or we are going to seriously hurt each other."

She got dressed, and we had a lingering soft good-bye kiss, and she squeezed my arm and said, "Tonight *our* restoration meeting was much, much better than my earlier meeting." With that, she left.

As I watched her taillights go down the street, I realized what she said to me was probably true. Maybe it was time to move on. And damn, the investigation, along with my affair with Harden, was beginning to make me feel like joining the living again.

The phone rang while I was having my morning coffee on the fly while getting ready to go to work. It was Karen, and she could hardly control her enthusiasm.

"Dirk"—she grinned over the line—"guess what? Tom asked me to marry him last night," she said before I even had a chance to say anything.

"He totally surprised me . . . well, maybe not totally. But when the waiter brought our dessert, on the tray was the most beautiful diamond engagement ring I have ever seen. Dirk, I was so excited I almost wet myself."

"Say, hey, Karen, congratulations! He's a very lucky guy. So Mr. Right surprised you with the ring. Just out of curiosity, did it fit?" I asked with a purpose in mind. "When I surprised your sister, I bought rings that were too big, and she had to have them resized."

"Actually, the ring is a little big, and we're going to Weatherford's tomorrow to get it resized. Oh, Dirk, I'm so excited, I really love the guy, and I can tell he loves me."

"I'm really excited for you guys, but you said Tom bought the ring at Weatherford's?"

"Yeah, why?"

"Nothing really, I was just curious. You know I don't trust Weatherford, and I wouldn't want to see anything put a damper on your excitement."

Then a thought struck me, and I said to Karen, "Are you off today?"

"Yes," she said. "But I can hardly wait to be able to wear my engagement ring."

"Can I call you right back, Karen?"

"Sure," she said. "What's up?"

"I just need to make a quick phone call, and I'll get right back to you."

"Okay," she said.

I hung up, and my sting was beginning to formulate in my head, so I looked up Darlene Highland's phone number. If there was anyone in this city who wanted to see the sinister six taken down, it was Darlene. In conversations with her over the past few years, she all but came out and accused them of being responsible for her husband's disappearance and most likely death. Even though she knew her husband was no angel, she felt like they had coerced him into taking more chances running cope from South America with more money than he would ever make at his catering business.

She was a really sweet lady, and we got along great even after a short-lived thing we had before each of us met our respective marriage partners. But she did like nice things, expensive nice things which is probably the reason Dick took on the shit, meaning drugs, he did. None of this mattered to me, because we had remained friends over the years. So as the genesis of my plan began to take place, in my mind anyway, I gave her a call.

"Darlene," I said as she answered the phone. "It's Dirk, how are you?"

"God, Dirk, is this really you? I'm good, really good," she responded in the same sweet voice I remembered. "And how are you? I haven't heard from you in a while. Let's see, I remember talking a bit at that silly fund raiser at the club but not enough to really catch up."

"I'm doing better lately, and I'd love to catch up, but first I'd like to ask you a favor, well two actually."

"You've got it, Dirk, shoot."

"Okay, first of all, I know you have some pretty nice jewelry, and I was wondering if you bought any of it at Weatherford's?"

"Actually, yes, I purchased several pieces from him, and I also have some gifts."

"Do you have any authenticity or certification papers or whatever they're called verifying their . . . well, authenticity?"

"Yes, I do. I keep them in my safe deposit box. But why do you ask, are you planning to marry me for my jewels?" she chuckled.

"No, Darlene, but it's tempting. What I'm after is well . . . I . . . I . . ." I stumbled.

"Spit it out, Dirk, you've never been one to beat around the bush, so come on, we're friends, are you in trouble financially, I mean."

"No, no it's nothing like that Dar, it's just that, well, can I trust you on something, because if I can't trust you on this, there's no one I can."

"Dirk, we've been friends along time. You can trust me with anything and something tells me it's about those asses at the club."

"Why would you think that, Dar, am I that transparent?"

"No, it's just that you mentioned Weatherford, and when you mention any one of those schmucks, you might as well mention them all. What's up?"

"Okay, I'll tell you the whole thing over lunch today, are you free?"

"Yes, I am as a matter of fact and I'd love to, where and when?" And then she added, "Didn't we dance to that song title back in high school?"

"Yes, we did, I think, a long time ago. How about that quaint little Mom & Pop Deli up on Main Street in Clarence Center. You remember, we went there a few times on the way back from the movies."

"Is it still there?"

"Yeah, I just went by it the other day, and it still had the cardboard open sign in the window."

"Okay," she said. "How about one o'clock?"

"Great, but I have another favor to ask, and if you say no, it's all right, I'll understand."

"What is it? You sound *so* serious."

"Could you bring one of your nicer rings with you, one with diamonds and its authenticity documentation?"

"But," I continued, "it has to be something you bought at Weatherford's and something you have had back to him for whatever reason since you bought it. It's a tall order on such short notice, I know, but trust me, and I'll explain it all to you at lunch."

"No problem, Dirk, I know just the ring and this is beginning to intrigue me. I'll meet you at one."

"Dar, I'd like you to actually meet me at Steinbeck's Fine Jewelry just around the corner from the Deli, same side of the street. And one more thing, my sister-in-law Karen is going to meet us there also. Not for lunch, just the jewelry store thing, okay?"

"Wow, Dirk, intriguier and intriguier, is that a word by the way? Well, anyway, sure it's okay, anything I can do to help. And if Karen wants to join us for lunch, that's all right with me. We've met before. I'll leave that up to you two. See you there."

"Thanks, Dar, I mean that."

"Of course you do."

Right after I hung up, I called Karen back and said, "Karen, can you meet me at Steinbeck's Jewelry on Second Avenue in Clarence Center at one o'clock. It's just off Main Street, right by Mom & Pop's Deli, and could you bring your engagement ring with you? It's kind of important we do this today. We'll be meeting Darlene Highland there and then we're going to go to the Deli for lunch. If you want to join us, you're more than welcome, in which case, I'll pick you up."

"We'll be coming from opposite directions, so I'll just meet you there and I think I'll skip the lunch, but why all the mystery, what's goin' on?"

"Trust me," I said, "Join us for lunch, and I'll explain it there."

Karen asked if this had anything to do with the thing regarding Baby and Rembrandt I'd been working on. "You bet it does. So can you and your ring make it?"

"If that's the case then, sure bro, I'll be there."

I called in to the *Journal* and left a message for Kristen. I guess considering the current state of affairs, I just can't seem to get away these plays on words, but anyway I was glad to talk to her machine because of the brevity of the conversation. I'd tell her more in-depth later—whoops, there I go again. I took Marie's wedding set from my drawer and headed out.

At about ten to one, I arrived at Steinbeck's. Karen and Darlene were already inside, and Karen was positively beaming as she showed Darlene her ring.

I said, "Hey" and went to peek myself. "Nice rock. Tom must be doing pretty well in the hotel management business."

Good for him and really good for Karen—she deserved something good in her life.

I gave both ladies a hug, and they looked at me with the anticipation of two kids ready to start their first Easter egg hunt.

"Well," I said, "let's do this."

Grandpa Steinbeck was at his spot at his jewelers' bench and as I approached he looked up and said, "So soon?"

I told him that actually timing was pretty important.

He said, "Well, let's have a look."

With that, I took Marie's rings from their box and put them in front of him. He looked at them and said without even using his loupe, "These are not the stones I sold you—what, twenty five years ago. These are CZs, cubic zirconias, and not really good quality ones either."

Although it felt as though I'd been stabbed in the heart, I was not all that surprised and said so. Now I asked Karen to show him her new ring, and he appraised it very carefully and smiled when he told her it was a fine gem of excellent clarity and color but just to be sure he tested it with a Ceres CZeckpoint XL tester, and after the light on the stylus turned green, he announced it was, without a doubt, a fine diamond and she should be proud. There she goes giggling again.

Next was Darlene's turn. She produced with pride, a diamond ring with several smaller diamonds surrounding a very large diamond. I don't know diamonds. but old Gramps's eyes did a little dance when he saw it.

"May I," he asked.

It was the most expensive looking ring I had ever seen and said, "Darlene, holy shit." She smiled and said it was a birthday gift from her husband Dick, the last gift her ever gave her.

Gramps then proceeded to evaluate the stones especially the very large one in the middle. He checked and checked using all of his gemologists skills and then announced that the smaller diamonds in the setting were indeed real, but he added that the large two carat stone in the middle was a not a diamond, but a simulant like the cubic zirconia, but Moissanite to be specific an actual jewel albeit not a diamond.

Darlene was speechless, so I said it looked more real than Karen's how could it not be real, it even passed that pointer thingy test.

"Aha, remember what I told you the other day. Moissanite especially, has more fire and brilliance than diamonds and is becoming popular as a substitute because of those qualities and its price, less than half of that of a diamond. And unless skilled gemologists assess them, it's almost impossible to tell the difference. The normal Ceres CZeckpoint test will not even distinguish the difference."

Darlene answered deflated, "But I have the GIA grading report that came with it."

"I'm sorry, young lady, you've been duped."

"But it looks so real."

"Unfortunately, looks can be deceiving my dear."

"That son of a bitch," Darlene spat, "He told me it was a two-carat diamond—one of the best Weatherford ever had the privilege of dealing with."

"Maybe it was when he bought it, but did you take it back to him for anything?" I asked.

"Yes, one of the smaller stones fell out, and I took it back and David replaced it for me free of charge."

"That's it," I said excitedly. Let's go have lunch ladies, and I'll tell you what I'm pretty sure is going on."

"Thanks for your time. Mr. Steinbeck."

"If you need me for anything else, especially to stop this illicit activity, which is a black eye for all honest jewelers, please *do not* hesitate to contact me. I'm afraid in today's world this kind of thievery goes on more than people realize. Good luck."

With that, and the tinkle of a little bell above the door we left, somewhat stunned, surprised and a lot pissed and walked over to Mom & Pop's.

Mom & Pops hasn't changed in twenty five years. It's a quaint little bistro, again like most of the businesses in this area and other ethnic pockets of the environs of Buffalo that are and have been family operated for as far back as I can remember.

This one is no secret especially to the people of Clarence Center. Saw dust on the floor with about six or eight tables nicely spaced so that when you get up or sit down, you're not knocking butt to shoulder with the person behind you. Fresh checkered tablecloths adorn each table with a small bouquet of real flowers in the middle of the table. There are no menus, but a chalkboard behind the counter announcing each day's fare. No prices either. The dining procedure is you come in, look up at the chalked in menu, and order at the counter, give your name, go back to your table and wait for your name and selection to be announced, and then you go up and pick it up. They have a small selection of wines, local bottled beers, and the usual soft drinks.

The menu mainly consists of sandwiches and the homemade soup of the day. The place is never empty, and no one is in a hurry.

There are two-and-a-half unique things about this place. The reason there are no prices listed is that if you didn't like your order, you don't have to pay, even for the drinks. How's that for customer satisfaction? The second thing is the proprietors, whether first, second or third generation, seem to never forget a name. The half unique thing is the homemade soup here was second only to Carla's at the Bridge Tender.

Just as we walked in, a young man was beginning to clear off a table in the middle against the wall that four others had just left.

"We're in luck," I said.

We slipped off our coats and studied the board, although none of us expressed much enthusiasm about eating. If you come in and find a seat, you have to eat something because there are most times people waiting.

We all agreed to split a turkey club, and each have a bowl of cup of chicken tortellini soup with spinach and thyme. Although I could have slugged down a couple of shots, we all opted for a glass of Riesling. I placed the order and went back to a very solemn table.

When I sat down and placed the wine in front of the girls, I heard Darlene say, "That son of a bitch. All the crap I put up with from him, and he tries to make it right by buying me a phony diamond."

"Darlene," I said, "Hold on. I asked you to trust me and I hope you do, and I think you should not rush to judgment on Dick's gift. Let me explain in twenty-five words or less what I'm pretty sure is going on. First of all—" And I was interrupted by "Dirk," being yelled to me from behind the counter by none other Mom herself.

"Mr. Crandell, how've you been? I was sorry to hear about Marie. I lit a candle for both of you. Isn't that Marie's sister, Karen, and is that Diane? No, wait, Darlene you're sitting with. Yoohoo, Karen and Darlene, nice to see you again."

I told you they never forget a name; scary, huh?

We all got our food, and when we were settled again, I continued. I told them about the letter and pictures from Rembrandt. I told them about the botched blackmail attempt. And I told them about my suspicions of Rembrandt's untimely death and/or murder.

I further explained, "I suspect, judging from the photos I had, Weatherford's actions in the alley behind his store and his well-known nose candy problem made it more than possible that our illustrious community's finest jeweler was swapping out diamonds for simulants and sometimes not very good ones. The average person can't tell the difference, hell, according to Mr. Steinbeck, even some jewelers can't, and besides, who would suspect that this was even a possibility? I mean that family has been in the fine jewelry business in Clinton for over a hundred years. Along with that, the GIA certification can't be forged. They maintain a record of who bought it."

Karen piped in between bites, "But mine is real. He said so."

"Mine were too, or Marie's, to be specific." I said, "I bought them from Steinbeck's, and they were real then, but Marie had them resized at

Weatherford's. I'll get to that in a minute. Now comes the difficult part to prove. I'm sure that the sinister six have to be in on this."

"Sinister six?" they said simultaneously.

"Yep, my new name for the not-so-good ol' boys."

"No arguments here," said Darlene.

"Me neither," said Karen.

"So the hard part is going to tie them in with Weatherford," I said.

"How do you know they're involved?" asked Darlene.

"Well, I'm sure that these guys are buying nice expensive jewelry for their wives, and how would it look if they weren't buying it from Weatherford. So they must know, who knows, they might be even getting a cut. Maybe after Weatherford takes his habit money, the rest is going to finance importing illegal drugs, which has been a rumor for a long time anyway. I can feel it in my gut, not my dick, like everyone thinks, that there is a conspiracy going on in Clinton and its hard-working people are getting shafted."

"So what's to do?" asked Darlene. "If David Weatherford is doing what you say or think he is, then I want my real diamonds back. That would mean that Dick was really trying to make up for his stupidity by buying the jewelry. Not the best way to do it but a start anyway."

"Tom and I are supposed to take my ring back to him tomorrow to get it resized, but now I don't want to take the chance," Karen said. "Dirk, I don't want to tell Tom because he'll call me paranoid. But the last thing I would want him to think was that I'd taken it somewhere to get it appraised and see how much it was worth or whatever. I wouldn't have cared if he got it out of a Cracker Jack box; it's the meaning, not the money."

"Hey, Karen, that gives me an idea. What if we could take your ring back to Steinbeck's and he could replace your real diamond with a really good CZ and mark it on its—what did he call it?—girdle, I think, with some jibber-jabber resembling the GIA inscription and then hope that Weatherford would just assume it was the same real one he sold you and make the switch. He's high most of the time anyway. He probably has no clue that anyone other than Rembrandt might even begin to suspect what he's been doing and Rembrandt's dead. Then your beautiful diamond would be in the protective custody of Steinbeck's.

"If we can get Steinbeck to agree to it, and he seems willing to help, we would have some solid evidence that Weatherford is a thief. If we could prove that, and that's a big if, I'll bet a fifty-five gallon drum of

Jack Daniels that we could get other people in Clinton to come forward too. Once it's out and people realize they've been ripped off and his shining armor has been seriously tarnished and that he's going down or up, as the case may be. If there's a link between him and the other good ol' boys . . ."

"Sinister six, remember," interrupted Darlene.

"Yeah, sinister six, anyway, once he gets squeezed, he might just squeal like the little rat he is."

"You know, Dirk," Karen said, "This just might work. Now if we can get Mr. Steinbeck to agree, if fact why don't we go back over there right now. If he could do it today, I could pick up the ring tomorrow, and no one would be the wiser."

"Would you be willing to put your ring in the sting?" I asked.

"Cute, real cute, Dirk, and yes, I would. Just to think of all the happy couples, including you and my sister, Darlene and Dick, and if we let it go, maybe even me and Tom being ripped off and deprived of having this memento from perhaps our happiest times, you bet your ass I will."

"Before we go back, I'd like to call Sheriff Chambers and give him a heads up to what we've got going. We worked a couple of charity things together a few years back before he was sheriff. Hopefully, if he has some upfront knowledge, we won't get caught with pants down when he does find out about it.

"He wasn't in on Rembrandt's drowning report because that was a city matter. So it was handled by our own Laurel and Hardy Harrison brothers' team and as a sidebar, maybe we could even prove Rembrandt was murdered for uncovering this charade. But before we get ahead of ourselves, first things first."

"I have a mobile phone, if you want to call him," said Darlene.

I was lucky to catch him in his office, said he just got back from working out at the Y during lunch. After a few pleasantries, I got down to it. It took about ten minutes, nonstop, for me to fill him in on our suspicions. He told me to go ahead and do the ring thing, but that he wanted to see my photos, the letters and any other evidence I thought I had, pronto. He would not act on anything until that happened. I also asked him to keep this all under his hat until we had a chance to do this.

"You bet your ass," he said, because this was quite a stretch for even Clinton's elite.

When I got off the phone, I told the ladies we had the okay to go ahead, but that was as far as we were to go with it until I could show him what we had so far.

"Can you trust that he's not friends with any of them?" asked Karen.

"Yes," I said, "When Wayne Chambers ran for Clinton County Sheriff six years ago, he ran as a democrat. He ran against Stanley Harrison, a republican. Harrison had all the backing of the SS—hey I like that, sinister six, SS, get it. Well, anyway, quite a bit of mudslinging went, on and it was a very ugly campaign, but Wayne won, actually by a pretty significant margin. After having drawn the line in the sand for who supports who, there is no love lost between our sheriff and our chief of police and his cronies. So we're in luck there, besides I can't say this about too many people in Clinton County, but I can about Wayne Chambers; I trust him completely. He's fair, and if he says we don't have a chance in hell, we don't. But we, or me at least, have to try. I promised Baby to follow this through, and her trust is in me. She needs me and you know what else, I need me."

We paid for our lunch said good-bye to Mom and went back over to Steinbeck's. It was starting to snow again. It was a very light, gentle snow with the kind of giant flakes that you try to catch on your tongue when you're a kid. So big in fact, that when they land on you, you can actually see their mystical, one of a kind shape and definition as they melt away before your eyes only to be followed by another and another.

We confided in Mr. Steinbeck as to our plan, and he said he would gladly help. As far as marking the CZ he could, with a micro-laser which would, to a lazy jeweler's eye, simulate the GIA inscription on all GIA-graded diamonds and that Karen could pick up her ring anytime after 10:00 a.m. tomorrow morning. He would also keep her real diamond in his safe, and when this all ended, he would gladly reset it for her at no cost.

As we walked back to our cars lost in our own thoughts, I said to both but neither in particular, "Hey, do I have that nice of an ass?"

Darlene said, "What did you just say?"

"I must have a pretty good-looking pooper because two people in the last half hour wanted me to bet on it."

No acknowledgment of my wit whatsoever from either of my companions.

JIM CONNERS

CHAPTER 12

I WENT TO THE Bridge Tender where I seem to do my best thinking and ordered my hydraulic dinner—a double JD up with a Labatt Ice chaser. I noticed the afternoon delight special was a Bridge Burger. This was a large medium rare Angus burger with bacon, blue cheese dressing lettuce and tomato. So I ordered one of those too.

I was feeling pretty confident that our little plan was going to work, and once we were sure Weatherford had switched stones on Karen's ring, I would go to Sheriff Chambers with our proof. That's when I would ask him about getting Rembrandt's body exhumed. Might as well go for the jugular while I was at it, kind of my *Tin Cup* philosophy.

The burger was great, the hydraulics were better. One more JD, and I went home and was anxiously awaiting a new day and a new dawn.

They both happened after experiencing an increasingly more frequent good night's sleep. I showered and shaved and scanned the *Journal* over wheat toast and coffee. I had to wait for Karen to call about her picking up the ring and taking it to Weatherford's for resizing. I'd left it up to her whether to tell Tom or not about the plan. I hoped she opted not to because the less people who knew about it, the better. But if she did, I would understand, in fact maybe after rethinking the situation, I ought to call her and tell she should include Tom because there should be no secrets when we're just starting a hopefully long-term relationship.

So I called her, and she told me she was glad I thought that way because that's how she felt. Too many lies and secretes had permeated her life, and since she was starting a new one, she wanted the innocence of truth to be at its foundation. I did tell her that when and if Weatherford did switch the stones out—to tell Tom not to do anything stupid like kick the shit out of him. There would be plenty of time for some brutal rectal activity if dickhead David went to jail. But yeah, I'm letting my hopes get ahead of me.

I went to my office to see how Melissa was doing and ask her if she was missing her doughnut run first thing in the morning and my cheery refutes. Judging by her appearance in her pantsuit, she wasn't missing too much of the dash for doughnuts and bagels.

She looked up when she heard me whisper, "No, missy, I don't care for a fucking doughnut, not today, nor will I want one fucking tomorrow either, thank you."

"Oh, Dirk, you're such a kidder." Something's never change.

"How's it going kiddo," I asked as I spotted the half completed crossword on her desk.

"Oh great, thank God, Clinton is the social mecca of the world, or I'd be bored to death," she joked.

"Seriously, how's it going, you keeping up with things, any problems?"

"Nope, just need a five-letter word for yup."

"Unhuh"

"Yeah, yup"

"Unhuh"

"Yup."

Oh shit, here we go again, I thought. "Melissa, a five-letter word for yup is unhuh."

"Yup, that works."

"God, I love this gal."

"Is Harden in?"

"I think so, but she's in a meeting with Mr. Foster"

"You mean TR?"

"The one and only."

"I wonder what he wants?"

Having just said that, Kristen jiggled into the newsroom with a little less enthusiasm than usual.

"Dirk, do you have a minute?"

"Sure, what's up." Damn, I keep opening myself up for these soft subtleties.

No comeback—only, "I just finished a impromptu meeting with TR Foster, and he point-blank asked me what you were working on since you weren't working on your usual 'trivial shit,' as he put it.

"Trivial shit, is that what he said? If it's so trivial then why am I even here?" I said as the anger in me began to rise.

"You're here, Dirk, my friend, and yes, my lover, because it's a favor to me, and before you go off halfcocked," with that came the scintillating smile I was used to which kind of crept into the corner of her mouth. "That favor was before you got your balls back and started this investigation. Now it's not a favor, it's your job as an investigative reporter and I frankly don't give a rat's ass what he thinks, even if it means my job. It's your life and your divine calling to do what you're doing. I don't think you realize how good you are at this."

"Your job," I asked taken aback. "What do you mean your job?"

"He asked what, to again coin his own words, 'was that useless drunk doing on the payroll if the doughnut girl could take over his job?'"

"What did you say to that?"

"I said that you were working on a story about someone who was purportedly trying to pass off their own counterfeit artwork as Rembrandt's now that he was dead and his paintings were worth more money. You had asked me as a favor, to look into it because he was your friend, and I said yes, since things were slow this time of year.

"I think he bought it, but he said if nothing came of it, which is what he suggested would be the results, you were gone and he'd have to take a serious look at me and my managing editor judgment."

"Screw him, the spoiled little shit."

"Don't think so, not that he hasn't tried."

Karen called at noon to say that she and Tom, her more than willing accomplice, had dropped off her ring at Weatherford's for resizing and that they could pick it up tomorrow.

Now if I could hope beyond hope that Weatherford had not changed his backdoor and window at his store, I had an idea. I have this little 35-mm camera with a pretty good zoom on it, and it also has a nighttime feature. It can also date each picture. If I could get a picture of Weatherford switching diamonds and have the photo dated as proof, well if only I could, it might be just enough proof to have Sheriff Chambers look into this. The only problem I could foresee was my plan would involve a stakeout, a stakeout in a Clinton alley with temperatures that were supposed to reach into the 'teens' tonight. I thought a trip to the friendly neighborhood liquor store was in order. I know that alcohol works just the opposite of what you think as far as warming you up, but you have to maintain a delicate balance here. You have to drink enough to not care about the cold, but not too much so as to not be able to focus the camera.

I made a quick trip home and picked up my trusty little 35-mm camera. While I was there, I thought it best to dress the part for my covert stakeout, gee I was even starting to talk the role I had scribed for myself, and changed out of my dressed-up work clothes into something really warm and unobtrusive that would blend into the night. Warm was easy. Everyone who lives in Western New York has warm winter wear. The best I had in the stealth department was an old camouflage, U.S. Army—issue all-weather coat. I don't know what they are called, but it's one of those that has three button-in layers, and of course, a hood. I had admired it on an old friend of mine who was in the Army Reserves and has since passed away. The next thing I knew he was knocking on my door with a brand new one. He'd even had a name patch sewed on it that said, "Crandell."

I added my pair of snowmobile boots which it seems I'd had forever and my artificial fur-lined gloves. Marie would never let me have real fur, always the animal rights lady. I filled my flask with some Christian Brothers brandy from my little wet bar and loaded the stuff in my car. I figured I wanted to cruise by the front of Weatherford's to see if he was even there and what time he closed up before I spent a bring-in-the-brass-monkey night in the alley only to find out he wasn't even there.

My plan was to park down the street at the Bridge Tender after dark and change into my warm stuff there. Since Weatherford didn't have any other employees, I figured if he was indeed swapping out diamonds for duds, he would most likely be doing it after hours. I was pretty sure he closed at five. It was 4:15 now and already well on its way to being dark so my timing couldn't be better.

Once I parked my car, I walked across Center Street that put me on the opposite side of the street from Weatherford's. Then I walked up the street to the next corner, re-crossed and headed back down past the store. If per chance Weatherford saw me strolling by, he would probably think I was just headed to the Tender to get drunk and pay me no mind. My guess was that he probably had other things on his mind anyway.

I was right. He closed at 5:00, according to the little open for business hours chart decal on the window and I could see him straightening some watches in a display case. Another interesting thing caught my eye as I went by. Another decal, only this one was an official GIA decal, and it was affixed to the window in plain view, announcing that he sold only GIA-certified diamonds. Well, if my luck held I was about to make a liar out of him.

I got back to my car and donned my clandestine garb, grabbed my camera and flask, and headed to my first and hopefully last stakeout. My luck was holding; neither the door nor the window had been changed yet. In all of my planning for this, I never even considered what I would do if there was no window to try and get a picture through.

I glanced in the barred window and had a clear view of his bench which was well lit. I could also see him locking the front door. I ducked as he headed back to his bench. It was now totally dark and really not that cold yet. I had to be careful not to get too close to the window. I didn't want my warm breath to fog up the window so I took a few steps back and waited.

I saw him piddle around doing close up stuff so I deduced if anything was going to happen it might be a while. I took up my position just far enough back that I could still see the bench but not much else. I took a healthy swig of brandy, and while my gloves were off, I got my camera out of my pocket and turned it on. I wanted to get the camera adjusted to the ambient temperature out here so that, as with the window, the lens wouldn't fog up when I needed to use it. I also made sure it was set to night photo mode which uses no flash.

After about a half hour, I saw him head back to his bench. Maybe this was it. I stepped in as close as I dared and took off my gloves and held the camera at ready. With no flash, I had to hold it very still. Actually, I should be using a tripod.

He sat down and pulled his opened his bench drawer and pulled out his supplies. Not the ones I'd hoped for. He placed his vial of nose candy on the bench and proceeded to draw two lines, and with his own little straw thing, he snorted up both white lines. He didn't put them away so I presumed it was going to be a long night—for me, anyway. I was about to do my own snorting when he got up and headed for the backdoor. I scrambled for cover under the fire escape on the opposite side of the alley. He opened the door and did a quick look around, probably to see if anyone was watching him.

I thought, "No, you bastard, you already killed the guy who saw you before."

Convinced the alley was empty, he went back in. I heard the metallic click of the dead bolt being turned so I snuck back up to about a foot from the window. He was back at his bench. His bench ran parallel to the display cases on one side of the store. I assumed his safe was probably behind him; anyway, the layout couldn't have been better for me. I was afforded a perfect profile of David Weatherford IV only a few feet away.

High and happy, he took a ring out of the drawer, which looked a lot like Karen's and inserted a loupe into his eye, and with the smallest pair of pliers, I've ever seen proceeded to remove the stone from the ring. He scrutinized the stone under the bench's light turning it around, back forth several times in smug admiration. He placed it in a small little envelope. He turned his chair around and rolled out of sight. Not before I shot about six rapid fire photos, again trying to hold the camera as still as death between shots.

When he came back into view, he reached into his bench drawer and removed another envelope and he shook out several glistening stones. He pushed and poked them until he selected one that suited him. Putting the other stones back in their envelope, he then replaced the stone carefully with an obviously skilled touch in the setting. Again, not before I took another bunch of photos at various stages of his course of action.

Once again, he held the finished ring up to the light under his gemologists practiced louped eye surveying his debauchery and smiled; hoax complete. The only thing left was to resize it. I remember that Karen had told me it was almost a perfect fit, but she wanted it just a quarter size larger to allow for well, whatever besides why else take the ring back to Weatherford in the first place. If it wasn't right, she could always take it somewhere else later.

Weatherford seemed to know what he was doing. It looked like he was placing the ring on some kind of tapered stand. He slid the ring down onto the thingy and took some calipers of a sort and measured. Then he stopped. He swiveled in his chair and drew two more lines of coke to snort up the old proboscis to happy land.

Once he began to feel its effect, he swung back and with his practiced hand, made a small saw cut on the back of the ring. Then he used what looked to be a small rawhide hammer and tapped the ring down on the taper.

Damn, I hope this is over soon because I was beginning to freeze my ass off out here.

I saw him then take a small torch and solder the ring back together only at its new size. After a few moments, he took a stick of something and began to polish the band. I was too far away but my telephoto lens served more than one purpose this evening. I was able to get a pretty good but not great view of his craft and take pictures along the way.

Once he seemed satisfied with his finished product, he replaced it in its original box, which as part of our plan, still had the little pink bow on it. Swiveling back to the safe once again, he came back and put away his tools, all except his dope.

I had all I needed as far as I was concerned, so I decided I'd better not push my luck any further and get the hell away from here. I looked around to make sure I was still alone, carefully replaced my lens cover, shoved my stuff back in my coat pockets and booked back on over to my car and its more than ample GM heater.

Ah, heat. Ah, brandy. Ah, you bastard David Weatherford IV, if these pictures come out and closely replicate what I actually saw, your ass is going *"duck up"* in the slammer.

Morning came without incidence. As my coffee brewed, I reviewed my plan of attack. First was to get the pictures developed, they were in fact critical to any solid proof I had. Second was to call Karen and tell her I had the pix, and she could pick up her ring from Weatherford's and for her and Tom to play it cool. Now was not the time to play our hand. Then we needed to go to Steinbeck's and verify the switch had been made. We could do all of that at the same time, if we went the same route I went the other day. Hell, we could even have lunch at the same gin mill across the street from the Rite Aid I had Rembrandt's photos done. I made the call to Karen.

She in turn called Weatherford, and yes, her ring was done. She then called Tom and they made arrangements to pick up the ring at 10:00 a.m. Since Tom was her boss, among other things, her getting the time off was not a problem.

We agreed to meet in front of the *Journal* at 11:00 a.m., which would give me a chance to check in with Harden. She was in a meeting, and as I peeked in her door, she looked up and smiled. I made the gesture with my pinky and thumb that I would call her later.

I went down and met Tom and Karen in Tom's Escalade; very nice ride, he must be doing *very, very* well for himself. Well, good for Karen, she deserves it. And then off we went.

I swear to God, they acted like two teenagers along the way with their demure little looks and squeezey-huggies, and the dreamy smiles and stuff. If I didn't want this kind of thing for Karen so bad, I think I would have puked. But it made me genuinely happy, for both of them.

It took us about an hour to get to the Clarence Center Rite Aid. I dropped off the film, told the associate I wanted the one-hour service and doubles. He said, "Cool, see you in an hour."

Tom had managed to find a place to park in front of the Dew Drop Inn. We walked in, and I spotted Rose, who to my surprise was actually tending bar.

I said, "Hey, Rose, how they hangin'?"

She turned to me and said with a warm, devilish smile, "Hey, Einstein, probably better than yours in this cold."

With that exchange, Karen said with amazement, "Is there a barmaid in the *entire* Western New York area you don't know on a first-name basis?"

Rose approached with the ever present bar rag in hand and said, "Cream Ale and chili?"

"Chili," I questioned, "Last time it was only pretzels and nuts, what's the special occasion?"

"Last time, I was watchin' *The Young and the Restless*, and the kitchen's closed then."

Karen, Tom, and I looked at each other and nodded and I said, "Is it canned?"

"Nope, homemade with these gentle little hands."

"Sounds good, make it three."

Another thing about Western New York is you can never go wrong with any gin mills' homemade chili, especially in fall or winter.

"Three green death drafts and three of Rose's specials it is then."

We sat at a table in the corner, and it only took about five minutes for Rose to bring us our winter gourmet meal. On her way back to the bar, she made a pit stop at the jukebox and announced with its plug in her hand, "Anybody here going to want anything else for the next hour, y'all better tell me now because Y'all know what time its gittin' ta be so think up, speak up, and order up and then shut up. Y'all know my afternoon delight policy. And yeah, for you, the hunk over there with Einstein, yeah you," she said as she pointed to Tom.

With a "Who, me?" expression, he quizzically and innocently looked up at her while she added, "Not even for you, stud."

I never saw a man get as red so fast as Tom did at Rose's remarks. He immediately looked down at his glass of ale, probably wishing he could hide in it. Karen just raised her head and laughed. I have never seen Karen enjoy life as much as she was now.

She just squeezed Tom's hand, laughed again, and said playfully, "Hey you big sexy stud, you're mine anyway, homemade chili or not."

We made small talk while we finished our chili and cream ale. The chili had a bit of kick ass to it, so we were all looking for another quencher, but none of us dared bother the not-so-young and restless Rose. So I walked up to the bar, grabbed an upside-down pitcher, and filled it backward from the tap. As I finished, I heard Rose say without even turning around, "That's five bucks, Einstein. Just add it to your tab."

"No sweat. Great chili by the way."

Just then, a commercial came on, and she turned and looked at our table and said with an impish grin, "If stud muffin over there would have tapped me as it were, it would have been on the house." With that, everyone in the place laughed, and Tom's blushing and Karen's mirth started anew.

We left the tab and tip plus the extra five on the table and headed over to Rite Aid. The photos were done. We paid for them and went back to Tom's Caddy to look at them. It was starting to snow again—this time, the really heavy wet stuff. Glad we were in a four-wheel drive. If this was going to continue—and according to the weather report, it was—no better place to be except maybe back at the Dew Drop Inn. I had the feeling that it might be a fun place especially since a sign in the window advertised live country-western music every Friday and Saturday nights. When this is all said and done, I'll have to bring Harden here to see her get down a little. Could be fun.

We looked at the photos, and I amazed myself. They all came out with such clarity and detail it was like I was standing right next to Weatherford while he was doing his devious deed. Now if we could get Steinbeck's sworn verification the stone now in the ring was not the original and had been replaced with a dud, together with these pictures we had Weatherford by the short hairs. Time to see the sheriff.

We checked in with Steinbeck, and he seemed to be as excited as we were. Nothing like a little jurisprudence to weed out the bottom feeders from the legit gemologists' pool to polish your stones.

The elder Mr. Steinbeck took Karen's ring from her finger and examined it very carefully.

"We have a wringer!" he said with enthusiasm. "This is not the stone I placed in this ring. I can tell without even taking it out of its setting. This undoubtedly is not the CZ I set in this ring. Granted it is of similar or even a little higher quality, but nevertheless I can see without even removing the stone from the setting that the mock GIA serial number I micro-lasered is not present. A switch has been made. And as you young people say, just to cover my own ass, I called the Gemological Institute of America informing them of why and what I was doing. They were extremely interested in the results of this fraud being perpetrated. The person I talked to, a Mr. Michaels. I believe, said that if all our activities were documented and it was indeed proven that an attempt to defraud the world-renowned GIA's authentication of diamonds reputation they would prosecute the perpetrator(s) to the fullest extent of the law."

This vice—again no play on words intended—was cranking tighter and tighter on Weatherford. I was beginning to have a sense for the part in the movie *The Replacements*, when Keanu Reeves talks about his fear of quicksand, only in this case it was Weatherford who was sinking. Hot damn, but it was only the third quarter, and there was a long way to go.

Tom dropped me off at the *Journal*, and since it was beginning to snow harder, they said they had better head back to the Marriot in case more planes got snowed in at the airport. That was always a busy time for them. I said thanks and that I'd keep them posted on what was happening.

I went to my desk to review the chain of events and to go over the photos again, only this time more carefully. I wanted to be absolutely sure that the details in the photos coincided with the elder Steinbeck's sworn testimony about Weatherford and his wrongdoing.

As I slowly looked at each photo, I tried to do so without prejudice. It was as clear as a starry winter's night what Weatherford was doing in the photos. These, together with Steinbeck's verification, were solid proof, to me at least, that dickhead David was diamond duping; time to go to Harden and then to the sheriff.

I called Kristen on the phone and told her what we had and that I'd like her to see for herself and if she thought the same as I. If so, I was going to go to Sheriff Cummings with my evidence and let him decide where things should go from here.

Kristen picked up on the second ring and had a smile in her voice. "Dirk, I was just thinking about you, what's up?"

God, does it ever end I thought although I beginning to hope not, not for a while anyway.

"Hey, Kristen, could we get together somewhere away from the *Journal* so I can show you what I've got." I regretted it as soon as I said it, and she didn't miss a beat.

"Dirk, honey, I already know what you have silly, and that's why I was thinking about you."

"Kristen, you're the only woman that can make me blush over the phone."

"You know, Dirk, blushing is caused by blood rushing to your head."

"Yeah, yeah, I know but this time I'm thinking with the big head. I need to go over what evidence I have so far with someone unbiased and see if I'm wishful thinking about this whole diamond deception or I'm really onto something and it's time to go to the sheriff. It has to be someplace where the walls have no eyes or ears."

"How about my place?" she said.

I knew this was wrong because if anyone in the office saw us together there might be a leak to TR Foster. Time and discretion was of ultimate concern.

"No, although I'd love to see your place again, if you get my drift, we need a place where no one knows our name."

I could hear the change from flirtatious girlfriend to her professional sagacity, almost as audibly as the flick of a light switch.

"No, Dirk, she said." My place is perfect. If we go to any restaurant within fifty miles and start looking at photos over dinner, our chances of being exposed by one someone who knows either one of us is much more probable than if you just come to my house for a late dinner. We'll go over the evidence and figure out our, or more accurately your, plan of action. Who care's at this point if people know we're seeing each other. Actually, it's probably better that people think we're having an affair than to think there is anything conspirative going on."

"You're probably right; I'll bring a pizza so you don't have to cook. What time should I come?" I said so idiotically naïve.

Click went the switch back. "After we go over the evidence. You don't mind cold pizza do you?"

"I, my dear Kristen even like pizza for breakfast."

"God, so I. How about seven then?"

"Deal, see you then."

"You bet you will, Dirky, you bet you will."

CHAPTER 13

B Y THE TIME I got home, it was almost five, so I called good old Umberto's Pizzeria and ordered a large cheese, pep and mush with green peppers and black olives and told them I'd pick it up at 6:30. I'd forgotten to ask how Kristen liked her pizza, but she could always pick and flick anything she didn't like, but somehow I didn't think pizza toppings were really going to matter tonight.

I went home and poured myself two fingers of Jack, went upstairs and showered, and put on a nice, burgundy V-neck and a pair of jeans, my only pair of jeans. Normally when I wear my jeans, I like to wear loafers without socks, but it was winter in Western New York so that was not an option.

It takes about a half hour to get to her house from mine, so by the time I finished preening in front of the mirror and gathering up my evidence and notes, it was almost time to go.

The back of my house has a screened-in covered deck, and my yard is pretty large for a city lot. I snapped on the spot lights as I savored the last of my Jack. As much as I bitch about the cold and dreary Western New York winters, the beauty and tranquility of its winter wonderland vistas never cease to amaze me. It was starting to snow lightly—adding to the white blanket of drifted snow covering almost everything and decorating the big twin pines like a Currier and Ives photograph. The footprints of the squirrels and birds dotted the glistening white coverlet highlighted in the aura of the lights. This all was a stark contrast to black night made even blacker by the abundance of pure white. Captivating.

I stopped off at our local Rite Aid and picked up a six pack of Labatt Ice to go with the pizza and went next door to Umberto's and picked up dinner or breakfast, be what it may. I arrived at Kristen's about 7:10. I wasn't exactly sure which house it was. I'd only been there once and in the dark and in the snow, all the houses on her street looked alike. On my third pass looking for numbers, I saw her entry lights flash on and off several times so I turned around and went back to her house.

I didn't even have to ring the bell because she opened the door as soon as I got to it. There I stood pizza and beer in hand with what I'm sure was a goofy look on my face.

"Didn't remember which house was yours, thanks for the beacon. Here," I said, "Take these please while I go get my briefcase."

She did and I did.

She looked absolutely fantastic. Her auburn hair was still damp from the shower. She was barefoot and wearing a light blue velour sweat suit.

She leaned into me and kissed me on the cheek, lingering just long enough to not be casual. She had put the pizza and beer in the kitchen while I'd returned to my car. She took my coat and hung it in the entryway closet and then turned and said, "Okay, let's see what you've got."

Subtlety not being one of her finer suits, I assumed she meant that first we would play then work. Again, I must have had an amusing expression on my face because she tossed her head back and laughed. She then put her hand on my arm and said with that twinkle in her eye, "I mean silly, let's see what you think you have on Weatherford."

I said, "For a moment there, I thought . . ."

"Later," she said.

At the dining room table, she was all business. She had a legal pad, and over the next two hours, I talked, she took notes, and asked questions, but only when I got ahead of myself either, because I was excited or just plain pissed. I placed my pile of notes down for reference. Then I showed her all the photos, both Rembrandt's and mine. Each time I talked about another phase of my investigation, she tore off a page and started a new one.

When I finally finished, she looked up at me and said, "Is that it?"

I was a little confused and somewhat annoyed. I thought all of this was more than enough to get the sheriff involved, and I said so.

"What, don't you think there's enough evidence here to nail at least Weatherford?"

She said very calmly and succinctly, "Yes, I do. If you had let me finish, I was going to say now we're going to organize my notes chronologically so that when we, and I mean we, go to Sheriff Chambers, we'll have everything honed into a nice little presentation, rather than—oh, and please forgive this it's just for a lack of better words—the ramblings of a man hell bent on crucifying some guy he's been pissed at for five years."

"We?" I asked.

"Yes, we. I'm pretty sure that if I go and support you, it might just tip the scales in your favor. But I really believe you have enough on Weatherford to have him brought up on charges. And who knows what other dominos might fall when his does. Now please, stop whining and go get us a couple of those beers while I try to put all of this in order. Then we'll go over it and try to fill in any blanks."

I did as I was told. We spent another two hours organizing what were now *our* thoughts and when we were finished she said, "Are you hungry?"

"No, I'm really too excited to eat."

"Good, let's go make love. It's Friday night, and we don't have to work tomorrow so after we do morning sex, we can get up have our pizza and review the presentation of our suspicions and evidence with a fresh set of eyes. I can get us tickets to the Sabres game tomorrow night against Boston, so we'll make a weekend of it. Let's really give those gossips at the *Journal* something to talk about."

"Sounds like the words to a country-western song. You sure you want to do this?'

"The weekend, you bet!"

"No, the *we* thing with the sheriff. Once Foster gets wind of it, you're going to lose your job."

"There's always another job for a woman like me, besides, Clinton is too nice a place and there are too many innocent people being taken advantage of. Call it a random act of kindness for helping clear your friend's name showing the hard working people of Clinton that as far as their community pillars go, looks can be deceiving. Now do you want to talk or fuck?"

Going to bed with Kristen Harden is a symphony of experiences. It's making love, having sex, giving sex, laughing, wrestling, cuddling, noisy, pleasing, being pleased, and oh, did I mention that she has a great body and she uses every part of it and mine and enjoys every minute of it.

I'm not sure what time we finally fell asleep in each other's arms, but I know when we woke up it was late morning. I woke to see her propped up on one elbow looking at me with the covers down around her waist revealing her beautiful rose-tipped breasts.

"It's morning, sleepy head," she cooed.

"Yes, it is," I said, suddenly wide awake; and with that, she kicked off the covers exposing the rest of her voluptuous body.

"Come to me, lover," she whispered huskily, and she reached for me and I gently rolled over onto her and she guided me and into her slowly. She was more than ready, and although I could already feel the fire in me beginning to consume me, I wanted to savor every erotic sensation we were sharing. We looked into each other's eyes as we began our slow rhythmic harmonious love-making and never changed pace. As we both drew near the crest of our passion, she wrapped her legs around me drawing me deeper and we both reached the pinnacle of our love-making at the same time.

We just stayed that way until she said, "If we don't get out of bed pretty soon, I'm going to hurt you in a pleasurable way which might cause you some trouble sitting at the hockey game tonight. Which reminds me, I have to call Vic from advertising about the tickets."

With that, we got up, and she went to the phone and arranged for our tickets to be picked up at the box office.

She peeked in the door and said, "Come on, let's shower. We can wash each other's backs, and I don't know about you, but I'm starving. So then we can eat that pizza and get to work." That's exactly what we did.

Turns out she likes her pizza the same way I do but added, "This is great, but how about anchovies next time." This woman was winning me over big-time.

We went over our notes from the night before. We went back over a few items and their significance to the case. Kristen was very organized. She had little colored sticky tabs and stuff like that to keep everything in its proper place. Drove me nearly crazy, but in the end I'm glad she did it. Now even I could keep it in order which is amazing in itself.

She rode along home with me while I changed my clothes and picked up a few personal things like my toothbrush and razor. Basically enough stuff to get me through to work on Monday. I didn't figure I'd need much, especially PJ's.

She just kind of wandered around while I got ready, and when I caught up with her, she was staring out the sliding doors from my kitchen onto my deck. She marveled at the serenity of the panoramic view of my own little winter wonderland.

"This is amazing," she said as she used her shirt sleeve to wipe away her breath from the window. Just then, small gust of wind stirred and a small drift of snow from somewhere up in one of the pines fell to the ground, a sparkling mist of snow crystals to plume up and glint in the fading sun.

We watched as a squirrel donning its winter coat, leaped, and bounded through the heavy snow up on to the fence and off into the neighbors' yard.

"Hey cool," she said. "Do you think they ever find any of their winter stash buried in the snow? If they don't, wouldn't they starve?"

"I think they probably find some, and besides, I'm positive they manage to get more than enough to eat from peoples' bird feeders."

We both took in the crystalline view for a few more moments before I said, "I'm ready if you are," almost regretting my choice of words before they were even out of my mouth.

Never missing a beat, she turned and smiled and said, "So soon, Dirky, my, oh, my, but I think if we dally any more, we'll be late for the game."

Changing the subject, I said, "I think I'll try Sheriff Chambers and see if maybe he's in his office on a Saturday. If he is, then I can set up a meeting with him as early this week as possible. In the meantime, why don't you think about where we can grab something to eat before the game unless you want to get junk food there, your choice."

I was in luck. I caught Wayne in his office. Actually, he'd left his hockey tickets in his desk and had just gone back to pick them up when his caller ID showed him it was me calling from home.

I gave him Kristen's and my theory and told him we had some significant evidence and could he see us officially ASAP to see if there was anything legally we could do.

He reminded me of his promise that if I had something substantial that would stand up in court he would look at it and then go from there. He added that if Kristen Harden was involved, because of his respect for her media and business acumen, he was really interested. He actually had a business lunch cancelled on Monday so he was available from 1:00 p.m. to 3:00 p.m.

I said, "Great, how about your office?"

"Fine with me, I'll hold all my calls, and, Dirk, this better be worth it."

"It is sheriff, I promise it is."

Kristen was looking at me with her big green eyes when I hung up. "Well, will he see us?"

"Monday, actually, 1:00 p.m. at his office."

"Wow, that was quick."

"Well, he had an appointment cancelled, so we're in luck. I can't get ahead of myself here. There's too much at stake. Kristen, I can't even begin to tell you how much your belief and trust in me means."

I reached out to hug her and held her for a long moment. The events of the last few weeks were like microfilm before my eyes; in a millisecond, it was all there.

"Hey, ya big lug, you're suffocating me here." She managed to mumble against my shoulder.

I let her go, but not before she grabbed *me* by the shoulders and looked up at me and said, "Dirk, I saw something in you from day one. I was hoping that a good old fashioned work routine might snap you out of your funk. I had a gut feeling," as she slid her hand down to my heart and held it there gently patting my chest, "that there was good in here and I was right. That you promised to your friend and his daughter from here," as she continued to gently pat my heart, "I knew you would see this through and you're doing it."

"I don't know if I could be doing this without you. Kristen."

"Yes, you could, Dirk, it's just that . . ." and she trailed off

"Just what?"

"Well, your right hand would be sore, and you'd be going blind stud," she laughed with her green eyes twinkling. "Come on enough serious stuff, time for that Monday. Tonight let's go to Frank and Teresa's Anchor Bar and get some hot wings and a couple of Labatt's on tap and then go watch the Sabres kick some Bruin ass."

"Oh yeah," she continued, "then we'll come back here and play house again, I'll call us in sick tomorrow for Monday so we can get to bed early and have our game plan set."

"Sounds like a great plan to me and Kristen, Thanks again."

Wings were really hot. Beer was really cold, so were the Sabres, they lost 6 to 1 but the sex was really, really hot, so all in all, it was a very good night.

On the seventh day, we rested and chilled.

It was still dark when I woke up with a start. I turned my head to the left to check the time and no clock illuminated my nightstand. What the hell, did the power go off? I looked around in the dark and a moment of anxiety stabbed at me because everything felt unfamiliar and I sat bolt upright. Now wide awake, I felt the presence of a warm body next to me and I realized I was not in my own bed but Kristen's, and my heart went back into my chest.

I glanced over the shadowed curves beside me and saw that it was 5:37 a.m. I fumbled for my Luckys and lit one. Weird, usually when I lit one in the dark like this, my hands were shaking so bad as an aftermath of the nightmare, I had trouble holding the flame to it to light it. Not this time; steady as a rock.

From beside me I heard, "Good, sex'll do that for you."

"What's that?" I said.

"Calms your nerves and helps you sleep better."

"Kristen, the sex is great!"

"No, it'll be great when you don't have to light one of those stinky things in the morning afterward," she said with a hint of distaste.

I took the hint and stubbed out my "stinky habit."

We both lay on our backs with our hands behind our heads not talking. I was pretty sure she was going through the rolodex in her mind the same as me concerning the events facing us today. After a few slow-mo minutes, she finally in one fell swoop rolled over and straddled me, leaned down and kissed me playfully on the forehead and said, "Fuck it. I've never been to one worry about things out of my control or to second guess my own ability."

She now had pinned my shoulders to the bed with her hands firmly and added with her face right in mine, "Dirky, we're as ready as we can be. You have done a remarkable job getting this far, and I have no doubt whatsoever that after meeting with our county lawman today, you'll get your exhumation and autopsy request, and a warrant to search Weatherford's store.

"With Sheriff Chambers and his departmental resources on board, we're going to kick some serious high society ass in the very near future. And speaking of asses, let's get ours out of bed, in the shower, and then let's go to the Marina Café for a couple of their to-die-for omelets—what say."

Now I understood two things completely. First, how Kristen Harden got to where she is in life and what propelled her there, and second, I'm sure glad she's on my side. I'm relatively certain I would not have come this far in this whole thing without her belief in me.

Obviously she wasn't really waiting for my answer as she dismounted me and headed for the shower without even turning on the lights, but I did so anyway, "okay, sounds good to me."

We arrived at the sheriff's office at the same time as Wayne did. He was just coming back from his daily workout routine at the Y so we rode up in the elevator with him.

Meeting casually with Wayne Chambers always made you feel like you had been friends for a long time. Don't know what it's like to be on the other side with him but his reputation as a lawman was just that. He was an honest, dedicated, by-the-rules enforcer of the law, good man.

On the ride up, we exchanged pleasantries and talked about the hockey game last night. Too bad the Sabres lost, but they still had a chance to make the playoffs.

Once we entered his outer office, he told his receptionist, Stephanie, to hold all calls unless it was a real emergency. We then entered the inner sanctum of his world. The walls were filled with commendations from the military, the community, and several diplomas.

He took his place behind a large oak desk which was very stark and neat. He placed his duffle bag by the side of the desk and took his seat.

"Before we start, can Steph get you anything, Kristen? Dirk?" he asked, making straight eye contact with each of us.

In unison, we said, "No, thanks, I'm fine."

Then he said, "okay," as he folded his large hands together and placed them on the high gloss surface in front of him.

"Well, it's your dime. Let's hear what this is all about. Take your time because I don't want you to leave anything you think is significant out. After hearing you, I'll make my determination whether or not I'll proceed with this. Fair enough?"

Kristen responded before me and said, "Fair enough." And I just nodded my agreement.

"I'm going to let Dirk explain what we've, or he, to be more precise, has uncovered about some pretty serious corruption—for lack of a better word, that is and has been going on in Clinton for God knows how long. I'm here for moral support for my employee and friend. Sheriff Chambers, may I be candid with you?"

"Certainly, it's what I'm expecting from both of you."

"We all know that Dirk has harbored a hard on for some of the members of our country club for a long time, and I just want you to know that when he first came to me with his suspicions, I, too, was skeptical as to his motives. He didn't pull any punches with me when he told me what he thought of them. But Sheriff, I sensed something in his demeanor when he told me of his suspicions and that he wanted to pursue an investigation to see if there was indeed some truth to the information he had received and his gut feeling. He basically told me he was going to pursue it with or without my blessing. My long story short is that I would and have staked my career on him in this pursuit of truth. I warned him in no uncertain terms that if at any time he let his personal feelings enter into this, it was over. He had made two promises that day, one which he'll tell you about as soon as I stop blabbering and the other was to me that he would be objective as possible in his investigation. I trusted him and told him to go for it but with caution and to keep me informed every step along the way."

"Okay, Dirk, your turn," said the sheriff. "I remember some from our initial conversation. You had uncovered some incriminating photos and were about to see if David Weatherford was switching diamonds in his jewelry somehow. Am I correct?"

"Yes, sir," I said, surprised but not really that he remembered.

"Drop the sir, Dirk, and this time, let's start from the beginning. Don't be offended by this, but now with such staunch support of your managing editor, the credibility of your suspicions has now got my full attention."

"No offense taken," I said. "It's no secret, especially to you, Wayne, I mean, sheriff, that I pretty much hate their collective friggin' guts. Oh, by the way, may I be candid here?"

He leaned back in his chair and laughed and said, "I guess you've already established your candor and Wayne is fine. Now let's get to it."

And so I began at the beginning with the heartfelt hope that the dark surreptitious saga of the Clinton Country Club's sinister six's cluster fuck of truth, justice, and innocence was about to become public and at least one of them would go to jail for it.

I started with the letter I'd received from Baby Hobbs-Mintz and consequent phone conversation pleading with me to uncover the truth about her father's death and in the process, having the people of Clinton remember him for who and what he really was not what he was made out to be in the end because of what he had accidentally stumbled upon.

I explained how the death of Rembrandt, her father whose real name was William Mintz, had been brushed aside as a drunken drowning by Laurel and Hardy, chief of police and county coroner without even an autopsy determining his actual cause of death.

"Stanley and Oliver Harrison," corrected my audience. "Remember, no personal agenda's here, Dirk, although I do enjoy the likeness."

"Okay," I said.

So then I told him of the conversation I overheard at the country club, and although I had no proof that it actually took place, the following chain of events and Baby's own story would prove it true. I told of Baby's visit and our conversation this time with Karen present revealing the story of Samantha Mintz, Baby's mother and her life, or what there was of it. How she had been given a new start by Doc Johnson only to have her young life, body and soul with new found hopes and dreams brutally raped by the good ol' boys at the country club, ultimately resulting in her slow mental and physical death.

I told of how Rembrandt's finding her battered, bruised and near death, and with Doc Johnson's intervening care again, helped her on the road to recovery which included the birth of Baby. All this kept secret because Doc suspected his son, Junior, was involved, along with his sanctimonious cohorts Should this terrible ordeal be exposed, other than fearing the obvious scandalous even criminal publicity that would surface, he also feared for the life of the young woman, Samantha. Knowing that she had been left for dead once and her being a transient of sorts, he had no qualms at all that they would make it all just go away for sure the next time. Little did he know as it turns out she was already dead inside, anyway.

I spared him the sorrowful details of Sam's life and death from that point on out of respect for Baby's wishes and Kristen's advice. He didn't ask, and I didn't tell.

Sheriff Chambers just slowly shook his head in what—sadness-disgust, maybe both as I spelled out the tragedy of life, heartbreak, and death that surrounded the entire Hobbs-Mintz story.

I continued, without even referring to my notes which Kristen and I had so meticulously organized step by step, because I knew the whole picture by heart.

I continued on about how with Baby's knowledge and aid of the keys to her parents' apartments, which I assumed she somehow must have gotten from her father, Rembrandt, I discovered the letter from Rembrandt written to incredulously enough—me. How it spelled out his accidental discovery of Weatherford and his criminal activity. Also writing ashamedly of his bungled attempt to blackmail Weatherford, hoping to garner enough money to join his daughter in California and become if not a family again at least be a bigger part of her life. He also included the negatives which I'd since had developed, of the photos of the subject of the blackmail attempt where Weatherford is actually switching out diamonds from his customers rings and other jewelry.

I passed these over the desk.

Now I was getting to the good stuff and after studying the pictures, I could tell I had his undivided attention.

I continued.

So now with the seed of Rembrandt's fraud conspiracy having been freshly planted in my mind, I told him that where I got those pictures developed was in the neighborhood of the jewelry store, Steinbeck's actually, where coincidently had bought Marie's engagement and wedding rings many years ago. I thought I would stop and ask them if it would be possible for a jeweler to switch diamonds from their original settings with stones of lesser value without the knowledge of the owners.

He said sure and then asked me why.

I told Mr. Steinbeck of my suspicions and that I myself had bought my wife's rings from him twenty five years ago, but in the interim, they had been cleaned and resized at the local jewelers because of the closer proximity to where we lived.

I asked him if I brought them into him if there was any way he could tell or verify if the stones in the rings were the original diamonds I had purchased from him at that time.

I now read from my notes and continued, Steinbeck told me, yes, it would. In fact, the high price of gem-grade diamonds has created a large demand for stones with similar characteristics known as diamond simulants or imitations. Diamond simulants may be artificial, natural, or in some cases a combination thereof. While their material properties depart markedly from those of diamond, simulants they have certain desired characteristics, such as dispersion and hardness which lend themselves to imitation. Trained gemologists such as him, with appropriate equipment, are able to distinguish natural and synthetic diamonds from all diamond simulants, primarily by visual inspection. However to the average person, they wouldn't have a clue as to the difference.

Then Steinbeck explained to me about the GIA Certification of Diamonds. The GIA Institute is probably the foremost authority of diamond grading and documentation in the world. Basically, he said, and he'll testify to this, that any jeweler of any repute sells only GIA-certified diamonds. These diamonds are certified both with paper and micro-laser inscriptions on the diamonds as to authenticity. These jewelers proudly display a decal in their windows and most certainly state in their ads as to that status. He does, and ironically, so does Weatherford.

Steinbeck had gone on to explain that if I were to bring in my rings he could verify that they were indeed the diamonds he sold me.

"Maybe," I confessed, "I do have a hard on for Weatherford and maybe that's what's driving me with this investigation. Maybe that affectation and my booze induced cynicism helped spawn my idea for setting a sting, if you'll humor me for my lack of a sleuthier word."

"Sleuthier?" quizzed Kristen.

"Yes, sleuthier, a term used by a not-quite-ready-for-primetime sleuth who doesn't have all sleuthing techniques down yet."

"Regardless as you'll see, our little web of intrigue caught the insect right in the middle of the web."

I spelled out after that conferring with Kristen, I had come up with a plan to, if it came to fruition, would prove beyond any doubt that my suspicions wedded with Rembrandt's were true indeed and that David Weatherford was fucking over, excuse me, stealing from his customers. For how long, I'm not sure but from my investigation, at least twenty five years.

I told the sheriff of how I contacted Darlene Highland who I knew to have a few diamonds from Weatherford's. I mean what country club wife doesn't and asked her to meet me with some of them known to have been purchased at Weatherford's and meet me at Steinbeck's. I told her to trust me I would explain later.

Then I found out my sister-in-law Karen's new boyfriend and now fiancée had just surprised her with an engagement ring and they were taking it to shithead, oops, Weatherford to have it resized. I asked her to bring her ring and meet me and Darlene the next day at Steinbeck's.

"Wayne, all the rings and jewelry we took in, including mine, actually Marie's, to be evaluated had been switched. Not one was authentic; good copies, but fakes all the same, except Karen's which had just been purchased.

That's how he is doing it, I figured. He sold authentic GIA-certified diamonds as advertised, Karen's case in point, but if they were brought back for any reason, which almost all were, he was switching them out for fakes.

How was I going to prove it and Steinbeck helped with this part of the plan. He was pretty pissed—my words, not his—that some dickhead—this time, my description—would do this kind of unscrupulous act—his term—and jeopardize the reputation of jewelers everywhere.

He suggested that he take Karen's ring and secretly laser-mark some gibberish on high quality CZ the same size as her stone and reset it in her ring, keeping the real baby in his safe. Then once resized, she could bring the ring back, and if it was not the same stone, we would have him.

So he did it, gibberized a CZ while we waited.

"Gibberized?" quizzed Kristen once more.

"Gibberized, the act of putting gibberish on something. Will you please stop questioning my vocabulary. Wayne knows what I mean."

The sheriff just looked at both of us rather bewildered and said with a half-smile, "Go on, please."

I explained to him how I played super sleuth and set up an under-the-cover-of-darkness photo op, trying to catch dickhead—oh, again, sorry—in the act of making the switch on Karen's ring.

"Along with him snorting a bunch of nose candy, I got shots of him in that very act, as you'll see in these," I said.

I slid the second set of photos across his desk, keeping my hand just barely on them while I concluded.

"One more thing. I think David Weatherford murdered Rembrandt and tried to make it look like an accident to cover up the fact that Rembrandt had discovered his charade."

Again, reading from my notes, I said, "I read somewhere that about 20 percent of all people die under circumstances that would warrant an official inquiry into the cause of death. The burden of determining the cause and manner of death usually falls to the first police officer to appear on the scene.

"Being part of *the* one big happy sinister six country club family, the chief of police and the county coroner never called for an autopsy. The chief, by the way, was the first police officer on the scene, according to the reports filed, which in itself was strange that he of all people should find the body. Consequently, in their joint statement to the press, being the *Clinton Journal*, which, as you know, is owned by none other than TR Foster, they stated the indigent discovered floating in the river was simply drunk, had fallen in the river and drown. The press, at the time being Brian Burke, the youngest brother of Melanie Foster, who is as you also know, TR Foster's wife. Brian was serving an internship of sorts at the *Journal* between semesters at Harvard. Soon after this, his first and only story appeared in print, he went onto finish his internship at the *Boston Globe*.

"I don't think Laurel and Hardy's conclusion was true. I think that son of a bitch Weatherford killed Rembrandt and those rat bastard cronies from the club, or at least a few of them, are helping him get away with it. Why? Because they think they're exempt from the law here they don't think or care if anyone in Clinton gives a rat's ass as to what really happened to the poor old guy anyway. Again, I don't know much about these things, but I read that if he really did drown, an autopsy would show there would be water in his lungs When someone is dead before they go in the water, their swallowing reflex stops, and so no water would be in his lungs if he was murdered before he went in the river, an autopsy would have discovered that. Gee, no autopsy, no more questions."

I let him have the photos.

I let him study them over, and while doing so, I glanced at Kristen who smiled and gave me the thumbs up.

"Okay, what else?" said the sheriff noncommittally.

Kristen must have seen me tense up because she reached over and squeezed my thigh until I thought I would yell out in pain. She must have known what I was thinking. This was the second time in a matter of seventy-two hours someone I was trying to sell this to had said what else.

What the hell, I thought, if this isn't enough to get him believing that Weatherford was a full-fledged criminal, how would I ever get enough dirt on the rest of the SS to even make them dust off their shoes?

Maybe I came to the wrong guy. Maybe he was one of the good ol boys himself, after all politics makes strange bedfellows. For as pumped up as I was when I came in here, I was now equally deflated as I sat there thunderstruck.

"Well, Dirk, here's how I see it. Now I let you talk without interruption so now I'd like the same courtesy, okay."

I could only nod. I sensed the same emotion from Kristen.

"I'm surprised at you Dirk, but I'm not," said Sheriff Chambers. I'm surprised you got through this for the most part anyway without letting your well-known repugnance for a certain group our community's self-proclaimed aristocracy get in your way of explaining your concerns."

"Concerns?" I almost screamed.

"Hold on there, Dirk. I said let me talk now," said the sheriff

With another slight squeeze from Kristen, I settled back down in my chair.

"I'm not surprised at what you've accomplished in bringing this corruption to the forefront. I am surprised that Weatherford, for all his family's community tradition, would commit the crimes you're accusing him of.

"But then again I'm not surprised he's doing it. He's a coke head and everyone knows it, but so far that fact hasn't presented any issues which would warrant any action on my department's part. That's more of a local police jurisdictional thing, and we all know who's in bed with whom, politically that is.

"You present a very good case against Weatherford, especially about the diamond-switching business. I think this situation needs to be looked into very seriously. You're sure your jeweler will testify to the facts as you've related them to me?"

"Yes, he will."

"Okay then, here's how it going to go down, officially. It's a police case now, not yours anymore, Dirk and Kristen, other than as witnesses if necessary.

"We'll start with a warrant to search Weatherford's store, including his safe, for stolen property as soon as possible. I'm confident that there is reasonable cause to believe there is stolen property on the premises. If he still has the stone from Karen's ring and your jeweler friend Steinbeck can identify it, combined with the photos, I'm confident we'll have enough to at the least bring him in for questioning for theft and fraud."

"That's all fine and dandy, Sheriff, and I'd really appreciate that, but I'd like more. I want to have Rembrandt's body exhumed also. Can you do that too, get Rembrandt's body exhumed and have an autopsy performed?"

"Hold on, I was just going to get to that. Since time is becoming of the essence with the state of Rembrandt's body, although the fact that it's still winter, Rembrandt's body should be in a holding vault rather than buried, so that's in our favor.

"I'm going to pull some strings with the DA and Judge Stuart to get both the body exhumed and the search warrant signed. Both the DA, Craig Scobelli and Judge Frank Stuart, are honest servants of the law and personal friends. Besides, we play racquetball together. In fact, we're playing tonight at the Y. I'll explain things to them then. I'm sure their cooperation won't be a problem. By doing it this way, we won't be tipping our collective hats until we are ready to dance.

"Again, since time is of the essence, I think I can get the paperwork processed and signed tonight or tomorrow morning at the latest.

"The only glitch I can foresee is that the coroner normally performs the autopsy. So if there is a conspiracy, we'll need someone other than Oliver Harrison doing it. I'll tell Judge Stuart to specify that there needs to be a reputable assistant present. Should be *no* problem."

CHAPTER 14

AFTER LEAVING THE SHERIFF'S office, we went to the Bridge Tender to have a drink. I myself really needed one, and Kristen did not object. Carla came over and took our order. Double Jack on the rocks for me, and Kristen ordered the same.

We looked out at the deserted windswept marina devoid of all life except a few brave seagulls soaring above the trickling steam of river meandering through the frozen winter ice-widened shores of the river.

We were lost in our own thoughts for a few moments until our drinks arrived. I lit up a Lucky, inhaled deeply and let the smoke out slowly through my nose along with my breath.

"Those things are going to kill you, you know," she said. "Besides, do you know how yucky they smell? One last thing, and I won't harp on your smoking because now would not probably be a good time for you to try and quit. When I kiss a man, I like to smell the man, cologne, his soap or even his own special his essence, not some stinky cigarette odor. Although I have to admit, you don't seem to retain the stink as bad as some."

Getting her subtle hint, I stubbed out my Lucky and moved the ash tray to the next empty table.

"You never said anything before," I said

"Lust."

"Lust?"

"Yeah," she said, "Lust can make you think differently or not even think at all.

"So now you're saying that the lust part is gone?"

"Not on your life, bub. It's just getting started. Ergo where there's no smoke there's a raging fire."

"Did you read that somewhere or did you just make it up?"

"I made it up, But it sounds pretty good, huh?"

"Kind of like thinking with the little head for a guy right?"

"Exactly."

"Okay then, prickly legs."

"Prickly legs?"

"Yeah, after a weekend in bed, tiny little hairs start . . ."

"Okay, let's let this go for now," she conceded.

"Sure get me all hot again thinking about them harrs and . . ."

"Dirk, shut up and drink up."

I picked up my drink and held it up to hers as she raised it to toast. "Here's to hope and justice," I said.

We clinked glasses, and each took a sip.

"Seriously, Dirk, you've done all you can do on this for now. What you gave Sheriff Chambers today was objective reasonable cause to do an official investigation into what could turn out to be the story of the century here in Clinton. But—and I can't stress this enough, lover—you have to let the sheriff do his thing. It's his case now. You just need to sit back, take a breath and let his investigation run its course. You yourself said he was a good man, and he says he's got some good men on his side too.

"So let's see what your friend Carla has on the menu and go back to your place and snuggle by the fire."

"Naked?"

"Of course, naked, silly."

The next morning, I woke up nightmare free and not hung over. This feeling was becoming more the norm than *the norm*, if you know what I mean.

I was beginning to realize, and I know this may sound parapsychotic if that's even a word, but the more I get involved with my mind and sense of justice in this case, then the inverse is true of three things. First and foremost, the nightmare. Second, my need to drink myself into oblivion every night, although an occasional oblivious state of being wasn't completely out of the picture. And third, which at times seems to go hand in hand with the booze, smoking like a chimney as they say.

So anyhow, I woke before Kristen. Seeing her laying there still spooned on her side, it took all the willpower I could muster to get up from our makeshift bed in front of the now ember only fireplace without awakening her. Although the thermostat would keep the house at 68 degrees considering her current state of dress or undress which was naked, I added a few small logs to the fire to duplicate the warm ambience last evening's sojourn of sleep with the cozy delight of the awaking to a new day.

I made coffee and retrieved the *Journal* from the front porch. A dusting of glistening of new snow blanketed the environs of my neighborhood. I went upstairs to take a shower. So unto my assumed solitude did a surprise arise when I opened the steamy shower door to see Kristen sitting knock-kneed on the john with a wad of neatly folded tissue in her hand.

"Good morning," she said, totally unabashed. "I really had to go; do you always keep it this cold in your house?"

"I'm usually too drunk or hung over to notice so it doesn't really matter much to me."

"Well, anyway, thanks for the new logs and hey, why we don't have our coffee in the living room this morning. I have the feeling today might be the first day in the rest of our lives, to coin an old phrase."

"Sounds good to me. By the way, thanks for not flushing while I was in the shower."

"No problem."

A short time later after I had dried off and got dressed for work, I joined her in the living room.

She'd toasted a couple of English muffins that I didn't even know I had and added some cream cheese on a little plate, again, the appearance and existence of which was news to me.

We scanned the *Journal* as we silently ate our breakfast.

"You know, Dirky," she said with a mouthful of muffin. "This isn't much of a journalistic experience is it?" she said, nodding at the paper. "I mean as a community communications medium, it pretty much sucks, doesn't it?"

"Pretty much."

"Do you think TR Foster keeps it this way or is Clinton just that boring?"

"Hey, boss. As managing editor, don't you have a say in what goes to print?"

"Yes."

"Owner or no owner?"

"It's in my job description."

"Good because, God forbid, that this whole deal with Weatherford should go down the shitter, I'm hoping to write the story about the allegations if and when he's brought up on charges.

"Worst case scenario, being that at least the citizens of Clinton will be made aware that all may not be well in Pleasantville."

"Dirk, my love," she said as she held my muffin chewing face in her hands, "I promise you, when you write it and I see it's objective and truthful, it will go to print. If not in the *Clinton Journal*, then in the *Buffalo News*, the *New York Times*, or wherever it takes to bring this travesty of justice to light."

"Good, I was hoping you'd say something like that because I have the feeling that once Sheriff Chambers starts his wheels in motion, it will be only a matter of time before TR gets wind of it, and you and me are going to be out of jobs. I can't help but wonder who, if anyone will print the truth, the whole truth and nothing but the truth, regardless of the political or otherwise forced pressure put on them by messing with the establishment here in Clinton. Hopefully it's a very near-sighted establishment."

"You made a promise and so do I. This will not be tossed in the river to be swept downstream."

"Thank you."

CHAPTER 15

A FTER STOPPING AT KRISTEN'S for her to change clothes, we headed for the *Journal*. We really didn't have much to say on the way and only after the elevator dinged softly at my floor did we speak.

"I'm going to keep Melissa on your old job for a while longer which will keep you free to do whatever comes up," she said with that mischievous smile of hers.

"I'll stay right on top of it," I re-punned with my own sly grin.

"Anyone asks, you're still on that special Rembrandt bootlegging assignment. That keeps you caught up on the surface in things concerning him, for now anyway."

With that, she gave me a small peck on the cheek and said to let her know as soon as I heard anything from the sheriff's office.

She got that last sentence in leaning sideways as the elevator door closed.

I headed over to the coffeepot and saw Melissa headed toward me smiling as usual.

"Morning, Mr. Crandell."

"Morning, Melissa."

"I don't suppose you want a doughnut since you've already had your muffin," she giggled.

No secrets keep here, I guess; it is a newsroom after all.

I grabbed my coffee and headed for my desk. I no sooner sat down when my phone rang. It was Sheriff Chambers.

"Dirk? Wayne Chambers."

"Just wanted you to know a search warrant is being executed at Weatherford's jewelry store as we speak and Rembrandt's body will be exhumed today as well and an autopsy performed ASAP, hopefully late this afternoon or this evening with two of my deputies, who both have medical experience from their time in the Marine Corps assisting. I made this a top priority legal action."

"Holy shit," I said, "You do move fast."

"I told you I'd pull some strings. We really need to, especially the autopsy part. The longer we wait, the more decomposition will take place. The fact that the body has been kept in a holding vault because of the season definitely would slow that process down.

"I'll need the name and phone number of the jeweler in Clarence to examine the diamonds we bag and tag as evidence from Weatherford. He's aware he's going to be called?"

"Yes, he is. He's also has a sworn statement and a notarized photograph of original diamond Karen brought to him along with another photo of the simulant stone and his counterfeit mark on it. I think he's as anxious to nail a crooked jeweler as I am."

I gave him Steinbeck's information.

"Keep me posted will you Wayne?"

"As much as I legally can, Dirk, but now this is an official criminal investigation, and you being a member of the press, the information you'll get will be in the way of official statements. So my unofficial recommendation is to hound my office for updates on the proceedings. Stay close—things are happening fast, my boy."

"Gotcha, and Wayne, thanks for listening to me."

"Give it until tomorrow morning, Dirk, and by that time, we'll have had time to gather and process enough information to make an official statement."

"I'll call my boss, and let her know," I said

"Oh, she already knows."

"What do you mean she already knows?"

"Since there was no family of record, as a courtesy, I thought that the young lady you mentioned yesterday from Los Angeles who had been taken in by Mintz many years ago should at least be notified so I called Kristen for a number I could contact her at. She said she didn't have it, but she would tell you and you would contact her. And then I told Kristen, as a heads up on the possible news breaker, what I just told you, being you two were basically working together on this story."

"Thanks, Wayne, I'll call her."

As soon as I hung up, I got a call for Kristen telling me the same thing and would I mind calling Baby and telling her what was going on. Better to hear it from me anyway.

I said, "Yes, and thanks for letting me be the one to tell her."

Then she warned me to stay cool and don't get too excited about this whole thing until the powers to be found something hard and fast to go on. I could tell something was seriously bothering her because there was no sexual innuendo added to the hard and fast comment.

"Hey, what's up kid," I said.

"It's just that with all that's happening with Weatherford and the exhumation of Rembrandt's body—well, it's just that if all of what you suspect is true, these guys are not only criminals but they are evil. How far does this web of corruption spread and to what end will they go to cover their tracks. If Rembrandt was murdered, then they can't and won't stop there. Why should they. You yourself said they all think they are exempt from the law, and well, Dirk, I'm worried for you. Be careful."

"I will," I said, "frankly I'm surprised I haven't heard any repercussions yet. You've got that Clinton Restoration thing tonight, don't you?"

"Yeah, it's probably going to be a long meeting so I won't be home 'til late."

"That's okay, I've got to call Baby and then make a few other calls, and I'd rather make them from home anyway."

"More privacy, I can't blame you, the walls are pretty thin around here lately."

"Yeah, well there's that, and then there's also more JD at home."

"I should have known, see you tomorrow." And she hung up.

When I got home, I poured myself a generous tumbler of JD over a couple of ice cubes. I placed my call to Baby and caught her just on her way out. I told her all that I knew and asked her did she mind not being here for the exhumation.

She said that was okay because she wouldn't be able to be here at this time anyway because she had some very time-sensitive things to take care of and to send her a copy of the official results if that was okay.

I told her I would get her all the information that I could.

She said, "Uncle Dirk, my dad was right about you. Regardless of the outcome of all of this, thank you from the bottom of my heart." With that, she said good-bye and hung up.

I had planned to call Darlene and Karen to keep them abreast of recent events and make sure they were still sworn to secrecy. There was however one thing niggling me about Baby. I'm surprised with everything going down, with the exhumation, autopsy and stuff that she wouldn't want to be here for it. Oh, what the hell, she probably had exams or something. As long as she was kept abreast of things, it was probably no big deal.

First call was to Darlene Highland. Although it was the middle of the day, I hoped I'd catch her still at home. She picked up on the third ring.

"Hey, Darlene, it's Dirk, do you have a minute? It's kind of important."

"Wow, Dirk, you sound so serious, yeah, I have some time. You still working on trying to get that thieving bastard Weatherford on his diamond switching thing? I certainly hope so."

"Yes, I am, and that's what I'm calling about. You haven't said anything to anyone about this yet have you, Dar?"

"Dirk, honey, I promised you I wouldn't so no, I haven't breathed a word to anyone, not even my mother."

I knew how close Darlene was to her mother, so if she hadn't said anything to her, she hadn't said anything to anyone.

"What I'm calling about you're probably going to hear or read about in the news in the next couple of days anyway, but I think we, meaning me and the sheriff have or will have enough evidence on Weatherford to bring him up on charges. They have a warrant and searched his store this morning."

"Wow, that's great. If he's switching diamonds on other people like what he did to us, he *should* be arrested."

"Okay, Dar, I know you have some jewelry from his store, and I imagine your mom does too. Once it comes out in the press that our illustrious Clinton jeweler is accused of ripping off his clients, I'd like to provide the DA with as much incriminating evidence as I can. Will you help me or better yet the case out here? It might mean you may have to go to court or at least make a statement."

"You got it, Dirk. After stealing Dick's diamond from me, I'll do whatever it takes to send David to jail."

"I was hoping I could count on you. Do you think you and your mom get together any diamonds in any settings, along with their GIA certifications, receipts of work he did, resetting, resizing, cleaning, appraisals—anything actually that Weatherford had to do with after the initial purchase, if you still have them. Anything even bought somewhere else that has authentication that went to him also."

"You know, Dirk, I know my mom has some really fine pieces my dad bought for her when he was alive.

"Oh my god!" she said, becoming livid. "It just occurred to me if that son of a bitch has been doing this crap for a while, he probably switched on my mom too. I'll kill him if he did."

"Let's hope, Darlene, that Weatherford only just recently started committing these crimes to support his drug habit. I can't imagine his father, who had the business before him, even remotely conjuring up a plan like this."

"I hope you're right, Dirk, for my mom's sake and a lot of other people whose life's mementos were entrusted to him. But he's been into drugs for a while that I know of. My husband, Dick, I'm ashamed to say, was involved with him for years."

Darlene went on to say, "Okay, so once it's out in public, I'll talk to my mom and try not to get her excited. She thinks the world of young David's dad. But she's never had too much good to say about David the IV. I'll help wherever I can Dirk, you can count on me."

I hung up with a heavy heart because if Weatherford had switched out the diamonds on Marie's rings, what twenty five years ago, he been committing this sham for a long, long time. My thought that maybe his deception had been a personal thing to get me was gone. I hoped for the sake of anyone in Clinton who had done business with him I was dead wrong. Hopefully, that last thought was not clairvoyant. But I knew in my liquor-saturated gut that I was right, and damnit, I was going to prove it.

Next, I called Karen. I told her the same thing about the search warrant. I told her I was sorry about her engagement ring and diamond being held by Steinbeck as evidence and asked how Tom was handling it.

She said he was fine with it, but he still wanted to "rip Weatherford's head off and shit down his neck," but he'd be cool.

"In fact, we went to Steinbeck's in Clarence and he bought me another ring so I'd still have a token of his love for me on my finger. Isn't that cool, Dirk?"

"Karen, no one deserves it more at this point in their life than you do," I said from the bottom of my heart.

"Hey, sis?" I said.

"Yeah?"

"This is all still staying quiet, right, at least until Weatherford is arrested right? Both you and Tom, okay?"

"Yes, bro."

"Thanks," and I hung up.

I poured myself another large tumbler of JD, donned my hooded sweatshirt, and went out on my deck. I lit up a smoke and thought about what Harden said about these things killing me someday. Well, it was probably a hell of a race between my liver and my lungs, with the winner opening death's door for me.

I don't know why I felt so morbid. Things were finally starting to fall into place with Weatherford almost certainly about to be brought up on charges. The mystery surrounding Rembrandt's death was about to be solved, good or bad. And me, I was having a pretty serious relationship with a gorgeous, sexy, smart woman, fifteen years my junior. What could be better?

My guts were telling me this deal with Weatherford was not going to be a walk in the park; not with Truehardt in his corner, which would be a given. I had a lot of faith in Sheriff Chambers and the good guys. But—and it's a bit of stretch—this conspiracy theory and the conspiring bad guys here owned this town for a long time.

CHAPTER 16

I GOT TO THE *Journal* early again for a change around 8:00 a.m. and decided to skip my usual coffee and went right to my desk. I no sooner hung up my coat when I got a call from TR Foster's office. He wanted to see me right away and his secretary emphasized, *right away*!

I called Kristen's office, but her secretary said she was also in a meeting with TR. This could not be good.

When I arrived at TR's office, the waiting room door was open, and I spotted TR as soon as he spotted me. He impatiently waved me in.

As I entered, I saw Kristen already seated in front of her boss. To the side, I spied none other than Allen Truehardt, the attorney; legs crossed who nodded at my presence after which he picked invisible lint from his $500 trousers. TR motioned for me to take the seat next to Kristen, and I did.

He didn't waste any time, nor did he ask his secretary to close the anteroom door.

"Just what the hell are you two up to?" he growled.

"What do you mean, TR?" I said, full of innocence.

"I just got a call from a hysterical David Weatherford that the sheriff's office was searching his store for stolen property. Then, I no sooner hung up with him when I get another call from Oliver Harrison questioning me, or better yet screaming at me, as to why that bum's body found drunk and floating in the river a month or so ago is being exhumed for an autopsy. As if that's not bad enough, he's ranting and raving that the sheriff's department is going to post two of his own deputies in the morgue to witness and verify the autopsy findings. So getting back to my question, just what the hell is going on here, Crandell?"

"Well, TR," I said, mustering all the blamelessness I could. "As you know, I *have* been looking into the rumor that someone was trying to sell off reproductions of the paintings of W.E. Mintz, locally known as Rembrandt or the bum, as you just called him, as authentic WEM paintings. The originals, since his death, by the way, are becoming quite valuable. So maybe the sheriff's department suspect that the bum, again as you call him, was murdered.

"Although to date, I have found nothing to actually verify that said reproductions have been sold or even exist for that matter. And since, to my limited knowledge, I don't believe an autopsy was performed when his body was found in the river. Maybe they just want to prove beyond a reasonable doubt that the man did in fact get drunk and fall in the river and drown. Just like the chief of police and his brother stated in their press release."

I knew it as soon as I said it, and I could hear Kristen' audible sigh, both of us knowing I had said way, way too much for him to buy into my explanation. He didn't get to be the head of his rather large empire by being stupid and gullible.

TR took it all in and then leaned forward with his hands intertwined as if in prayer and said, "You know what I think. I think that you have had a giant hard on for almost everyone in this city except your favorite bartenders, liquor store operators, your whore of a sister-in-law and your new whore who is at the moment sitting next to you and who incidentally is now fired."

He rapid-fired on, "The only way to justify your vengeful conduct is for you dream up some cockamamy story and get your old buddy, the sheriff, to listen to you over a half gallon of Jack Daniels with some sob story about since your poor drunken slut of a wife died. Nobody loves you anymore, boohoo. So you want drag everyone who leads a decent life and made something of themselves down in the gutter to hell with you.

"Sorry, asshole it's over. No one is going to give a rat's ass about any of this. For one thing, none of it will ever be published by this newspaper so the story ends before it begins."

Raging, and on fire inside, it was all I could do to control my anger after his descriptions of my wife and family, I said, mustering as much control as I could, "I'll just take it to the Buffalo papers, more people read them here in Clinton anyway, way more credibility than this rag."

"No, you won't," piped in Truehardt, "By law, you can't feed this story anywhere but here because you're in its employ, and therefore, the *Journal* has literary privilege to the story unless we sign off on it, which we're not going to do."

I'm not familiar with the actual law in matters of this kind but, with Truehardt here, I suspected it may or may not have some validity to it but I was in no position to question it.

"I thought I was fired?" I quizzed.

"You are now, but you weren't when you began this debacle. Yes, you drunken piece of shit, both you and your girlfriend here are done here and with my influence, which I can guarantee you is substantial, I'll see to it that neither of you will ever work for a newspaper again, not even selling them on a corner, where I expect to see you drinking your lunch from a paper bag while you're pimping out Miss-easy-lay here."

Kristen never said a word, but I could feel the internal seething during TR's entire tirade. Finally she spoke as TR leaned back in his mammoth chair like the little tyrant that he was and Truehardt continued to pick invisible lint from his trousers.

"I do not like or deserve your vulgar name-calling but it's nothing less than what I would expect from a little man in a big chair, however on what grounds are you terminating my employment? I have done nothing outside of my job description to warrant dismissal."

Actually, she was right on this. She just backed a writer who thought he had a story. But we both knew differently.

"And even if I had, which once more I haven't, I have a contract and it spells out that I'll receive one year's salary as my severance pay."

"Read it closer, sweetie. Read the morals clause. Among all your blatant, salacious behavior out in the open here in this building for all to witness, and by fucking numb nuts here in the elevator constitutes a lewd and lascivious behavior. That's breech, baby, and you're fucked again; no severance, right, Allen?" he asked as he looked smugly at his attorney. Truehardt nodded in agreement.

"That never happened, and you know it, TR," she said, calmer than I would have. "And even if it did, you have no proof."

"Aha, my nephew Brian said when he was interning here, he accidentally caught you one evening while he was working late."

"That's a lie, a bold-faced lie. It never happened."

"I have his sworn statement here," he said, as he waved an official looking piece of paper at her. "You're done here Harden, pack your things, and I'll have a security guard escort you out. And by the way, you, too, have a legal obligation not to use any information you obtained while you were in our employ without our consent, subject to a lawsuit. Now get your sorry asses out of my sight."

Kristen and I stood up and turned around and headed for the door without another word until we were almost out when I turned and said to the little man sitting in the big chair. "You and *your* girlfriend here, nodding at Truehardt may think this is over, or that you're just going to make it go away like you always have, you little prick, but this time, you're not, not by a long shot." And we left.

On the way down in the elevator, I said to Kristen, "I'm really sorry I dragged you into this. I never expected he'd fire you. I'm really sorry. Anything I can do?"

"You didn't drag me into this, Dirky Boy. I'm a journalist and I saw the possibility of a story and I did what I felt was right. That includes you and me."

"What happens now?" I asked.

"You keep digging on this. You have the sheriff on your side so they can't do anything to you, but make your life miserable."

"Been there, done that," I said.

"Me," she said, "I have a sister in Florida that I haven't seen in a while. I think I'll go and see her and enjoy some warm weather."

"When?"

"Tomorrow morning. TR has been a busy little boy. I've been dismissed from all my board positions in Clinton."

"Why so soon, what about us?"

"Dirky, I'm finished here in Clinton. I won't be able to get a job doing what I do anywhere. You heard TR. He means it. Time to move on. But Dirk, promise me you'll finish this and I mean finish it. You—given what's just happened—won't be any good to yourself or anyone else for that matter until you do. I'll be fine. I'll give you a call when I'm settled. And just so you know, this is not easy for me, but it's best."

With that, we got to her floor, and she turned and gave me the softest kiss on the lips I ever experienced and turned and walked away. "Fuck," I said to myself. But even as much as I cared for her which was becoming a lot more than just care, I knew she was right. There was more involved now than my promise to Baby, way more.

CHAPTER 17

THE DARK ROOM WAS filled with flashing red lights, the wail of sirens, the sound of sleet pummeling the windows the deathly pounding in my chest . . .

I snapped awake, and once my brain went from subconscious to conscious, I was perplexed. I'd thought the déjà vu nightmare and my time-looped reaction to it was gone. Ever since I had met Kristen and got involved in this case, the terrible dream had *almost* become extinct. Surprise, surprise. So instead of my normal reaction of booze and butts, I got up and went downstairs and made some very strong coffee.

So having not slept all that well, Wednesday morning came way earlier than I would have liked. I retrieved the *Journal* from the front porch and actually read it to help pass the time until the normal world woke up. While having my third or fourth cup of coffee and having finished the paper, even the friggin' want ads, I got a call from Sheriff Wayne Chambers asking me to meet him in his office right away. He had some important information for me concerning the Mintz/Weatherford case.

I grabbed my coat and was gone. I let the windshield wipers do their, job and they really struggled to clear the window. I figured if I drove fast enough, the goddess of winter wind would take care of the rest of the previous night's snow accumulation. It worked, somewhat.

On the way to the sheriff's office through the blizzard of the goddess's work in progress, I thought that if Chambers didn't know I'd been fired, maybe it's best not to say anything. I wasn't sure what the repercussions would be, but I'd worry about that later. It was still my investigative story, and I was damn well going to see it to fruition.

Once I got there, I was greeted by his receptionist, Stephanie, and told that the sheriff was expecting me. I went in and sat down. I figured if he didn't say anything about Harden not being there, again, all the better.

"Dirk," he smiled, "you're going to friggin' love this. We got us a double header. I've not only got the official results of the William Mintz autopsy, which proves he didn't drown but was murdered, and the results of the search warrant from Weatherford's Jewelry Store. And the evidence from which justifies that he be picked up for suspicion of grand theft and fraud."

"Holy shit, really!" I gasped.

"Wait, there's more on Mintz' autopsy, and this is something I never expected. Mintz actually died from a gunshot wound to the back of his head, not drowning as first reported. There was no water found in his lungs which means that he was dead before he went in the water. Toxicology couldn't tell about alcohol in his system because of the time frame since his death, but his liver had been perfectly healthy. That means your theory and information that he was not the drunk everyone portrayed him to be was accurate."

"Goddamn!" I said.

"And the really surprising part of this puzzle," he went on, "is that during the search of Weatherford's store, a .22 caliber pistol was found in his safe and the ballistics from that gun match the bullet taken from Mintz' skull."

"Holy shit, this just keeps getting better and better."

"Yes, it does, and the beat goes on," continued the sheriff. "Mr. Steinbeck was asked to be along as an expert, all legally spelled out on the warrant, and he verified a ring, Karen's, found in the suspects safe as being the one brought to him at his store in Clarence and that he had switched the real diamond for a simulant and specially it marked at your request at his store. The diamond simulant in that setting from Weatherford's safe was not the same one that was brought to Steinbeck. It had been switched. Steinbeck will testify to this. Now based on this evidence and other pieces of jewelry found in Weatherford's safe, we expanded our search to Weatherford's home office. Being listed on the tax rolls as a satellite office of the downtown store, the warrant covers the house too.

"It appears that some of Trisha Weatherford's jewelry has diamonds which aren't authenticated for the settings they're in, which in itself is not a crime. However, the Weatherfords' have no records of ownership of the diamonds. Steinbeck says they're GIA-certified diamonds, but there are no certificates to prove ownership or bills of sale justifying the Weatherfords' having them. He also said with a little back check, he can trace their history and see if the path leading them to the Weatherfords' was all above board. He said it might take him a couple of days. but he's going to be on this like white on rice. The old guy is really pissed that a seemingly legitimate jeweler would try to rip off trusting customers."

"Gives us all a black eye," he said.

"So based on all of this evidence, we've issued a warrant for David Weatherford IV's arrest on suspicion of murder along with the fraud and theft charges."

"I can't believe this!" I said excitedly. "You nailed his ass. Unfuckingbelievable!"

"The only problem, Dirk, is that Weatherford has Allen Truehardt for an attorney, and he's questioning the jurisdiction of my department over the city police in this matter because of the location of the alleged crime."

"But the local chief of police is in on it!" I exclaimed rising from my chair.

"Whoa, boy, the DA is a county position, and he ordered a grand jury to look into a conspiracy to cover-up a murder on government property under which the Clinton River falls. The New York State Thruway Authority has legal responsibility and jurisdiction for the river and the river's rights of way, and the DA has sought an injunction to take this case away from local authorities since they're all named as co-conspirators. If this goes well, it's going to shake a lot of rotten apples from the old tree, but let me caution you, that's a big if. Truehardt is a tried and tested criminal defense attorney and these are his friends."

"But the evidence speaks for itself, doesn't it, Wayne?"

"Maybe and maybe not, but we at least have enough to try Weatherford for larceny and fraud. We need motive for the murder. Weatherford insists that he only got possession of the gun about two weeks ago from a botched robbery attempt, which by the way he didn't report. It'll be hard to prove Weatherford murdered Mintz with no witnesses and his explainable fingerprints on the weapon. Truehardt will probably be able to get that charge dismissed with reasonable doubt unless Weatherford is lying about the gun and the New York State Police report verifies his ownership. That would prove him lying about how and when he obtained possession of the gun. But again, with no witnesses to the actual murder, too many possible explanations will be available to Truehardt to, pardon my pun, but to shoot holes in. I'm sorry to tell you the DA may have to concede that evidence as reasonable doubt to make all the rest of what we have on Weatherford stick because on the other charges, we have him dead nuts.

"I've talked at length with the DA, who incidentally is Lou Scrobelli from the Falls and originally from the law firm of Scrobelli, Scrobelli, and Dimaggio. They are a definite force to be reckoned with. Needless to say, they have some very good and not so good—if you get my meaning—connections, and word is they really don't care much for the faggot forces in Clinton, as they call them. Add to that the fact that the DA is an elected county position, not a civil position. He cannot be removed from office by city or county officials, so no fear there."

I looked up in surprise as the sheriff continued. "Hey, what can I say, Truehardt, TR and the rest of the good ol' boys reputations precede them both in and out of the locker room, if you get my drift. Dirk, Me, Lou and Tony Scrobelli and Mario Dimaggio play racquetball together and guys talk. We have quite a battle on our hands, but the DA is a legitimate honest, justice-seeking citizen who's just as fed up with these upstanding citizens running this town as much as you or I."

"Holy shit!" was all I could muster. This was beyond, way beyond my wildest expectations from when this whole thing started. I sure didn't want to muck it up now so I decided to come clean with the fact that I was no longer working for TR and the *Journal*, so I told him.

He looked stunned for a moment, leaned back in his chair, and rubbed his clean-shaven face with his hands.

Uh, oh, I thought to myself. I hope this doesn't change anything.

"Dirk, this could be a plus for us actually. With TR officially taking you off this story and Ms. Harden gone, neither of you will be able to exploit TR's restricted literary privilege when this goes to trial, the potential jury pool will be totally unaware of any press bias influencing the trial. One question though, since you can't officially write this story now, do you have someone you can really trust who would and could take your background material and under the table collaborate with you to write this story, or should I call it an exposé maintaining the integrity of its authenticity without fear of repercussions from the *Journal*'s powers-to-be. It sure would be nice if these assholes, pardon my French, could be all exposed first-hand for what they aren't."

"I'm pretty sure." I said. "But I'll have to check to see if she signed a contract like Kristen and I did. Then I'll try and use my wiles to convince her it's the right thing to do and working for the *Journal* really isn't journalism in truth, but Foster's own agenda. A fact she has already been subjected to through the obit on old Dr. Johnson. Besides, working here under the present circumstances sucks, and she could do a lot better elsewhere, especially with an epic corruption story like this one under her belt. And if not, I'll take the lawsuit. The whole story is too important not to be told."

I wanted to call Baby and give her the news that her father had been murdered like she had suspected all along. All I got was her machine. I didn't want to leave a lot of detail on a message so I told her to call me as soon as possible.

Later at home on a Buffalo TV station's six o'clock news was a short story about the arrest of a prominent Clinton jeweler for possession of suspected contraband diamonds. Allen Truehardt spoke briefly outside the county courthouse on the fly.

"This has all been a gross misunderstanding. And the absurd charges against my client, Mr. Weatherford, will be dropped once the truth comes to light. These ridiculous charges have been fabricated and brought against my client as a personal vendetta based on absolutely no viable evidence whatsoever. Neither I nor my client will have anything further to say in public on this matter."

With that, Truehardt turned his back on the cameras and whisked his smirking client away.

The reporter said, "And now onto sports."

That was it?

No murder charges, no mention of the gun linking Weatherford to the murder, no fraud or conspiracy to commit fraud or grand larceny? This was pure and total bullshit. And later, I found out he was out of jail on his own recognizance. This was TR and Truehardt and their political machine at its finest.

I called Sheriff Chambers, and before I could say two words, he said, "I saw it, and don't worry about it yet. We're still in the game. Trust me, Dirk, we're going to get him."

I tried Baby again; still no answer.

So I went down to the Bridge Tender for a bite and some booze. I tried Kristen from the pay phone when I got there, but her line was no longer in service. Wow, I knew she believed in clean breaks, but holy shit. Well, maybe this was for the best. I must have been fucking dreaming to think a beautiful, sexy woman like her could ever fall for a bum like me. It was fun while it lasted, but it's over. Deal with it, Dirky Boy.

I took my usual table by the window and flung my coat over a chair and took a seat. Carla was still in the kitchen, so she came over smiled and said, "What are you gonna have today, Dirk?" I had the special of cabbage soup and bratwurst and, of course, a Labatt with a double Jack chaser. Then I went home.

My dinner was flatulence waiting to roil. Didn't much matter if I farted myself to sleep tonight since I was going to be alone anyway. Kristen used to get so mad when I farted. I still can't believe the old "pull my finger" trick worked with her. She got so mad, but I could tell she was really smiling under the angry façade. Oh well, life goes on. It did after Marie, and although it sucks big-time, it will again, I guess. Kristen was right though; I really needed to finish what I'd started here, or I wouldn't be worth squat to myself or anyone else.

I turned on the TV and caught one of the early rounds of March Madness. Always had a fondness for the North Carolina Tar Heels and the Duke Blue Devils. But instead, I got to watch Notre Dame and Indiana. Notre Dame, there's a young lad's dream college, With all of these pedophilia accusations surrounding the Catholic Church, it's priests and the cover-up contiguous with the whole mess and, since cover-up seems to fit right into their lifestyles, maybe Truehardt or TR would send their boys there as sort of a gay prep school. Anyway, with nothing much going on probably because my mind was elsewhere, I finally went to bed.

CHAPTER 18

I WOKE UP THE next morning to the news on the radio. "Dr. Bernard Johnson Jr. was found shot to death in his office late last night. Chief of police, Stanley Harrison, suspected that the perpetrator was after drugs and was surprised by the victim while in the act of the felony. It appears Dr. Johnson was shot three times, two in the lower torso and once in the head. He was discovered by his maid. 'This investigation will warrant all of the law enforcement resources at our disposal to bring this heinous criminal to justice. People just don't commit murder in my town and get away with it,'" he said.

Well, I guess that depends who is the murderer and who is the victim, I thought to myself. The weather said another cold front was coming in, and since the lakes were finally pretty much frozen, the lake-effect snow should only be a couple of inches.

I went out to get my paper and found it under some snow on the porch. I looked out at the drive and was actually glad I didn't have to battle being plowed in because I didn't have a job to go to for now.

I scanned over the paper, and there was nothing, nada, about Weatherford in the news. Why didn't *that* surprise me? Evidently, Junior's murder happened too late to make the morning paper.

Too bad for his wife and kids. Losing old Doc Johnson such a short time ago, and now Junior, I don't want to speak ill of the dead, but Junior was one of the sinister six and did have a hand in Samantha's beating and rape, so maybe what goes around comes around. Karma or some shit like that. Anyway, I feel bad for the innocents in the whole thing.

I wanted to try Baby again since I hadn't heard from her, but it was too early with the time zone differences and all, but I was beginning to get worried that she hadn't answered my call. I'd try her again at noon that should be about 8:00 a.m. there. Unless she had early classes, maybe I'd catch her at home.

I decided I'd go and shovel out my drive, but I heard the soothing familiar sound of the dummy next door firing up his truck and figured better him to do the snow removal than me.

So I showered and shaved and just kind of straightened up until noon, and then I tried Baby again. No answer.

I dug around in my piles of organized clutter and found the number of her aunt Kathleen and tried her. I caught her on the third ring. She was just on her way out the door herself and told me that Baby had decided to take some time off and went back east. She was really surprised that she hadn't contacted me or returned my calls because according to her aunt, I was all she talked about lately. She even had referred to me as Uncle Dirk. Kathleen said she was looking forward to meeting me on her next trip to Toronto in a month or so, and said we should do lunch or something. But on a more serious note, she and I agreed that if either of us heard from Baby soon, we'd let the other know. She didn't seem too worried because sometimes Baby took off to see friends and wasn't real good about letting her know everything.

I don't know why, but I decided to clean house a little. A little vacuuming, a little dusting, just a lick and a promise, as my mother used to say.

Sometimes, during a full moon, I still talked to Emily. Great Gal. Even after all these years, I still missed her. But during a full moon, I felt especially close to her, maybe because she crossed over during a full moon.

I ordered a small Umberto's white pizza with spinach and anchovies and then watched the Sabres tie the Chicago Blackhawks one to one on TV. Watching sixty minutes of hockey only to have a one-one tie is like kissing your sister, although I've never had a sister. Come to think about it, I've known some guys whose sisters' I wouldn't have minded kissing but hey, what the heck. Oh well, I only half-heartedly watched it anyway. The only good part besides the pizza was my faithful companion Jack at my side.

When I finally woke up, it was 9:00 a.m. It didn't take long to break the habit of getting up early for work. I was about to put the coffee, on but decided what the heck, maybe I'd treat myself to breakfast out.

Probably a good choice, since I didn't have a lick of food in the house. Groceries were never one of my domestic strong suits anyway.

I went down to Elaine's Diner, a little place we used to call the Greasy Spoon, open 24/7. Last of the short-order cooks worked there. A very large woman with yellow hair manned the grill. I sat at the counter, and when she came over to me, she filled a coffee cup that came from a shelf behind her and said, "What'll it be sweetie?" as she took the pencil from somewhere behind her ear and out of her hair. She licked the tip and poised to take my order.

"I'd like a cheese omelet with sharp cheese, home fries—extra crispy and wheat toast."

She took my order, and while I was waiting I unfolded the *Journal* I had scooped up from my porch as I left home. The front page was dominated by the murder of Junior or Dr. Bernard Johnson Jr. A picture of him taken professionally centered the page along with the article reporting that according to Chief of Police Stanley Harrison, the investigation was continuing with all of the resources available to him. He reported that Dr. Johnson must have put up quite a struggle with his assailant judging from the condition of the office where the crime was committed, but had been overpowered because of the nature of the wounds. It appeared that the victim was shot twice in the groin area and then in the head. This, according to the chief, indicated that the doctor had tried to wrestle the gun away from the assailant resulting in the two gunshots in the torso. The victim must have been lying wounded on the floor when the assailant fired point-blank into the victim's forehead. Chief Harrison said an autopsy showed the headshot killed Dr. Johnson instantly.

A pretty gruesome account of a crime by the *Journal's* standards. I suspect this was done to try and add effect to the crime for down the road trial purposes. Again, Harrison reiterated his promise to catch the perpetrator swiftly.

My order arrived just as I put the paper down.

"Quite a thing we've got going here in sleepy little Clinton," said Amy, according to her name tag.

"You mean about Dr. Johnson being murdered?" I asked.

"Yeah, that and Carl Southerland being gunned down outside the Crypt late last night."

"What?" I said, astonished as I dropped my fork on the floor.

"Yeah, I was talking to two cops who just left here a little while ago who worked an all-nighter at the crime scene. Overheard em' sayin' he was shot in the balls twice, same as young Doc Johnson. Sounds like they was both tappin' the same well, and the lady got real pissed off. Either that, or a poor clueless husband found out and fixed it so it wouldn't happenin' no more. Although from what I've heard, Doc. Johnson weren't the kind of guy to be doin' that kinda a thing. Gittin' kind a scary around here."

I absently said thanks and threw a twenty on the counter and left. I went straight back home and called Sheriff Chambers. Stephanie said that Wayne had been trying to call me and put me through to him.

"Wayne, what the hell is going on?" I said in bewilderment.

He said, "I want to ask you the same thing. Nothing goes on in Clinton Country for all this time, except some old guy killing some poor old lady's poodle for shitting on his front porch, and now two murders in two days, and somehow I think your investigation is at the center of it, but there something missing. Fill me in, Dirk, or I'm going to begin to think you're involved somehow, taking out your revenge on these country club guys."

Bingo! A light and sirens went off in my head when he said that.

"Wayne, I have no idea," trying to conceal my racing thoughts. "But I guarantee it's not me. Trust me."

"If I didn't know about this corruption scam going on and that its tentacles may be farther reaching than what we've uncovered so far, Dirk, I'd ask you where you were last night and if can you prove it."

"Again, trust me on this, and by the way, I was home alone and, no I can't prove it."

On the way home for some unknown reason, probably my brain was trying to white out the reality of what was really going on here in Clinton, my thoughts drifted to the fact that, I know it seems comical to some, but obviously not so for Mrs. Green, whose beloved poodle Fifi or Fufu was shot. The poor little thing must have finally pissed off or obviously worse, Mr. Wiley enough that he shot the little bitch. I always thought that this quarrel would end mortally for someone involved. I'm just glad it was the dog and not one of the disputers who got whacked.

When I got home, the realization of what was really going on here was coming to the forefront of my thoughts, loud and clear. Revenge, pure and simple, that was what the warnings and sirens were all about. I decided to call Karen. She picked up almost on the first ring.

"Dirk, what's up?"

I still can't get used to caller ID, but I went on.

"Karen, do you remember Baby?"

"Sure, bro, why do you ask?"

"Is she staying there at the Marriot by any chance that you know of? Have you seen her at the bar or in the restaurant in the last couple of days?"

"Yeah, sure, in fact we had a drink last night about seven just before I started my shift."

"Really, did she say why she was here, or better yet, what she was going to do last night?"

"Actually, yes, twice. She said she was here to tie up some loose ends concerning her father's belongings and she had heard that the Crypt was a cool place to go for night life and I told her it was because until recently, I worked there. She asked me why I wasn't working there anymore because I seemed so personable for a bartender that she couldn't understand why I'd left."

"What did you tell her?"

"I told her the reason I left was because Carl Southerland the owner, was a groping pig, and I'd had enough of his grab ass, so I quit."

Then she said, "Oh, does he do that to all the women in there?"

I said, "No, Southerland, seems to only grab employee's asses; it's like a power trip or something for him. I hear he does the same thing out at the Clinton Country Club with the waitress, but they make good money so they let it go."

She said, "thanks, maybe she'd check it out anyway."

"We finished our drinks and she left."

"Did you happen to see her before last night?"

"Yeah, she's been here a couple of days, why do you ask?"

"Oh, no reason," I lied. "I've just been trying to get a hold of her because I have a picture of her painted by her father that I wanted to give to her, but I've been unable to reach her. Hey Karen, how's everything else going?"

"Oh, Dirk, I feel like Cinderella with Tom. I never knew there were men like him out there. I'm so happy."

"That's wonderful, sis, he seems like a really nice guy. By the way, does Baby stop by the bar every day?"

"Yeah, actually, I see her coming in now."

"Do you think you could keep her occupied for a while, for like forty minutes or so or at least find out what kind of car she's driving?"

"Do you just want me to tell her to wait here for you?"

"No, no, I want my gift to her to be a surprise."

Not a very good explanation, but it was the best I could come up with without drawing any suspicion from Karen and thus not alerting Baby to my queries.

My plan, if that's what you'd call it, was to follow Baby to see just exactly where and what loose ends she was tying up. I was hoping to God that my suspicions were way wrong. But oh, sweet Jesus, what if they were right?

I took off for the Marriot as soon as I got off the phone, and about twenty minutes into my ride, I got a call on my Journal cell phone, which I hadn't turned in yet, from Karen.

"Baby just left. She said she was going back to Clinton today and then she was scheduled to fly back home tomorrow. I asked her how she was going to get there, did she need a lift because I got off work in about an hour. She told me thanks, but she had a rental car, and she was fine.

"I asked what kind she had because they always seemed to want to upgrade me whenever I rented one from the airport. She told me no, the rental company actually told her she would get a Toyota Camry and that's what she got.

"So I asked, I'll bet it's white, it seems like all rental cars are white. She told me no, it was actually dark blue, which was a surprise to her as well. Did I do okay, bro?"

"Oh, Karen, you did great. I'm going to have to take you and Tom out for a celebratory dinner at Salvatore's, or someplace of your choice really nice."

"Deal," she said, and we parted phone ways.

I no sooner hung up when a Dark Blue Toyota Camry went past me in the opposite direction. No doubt in my mind that it was Baby behind the wheel.

I did an immediate turnaround and went after her. I finally caught up with her just outside of Clinton. I'm not good at tailing people because I've never done it before, but I don't think it made any difference because she had no reason to believe anyone was tailing her. She went down Center Street and found a place to park about a block from Weatherford's Jewelry and got out of the rental. I found a place to park about a half a block away. It was in a handicapped place, but what the hell, I'd deal with those consequences, if any, later.

I walked down the street to Weatherford's and saw that the We're Closed sign was spun around on the window. I tried to peer in because I was pretty sure I'd seen Baby enter the store in my rearview mirror just minutes ago.

I tried the door—locked.

I felt in my gut this was not good.

Fearing the worst, my adrenalin was going into overtime urging my out of shape legs on as I ran around to the back of the store, hoping beyond hope that my fears were wrong, and if they weren't, I wasn't going to be too late. As soon as I reached the backdoor and turned the handle, two things happened at the same time.

The door opened, and I heard the unmistakable retort of a gunshot.

I charged into the store and saw Baby with a smoking gun in hand standing over a whimpering, bleeding David Weatherford.

She must have heard me come barging in because she turned on me with vehemence in her eyes and the gun aimed at my head. As soon as she recognized me, her eyes softened somewhat but not all together, and she turned the gun back on Weatherford.

"Dirk," she almost hissed. "Go away, this is not your business any more. Just turn around and go away."

"Baby," I said, out of breath and foolishly heroic, "I can't, and I won't let you do this."

"Yes, I can, and I'm going to."

With that, she fired another round into the prone Weatherford's groin area.

I started after her, but she spun on me and again pointed the gun at my forehead.

I, not wanting to be a dead hero, stopped dead in my tracks, hoping that this was not going to be my last pun.

"Stop, Baby," I said. "Think about what you're doing. He's not worth it. He's going to jail for a very long time for his grand theft and fraud charges and if we're lucky, even the murder of your father."

Weatherford lay bleeding on the floor and crying like a little girl, moaning. "She's crazy, she broke in here and shot me for no reason. Call me an ambulance, call 911, you asshole, call the police. Don't just stand there, you drunken fool, do something!"

Baby looked momentarily at the sorry sight on the floor with the pool of blood slowly spreading around his wounded area and then back at me.

"Dirk, don't move, I mean it! He's going to die right here, right now just like Dr. Bernard Johnson Jr. and Carl Southerland did."

"You did kill them then, I thought it was you, but why? And why Weatherford, I already told you he was going away for a long time. Why throw your life away, you're so young and you have so much going for you. Why toss it all away for this scum."

"You want to know why, I'll tell you!" she spat. "Southerland and Johnson raped my mother, along with the others, but they went on to beat her senseless and tossed her in the river to die, which she did. Not physically right away, but that night they killed her inside. It was just a matter of time before her physical death caught up with her emotional death.

"They got away with it, or so they thought. When I read about my father's death and the bullshit circumstances surrounding it, I vowed to get revenge for both he and my mother, at any cost. Between his last letter and your help, we now know what really happened. Why Weatherford? Because was he not only in on the rape, but after all this time, my father found out what this scumbag was up to with his diamond switching. And since he couldn't make anyone but Weatherford atone for the crime against my mother, at least he could make *him* pay, if only monetarily for his part. So Dad was going to blackmail him.

"My poor, kindhearted, naïve father didn't have a clue how to do it so when he tried, this bastard killed him and made it look like an accident. Since he was one of the boys, I'm sure everything was hush-hush, and nothing at all was done about it. I decided to take matters in my own hands."

She went on despite the pathetic moaning from Weatherford. "Who better to do it than me? No one in Clinton even knew about my existence, except old Doc Johnson and he took that to the grave with him. I was really sorry to hear about that. He was like a second father to me.

"This town, run by these guys, never gave my mother a chance. They never cared about my father either despite all the community spirit he added with his artistry. They didn't give a rat's ass that he died. They didn't even give him the courtesy of an obituary. Jesus, Dirk, they didn't even know his name."

With tears in her eyes, she went on.

170

"Then this shit and his crony friends just disposed of him like a piece of garbage and went on with their country club lives."

I looked at Weatherford and could see he was bleeding a lot but it didn't look imminently mortal.

She saw my glance and said, "Don't worry, Dirk, he's not going to bleed to death; oh, but today is the day he's going to die."

"Baby, I told you the sheriff's department thinks they may have enough evidence to convict him for your father's murder."

"Thinks! Thinks may have! I know, and so do you, that he did it. I'm not taking any chances that he may get off. Truehardt is a very good lawyer so I'm going to kill this one now and then just walk away.

"I wrote you I wanted my mother and father's names cleansed and thank you for all you've done. I don't think I'd have known what really happened without your help. You filled in the gaps from all the stuff my father told me. But that was a long time ago."

Still trying to get her to walk away from this, I said, "I thought you told me to let the rape go that night at the Marriot."

"That's right because I knew then that I was going to kill Johnson and Southerland."

"Why not Truehardt and TR, why not them? They were there too."

"Don't worry they'll get theirs too. Just not now. Let them wonder about it, and if they're too stupid or arrogant to realize what this is about, then that's the way they'll die after a while, stupid and arrogant. Unless, of course, you're going to warn them. You're not, are you, Dirk?"

"You know this puts me in an awkward position, don't you," I said. "Up until now everything that's happened will go unsolved, like you said, no one knows you therefore you're beyond suspicion."

"I'm afraid for you, Dirk. What if they blame you for this, everyone in this town knows you hate these bastards and you would most likely be the prime suspect especially with this one dead. We can't have that."

From the floor came a snarl from an ever-paling Weatherford. "Take the gun from her, Crandell, you drunken coward and call 911. Jesus, I'm dying here. I'll tell them you had nothing to do with this. I'll tell them anything you want, just call 911, *please!*"

At that Baby looked down at the pathetic coke head on the floor, which was what he'd been doing while she came into the store completely unnoticed.

She told him, "He doesn't deserve that especially from you, you shithead," and then she shot him right in the middle of the forehead. Bang! Dead!

"Ah, Baby, why'd you do that."

"He deserved it. And besides now we don't have to wait for justice to be served."

"Ah shit, Baby, this is so wrong."

"Listen, Crandell, you can stand there saying ah shit, or you can help me finish this before someone reports gunshots or looks in the window."

With that, she went over to the front window and pulled the sun shades.

"I've scoped him out. He usually does this closing thing for his drugs bit about this time every day anyway, so no one should get suspicious, for a while. If you want to walk away from this, just do as I say."

"You talk like you've done this before."

"I read a lot of crime stories. Okay now," she said, "take all of the money from his open safe and then clean out a couple of his display cases and put the stuff in his bank depository satchel. We're going to make this look like a drug deal gone bad."

"Shouldn't we take the diamonds from the safe then?"

"No, a respectable druggie wouldn't have a clue how to get rid of diamonds, but watches and rings, and that sort of stuff is easily fenced. Make sure you mess the cases up some to make it look like the thief just grabbed the money from the safe some fancy jewelry and ran.

"We also want to take his stash of coke and rip the bag open and spread it around his body and put the ripped bag in his hand. Hopefully it'll look like a struggle and it resulted in him being shot. Just like Dr. Johnson."

"Ah shit, Baby." But I did as I was told.

When we had this all done, she turned and took a look around and told me that the scene looked good.

I looked at the dead body of Weatherford on the floor and said, "Even though he was a prick, he still has a family."

"So did I. So did I," she said softly.

We went out the back door and into the alley. I said, "I wonder why no one reported the gunshots."

She said, "Since there is only an empty appliance store on one side and an empty Army Navy surplus store on the other, I doubt anyone heard them unless someone happened to be walking by when they happened."

"Doesn't look that way," she said.

As we started out of the alley, I said, "You're so calm and that scares me, Baby, it really scares me. You've killed three people, and I saw you shoot this one in cold blood. When I first talked to you on the phone, you sounded so timid and then when I met you at the Marriot. I would have never guessed that you would be capable of calculated cold blooded murder."

"Looks can be deceiving, Dirk. Looks can be deceiving."

"What do we do now?" I asked. "I heard from Karen that you're flying out tomorrow morning."

She stopped me just before we got to the end of the alley. "We need to talk some more, but not here. How about at the Marriot?

"Yeah, I think we definitely need to talk more."

"Karen's still working right? So maybe she can say you were there all afternoon. What do you think?" she asked.

"Since I was already at the Marriot earlier, I'm pretty sure that when I explain to Karen that regardless of what she hears, I'm innocent and I need an alibi for the day, no questions asked, she'll say no problem. No love lost between her and Southerland and Weatherford, anyway."

"Great!"

"Since the Bridge Tender is only a stone's throw from here and I frequently park out on Center Street when I go there, I'll just go and get my car and head to the Marriot. You turn right and go down to the bridge and look at the river for a few minutes and then head for your car. Since like you said, no one knows you here, you should draw no suspicion. I'll meet you at the bar in about forty five minutes to an hour. Deal?"

"You're acting like you've done this before, Dirk. And yes, deal," she said with a slight smile on her lips.

Then she said, "I'm sorry I got you involved in all of this but, well, I love you for what you've meant to me and what you've done to help my father we're going to cover your butt on all of this, and don't worry, remember you didn't do anything"

Yeah, I said to myself that's my problem, I didn't do anything to stop her, not that I could have anyway.

CHAPTER 19

ON THE WAY TO my car, I thought, still no sirens. Maybe we're going to get away with this. Still a long shot; Okay, Crandell, stop with the puns already. There's a good chance that I could still wind up some big dude's bitch in jail for the rest of my life, and I'm cracking jokes. If we can just make it to the Marriot undetected, maybe I can figure out just how to avoid jail.

Once I got to the Marriot, I parked out in the parking lot myself, not using the valet like I normally do. That way, should my time being here come into question, at least there wouldn't be any kind of paper trail to tie me a specific time frame.

I didn't even check my coat. When I walked in the bar area, it was already pretty busy for happy hour. I spotted Baby at the bar sipping a chardonnay. Karen was still behind the bar smiling and laughing like her old self. God, I was happy for her. I almost hated to ask her to get involved with this. But come to think of it, she already was. Her ring had been part of the sting to catch Weatherford so that meant she was involved.

Baby spotted me as I approached her.

"Hey you, how y'all doin'?"

"Just great," I said with more than a hint of sarcasm. "Hey, Karen, how about a double Jack on the rocks?"

"Sure, bro," and she proudly flashed me her diamond again.

"She looks really happy," said Baby. "I envy her. It must be a really nice feeling to have someone in your life that loves you and you can love back."

"It is, or it was, I should say."

We both looked at each other with knowing looks and nothing more needed to be said.

When Karen brought my drink over, I asked her if she could talk with us for a few minutes and that it was pretty important.

She said she had a break in about ten minutes; we could talk then.

"Somewhere private?" I asked.

"Yeah, we can use Tom's office. One of the perks of sleeping with the boss," she smiled.

While waiting I asked Baby just how much she wanted to tell Karen, and she answered saying, "How much *do you* trust her. Do you trust her with both of our lives? As it stands now, only you and I know what happened to Weatherford. You don't even know for sure what went on with Johnson and Southerland. If we just tell her to give you an alibi for today, no questions asked, and the whole ugly murder thing comes out, will she freak? Especially if you're the prime suspect?

"If we tell her the whole sordid story, will she freak and not want any part of it, particularly now that she has her life together? Do you want to take the chance of ruining that for her?"

"You know," I answered, "I don't know. The chance of getting a conviction for your father's death on Weatherford looked pretty good, but that's shot now."

"Funny, Uncle Dirk, very funny."

"Anyway, I don't know how much she knows about that charge, Truehardt kept it out of the media so she may not know about it at all. The sheriff and DA thought that the murder conviction was a long shot, but maybe enough to get him to cop a plea to save his own ass and implicate some of his business partners if there were any. But now with Weatherford dead, there's no way to connect him to anyone else. The conspiracy theory revolved around the hope that aside from his own personal financial and domestic gain, Weatherford was selling his pirated diamonds to some of his cronies at the Clinton Country Club. Far reaching as it sounds, I was even hoping to tie them to drug running with Dick Highland, throw in a Weatherford plea deal and Highland's wife's testimony. A long shot at best, but a shot nonetheless. Weatherford's death changes all that. She obviously knows about Weatherford's ring sting thing because she is a part of it."

"I'm sorry for that, really sorry, but as you said, it was all a long shot. Not now, three of them are dead. The other two, well, time will tell on them if I go home now. I know you and the sheriff wanted to take them down in front of the community. Again, I'm sorry it didn't work out that way. But it still could if you were to try and stay with the diamond switching thing. You still have that jeweler trying to right Weatherford's wrongs, don't you?"

"Yeah, that's right. I almost forgot about that, I think he'll still want to take the tarnish off the jewelry profession inflicted by Weatherford. I'll worry about that later; right now, what about Karen? You know what? I'll ask her how much she wants to know. She's a big girl, and life has dealt her share of crap here in Clinton. We'll let her decide."

"Now, Baby, *you* have to decide if you can trust her. Let me help you with that. If you feel you can trust me, you can trust her," I said emphatically.

She thought for a minute and stared at me as if trying to read my soul. "My father said in his last letter to me if he wasn't around, I could always trust you, so okay, let's let her decide and then I'll go home."

Karen came over to the table and said to follow her. We got to Tom's office which was just off the lobby. It was very plush and done in the same regal décor as the ballroom. He indeed was doing very well for himself and for Karen now for that matter. I was having second thoughts and a quick look at Baby and I could see she maybe was also. We all sat down.

"What's up you guys? You look so serious," said Karen.

"Karen," I started. "Will you do me a favor? If anyone should ask, would you tell them I was here all day from say around 11:00 a.m. until closing."

"Sure, Dirk, but again, what's up?"

I took a deep breath and reached out my hand and took hers in mine. "Sis, Let me first tell you what you already probably know. Dr. Bernard Johnson was killed in an apparent burglary at his home office. Last night, Carl Southerland was gunned down outside of the Crypt just after closing."

"Yes, I knew about that. Can't say I'm surprised about Southerland. He was a slime ball, has been for years. I already told you about him and that he was the reason I left my job at the Crypt. I got tired of his ass-grab all the time. I heard a rumor he was shot in the balls, is that true?"

"Yes, it's true," I said.

"Anyway, this afternoon David Weatherford IV was killed in apparent drug deal gone bad."

"No, shit, I hadn't heard that. Wow, Clinton beginning to look like Dodge City," Karen said, bemused.

"Yeah, well, not everyone knows about Weatherford yet. Here's the sticky part. If you're asked about me being here all day, you'll have to kind of like lie. But I'm going to tell you on Marie's grave, I did not kill any of those men."

"And you're telling me this why?"

"Because I think the chief of police and possibly even the sheriff may or may not be going to try and pin these murders on me. And the thing is I have no alibi for the time of their murders, and according to almost anyone who matters in Clinton, I have plenty of motive

"So I hesitate to ask you because your life is your dream come true now, and I wouldn't want to do anything to change that. If you want me to just walk away, I will. I know the sheriff was in my corner up until now, but with Weatherford, I really don't know anymore."

"Bro, if you tell me you didn't do it. I believe you. I believe you. But if you want me to perjure myself for you, I'd kind of like to know the whole story. I don't like surprises, you know that."

"Karen, are you sure because once I tell you, I can't untell you."

"Fire away, bro."

"Well, you know Baby's story here about her mother and father and . . ."

At that point, Baby interrupted me and said just as calm and collected as can be. "I killed Johnson and Southerland because sixteen years ago they helped rape, beat, and eventually kill my mother, so I shot them dead. Then today, despite Dirk here trying to talk me out of it, I shot and killed Weatherford because he was in on the rape of my mother and he killed my father. Shot him in the head and tried to make it look like an accident by pouring whiskey down his throat when he was already dead and dumped him in the ice cold river. I shot each one of them twice in the balls to make them suffer for the rape and then in the head to make them dead. End of story."

"So you shot them in the balls?" she asked Baby incredulously.

"Yes, I did!"

"You go, girl," and she leaned over and high-fived Baby. "Live by the sword and die by the sword, sort of. Can't say I wouldn't have done exactly the same thing if I was you."

Baby smiled and said, "Karen, I want to thank you for this, but I don't need anything from you, Dirk said I could trust you, so I do. No one here in Clinton even knows who I am so I'm going home for now. However, I'm giving you both fair notice. It's not over between me and the men who killed my mother and father. Foster, Truehardt, and McNeil still owe me a debt and I will collect on it in time, just not right now. That's the plan. Make them realize what they're facing, make them sweat and then make no mistake about it, I'm going to kill them too."

"McNeil," I said, astonished looking back at Baby. "Why him, he was only the club manager, he didn't have anything to do with it."

"Yes, he did. He knew what those guys were doing and just looked the other way. That, in my opinion, makes him equally guilty."

Then she added, "Karen, if push comes to shove, tell the truth about me, just leave Dirk out of it, okay. His only crime was doing me a favor and reinforcing what I already suspected went on here concerning my mother and father. If it comes to that, tell them I'm the guilty one. What the hell guys, they can only execute me once right. Promise."

"Promise."

"Baby, these guys were scum and deserved exactly what they got, but you giving up your life, they just weren't worth it damn it," I lamented.

"Dirk, this has been my decision all along, and I'll take whatever consequences come my way. Besides, what done is done, my only hope is that I'll get to finish it."

"The sheriff knows of you," I said solemnly. "He knows your whole story. Kristen and I told him the whole, sordid account, but then again, he doesn't know you were here in Clinton. He's not a stupid man. He's going to put two and two together. If it wasn't me committing the murders, he's going to look elsewhere. And talk about motive, you've got motive up the ying-yang. So unless you can prove you were there and not here, you're going to be someone of interest, he's going to want to talk to in a lot more detail"

"Well, I'll deal with that if and when it happens, but for now," she said to Karen, "Dirk needs the alibi for this afternoon."

"What about last night when Southerland was killed? I can help there too."

"How?" I asked.

"Easy, Tom and I went to the hockey game, I'll just say you went too and then we stopped off here for a drink afterward, and you slept here because you were too drunk to drive home. No one who knows you can question the probability of that happening."

Baby said, "You would do that? Do you know what you're possibly setting yourself up for?"

"Dirk would do the same for me."

"What about Tom?" I said.

"He'll be fine with if I ask him. Dirk, you're going to love this guy when you get to know him."

Baby stood up and said, "It's settled then, right, Uncle Dirk?"

"Ah shit, Baby."

"Uncle Dirk?"

"Yeah, it's settled."

"I'm going home now. Thanks, both of you, I mean that."

"Before you go, I have this painting for you. I found it in your mother's studio apartment, and I thought you would want it."

I handed her the painting wrapped in brown wrapping paper. She opened it and stared at it for only a few moments. I could see tears welling in her violet eyes. She said thank you so low it was almost inaudible. Without looking up, she rewrapped it and kissed both Karen and me on the cheeks and left the office.

The next morning, Baby went back to Los Angeles; business as usual.

CHAPTER 20

ABOUT 10:00 A.M., I got a phone call from Sheriff Chambers asking me if I knew anything about Weatherford's death and just out of curiosity could I tell him where I was yesterday afternoon.

I told him I was having a few drinks with my soon-to-be-wed sister-in-law at the Marriot and then she, her fiancée and I went to dinner at Salvatore's Italian Garden. I added, "Have you ever tried their Chicken Marsalis? It's to-die for," I said.

"And again, just out of curiosity, where were you the night before?

"Hey, Wayne, didn't I tell you yesterday morning when I saw you that I'd gone to the hockey game Tuesday night. A tie, how boring is that? That doesn't really help the Sabres' chances of making the playoffs, does it?"

A few second silence on his end and then he said, "No, Dirk it doesn't."

Another pause and then, "Have you ever considered retiring to say, I don't know, Florida or Arizona maybe, might be good for your health. Think about it." Then he hung up.

Later in the day standing on my deck having a smoke and a slow-soothing Jack Daniels straight up and reflecting on the current events, the phone rang. I went in to answer it, and it was the chief of the Clinton Police Department, none other than Stanley Harrison. He said he wanted to see me at his office at my earliest convenience as long as that convenience was right away. Such a smooth operator. I feel better knowing my city is protected from evil by him and his band of merry men.

I walked into his office and sat down. He took his time fidgeting with stuff on his desk until he finally looked at me and said,

"I'm sure you're aware of the recent deaths of three of our city's most honored and distinguished citizens—Dr. Bernard Johnson Jr., Carl

Southerland, and David Weatherford IV. It's common knowledge that you've had a hard on for these fellows for quite some time. It seems you went around me with accusations concerning Weatherford's honesty and me and my brother's competency concerning the death of some transient found floating in the river a while back."

"William Mintz, William Edgar Mintz. That's the name of the transient, as you put it that was murdered and dumped in the river. And just for your information chief, he wasn't a transient; he lived here his entire life and helped add some class and beautification to this otherwise dead burg."

"TR was right!" he retorted. "You are a wise ass. I'd like to know for the record where you were the night before last and yesterday."

"Am I a suspect or something? Do I need a lawyer?"

"Just answer my questions, smart ass."

"Okay, Oliver."

"It's Stanley, and you know it, shithead."

"That's right, I have trouble keeping Laurel and Hardy separate."

"I'm warning you, Crandell, regardless of your present rapport with the DA and the sheriff, you're on thin ice with me. Where were you?"

"Let's see. Night before last, I was at the Sabres-Blackhawks game, and I think I still have the stub," I said as I reached in my coat pocket and produced my ticket stub. "I was with my sister-in-law, Karen O'Donahue, and her fiancé, Tom Gardinier, hotel manager at the Marriot in Williamsville. Then we went back to the Marriot for a couple of drinks afterward. I got drunk and spent the night in the penthouse suite there, compliments of Tom. Yesterday I had breakfast at Elaine's here in Clinton on Boardwalk—a cheese omelet and home fries, extra crispy, I believe . . ."

"Just get on with, Crandell."

"Where was I? Let's see, I talked with the sheriff. Then I went back to the Marriot to see Karen about taking her and her fiancé, Tom, out to dinner at Salvatore's later that evening. Have you ever tried the chicken Marsalis there, Oliver? It's to die for."

"Stanley! Stanley! You asshole. I'm going to check with these people and Salvatore's, and you better be telling the truth, or I'm going to arrest you on suspicion of multiple homicide."

"Be my guest, do you want to make a copy of the stub? Perhaps you'd like the name of the couple who were from Chicago who were sitting in front of us, Ethel and Fred Hertz, or maybe Mertz, I can't exactly remember. Maybe you'd like the name of our server at Salvatore's. It was—"

"Shut up. Just shut up. Get out!"

"Are we done?"

"Yeah, for now, but you haven't heard the last of this from me."

"I think I have, Oliver, and it's no wonder you don't have any clues on these three murders. You didn't have a clue about the murder of William Mintz, and you know what else, Stanley, Oliver, Laurel—or whatever your name is? I don't think you've had a clue about anything around here for a long fucking time. Now unless you're going to arrest me, I'm out of here."

I left.

Maybe Florida doesn't sound so bad. But first I needed to stop at the *Journal* and talk to Melissa.

SIX MONTHS LATER AT A RETIREMENT COMMUNITY IN FLORIDA

I WAS JUST COMING OUT of the shower after a torrid round of 95 on our community's championship golf course when the phone rang.

"Guess who, stud?"

"Kristen?"

"None other than. Do you have a minute?"

"Actually, I'm standing here butt naked. I just got out of the shower. What's up?" I said, regretting my choice of words almost as soon as they left my lips. She didn't let me—eh, down.

"Still got it, huh, stud?"

"I don't know, Harden. It's been holstered since you went away."

"Maybe we can fix that, Dirky."

"That would be nice. Where are you?"

"I'm having a glass of wine at the Cypress Springs Bistro, overlooking a lake with an Indian name that I can't pronounce. It's just a few miles from where you live. A little birdie told me you were living here now. So I thought since I was here on assignment for my magazine, *Sunbelt Living*, I'd call and see if you were okay."

"I'm fine, Kristen, seriously. How about you?"

"Actually, Dirk, believe it or not, I'm missing you. You're not in jail or a rehab center, so I gather things in Clinton must have been settled to your liking, or you wouldn't be here. Am I right?"

"Yes, you are, not exactly as planned, but more than right. You didn't leave me any forwarding address, no way to get in touch with you. You actually pissed me off the way you left."

"I'm really sorry about that. That's really not my style. Tell you what, Dirk, if you have no plans for dinner tonight, I'll meet you at your country club restaurant at, say, seven, and we can catch up. Are you free?"

"No, but I'm still easy. I'll make myself free and see you at seven."

At seven, I pulled my Candy Apple Red '57 Chevy golf cart into the parking lot and went inside the restaurant. I walked up to the hostess and inquired about a Ms. Kristen Harden.

"She's out on the patio sir, follow me."

I went through the glass doors to the patio overlooking the pool and the golf course. It was a beautiful evening, and it was going to be a gorgeous sunset. I spotted Kristen at the same time she saw me.

What a sight for my lonely eyes. Her auburn hair was streaked lighter from the sun. She wore no makeup as usual and sported a golden tan covered only by a light lime green sundress. As she stood to greet me, the sun silhouetted her perfectly sculpted, voluptuous body through the shear fabric. Her beauty never ceased to take my breath away.

"Dirk," she said with a seductive smile, "how wonderful to see you again." And with that, she hugged me lightly and brushed her soft lips on mine.

I couldn't help but feel that all eyes were on her. I had this scene from *Pretty Woman* flash through my mind. We sat down.

She took my hands in hers and looked deep into my eyes looking from one to the other and smiling all the while.

"Damn it's good to see you again. You look good with a tan, and you look like you might have lost some weight."

"Yeah, I shed a few pounds, but you, Kristen, you look amazing. Seeing you in this fading sunlight and in that dress, you are absolutely dazzling."

"Stop it, Dirk, you're making me blush."

The waiter came up then asked if we wanted something to drink.

Kristen said to him, "Two Jack Daniels on the rocks please."

Then she looked at me and said, "That is still your drink of choice isn't it?"

"Yep, and you know what else, everywhere here in Stone Hills at dinner time, it seems it's happy hour. A lot of happy retirees racing around in their golf carts."

We chit-chatted for a couple of minutes until our drinks arrived. We toasted to renewed acquaintances took a sip and put our drinks down.

After a quiet moment, she looked up at me and said, I read Melissa's exposé on the Clinton scandal. She did an incredible job. I never would have guessed she had it in her."

"I guess looks can be deceiving, Kristen."

"She had some help with the facts, I'd assume."

"Yep."

"Still, she did a remarkable job."

"Yes, she did."

"Dirk, please tell me you're finished with it, and it's closed for you. I really meant what I said when I walked away that day. I'd really like—no, wait—love to pick up where we left off, but I have to know I have all of you. I don't expect you to ever totally get over Marie, well maybe in time, but this other thing, look me in the eye and tell me it's over."

"It's over for me, Kristen, I promise you that."

"Great, how's your drink? By the way, do you want something to eat?"

"I need a refill because I get the distinct feeling you want the skinny on what went down, am I right?"

"As you so eloquently put it at times like this, yep."

When the waiter came back with our drinks, I told him, "We'll share an order of your mussels in white wine sauce. And then just keep an eye on our glasses. When they're empty, please bring another and please, Chris, is that your name? Well, Chris, please don't bother us until we call for the check. Deal?"

"Yes, sir, deal."

For the next hour as the sun set in it's typical Florida pinkish-orange, I told Kristen I didn't remember how much she knew or read but "I'm going to tell you what happened in 'sleepy hollow' to shake the hollowed walls of the Clinton Country Club elite."

So I started or finished, according to one's point of view. "If I remember right, Sheriff Chambers had just got a warrant to search Weatherford's store and an exhumation order for Rembrandt's body and a proper autopsy.

"Well, the autopsy proved beyond a shadow of a doubt that Rembrandt was murdered by a .22 caliber gunshot wound to the back of his head. One mystery solved.

"The search warrant not only turned up diamonds that Weatherford had pirated but especially the phony stone from Karen's engagement ring

185

in the process. One other small item was the discovery of a .22 caliber pistol which later was proved to be Rembrandt's murder weapon.

"With my trusted jeweler friend James Steinbeck—turned-GIA-certified diamond expert, the subsequent search of Weatherford's home turned up more ah, pirated treasure in Trisha Weatherford's private collection of fine jewelry. So with Sheriff Chambers and DA Scorbelli smelling blood in the fraud case, plus a timely placed phone call from Darlene Highland, one of Clinton's socialites, regarding rumors about the possibility of her and her very wealthy mother's jewels being compromised by Weatherford, she demanded a full investigation and financial retribution concerning this matter.

"She was going to also inform all of her friends, be they many and rich, to be forthcoming with their dealings with Weatherford. Apparently, not all the wives of the sinister six were aware of Weatherford's fraudulent ways and were pissed that their loving husbands were giving them stolen diamonds and were willing to help anyway they could. Basically covering their own, pampered asses.

"Steinbeck actually got the support and assistance of the GIA Institute when he requested GIA diamond dossiers on the stones coming into question. I'm not quite sure of all the semantics, but it seems the entire diamond credibility community became involved and are working with the whole Steinbeck family diligently to get the as many of the diamonds Weatherford pirated back to their rightful owners. It appears between Weatherford's insurance and his estate, the funds to complete this should be adequate. Unfortunately a lot were already sold for his personal gain; apparently Marie's rings were included in that group.

"Bob McNeil, the club manager really panicked at the investigation after taking the spoils from his friends, but not wanting to become implicated or even investigated. Seems he had a rather seedy past involving altar boys when he was in the seminary years ago which was omitted from his job application.

"At some point, he caught Truehardt and Foster in some rather compromising situations in the massage spa at the club and even photographed them for, I don't know, for future security maybe, who knows with the kind of a kinky history he had anyway.

"Then when the three stooges, Johnson, Southerland and Weatherford turned up dead and Weatherford's diamond switching came to light, things in the inner circle got a real antsy.

"Now I can only speculate from here, but my guess is Melissa's story brought this country club shit to light. Foster and Truehardt could do nothing about the story being printed because McNeil had them compromised. Again, I can only hypothesize that, since McNeil wasn't involved in the actual Mintz-Hobbs scandal, only by proxy, he was publicly not going to be implicated anyway, so he had the Bobsey Twins over a barrel, so to speak.

"Truehardt and Foster were scared shitless because they suspected someone knew what happened years ago and were exacting vigilantism on their circle. Combined with McNeil's cover-his-own-ass photos, they were seeing their self-made untouchable social fortress come crumbling down around them.

"McNeil is now a board member and CEO of the Clinton Hills Country Club and bought a very expensive home on the Niagara escarpment. Methinks, compliments of Truehardt and Foster and some photos.

"TR Foster has purchased a very large and very expensive yacht and is taking his wife on a long cruise around the world. When they return, they'll set up home in the condo he bought in Malibu.

"Truehardt and his wife are being divorced, irreconcilable differences, and he is moving to California to set up practice there as lawyer to the criminally, substance abusing, spoiled rich and famous Hollywood set.

"It may seem like they all landed on their feet after the Clinton scandal, but if I were a betting man, and knowing they are both living in California, and so is Baby. I'd say the odds are pretty darn good that their balls are going to drop way before New Year's Eve.

"Oh, I think I may have left out the part where Baby shot and killed Dr. Johnson, Carl Southerland and David Weatherford IV. Shot em' in the balls and then the head. She made them look like drug deals gone bad. Weatherford was done in with me standing there. And then she just walked away."

Kristen asked, "What happened with Baby and the sheriff? He knew about her, and he had to suspect she was involved. Even though the crimes were staged to look otherwise, he had to suspect she murdered these guys out of revenge for her mother and father."

"Here's the kicker, Krissy. Stanley Harrison was so intent on pinning this whole thing on me that when the sheriff suggested to him he might want to look elsewhere at a more viable suspect, Harrison got this huge bug up his ass and wouldn't hear anything of the sort. When the sheriff went to the chief's office to present him with the evidence about Baby and her possible involvement, Harrison screamed at him to mind his own fucking business. This was not his case and not his jurisdiction and he, Harrison, would solve it.

"The sheriff stood there in disbelief and said 'fine,' and then something on the order of get this; 'Oliver,' just like I used to rag on him, 'you handle it then!' and he put his file on the murders of Johnson, Southerland and Weatherford back in his briefcase. He added just before he left Harrison's office, 'you know, even though you're clueless in more ways than one, you have my blessing, you solve it then.' And he walked out.

"That afternoon, I got a phone call from the sheriff. He told me that he was pretty sure that my friend, Baby, was responsible for the deaths of Johnson, Southerland and Weatherford. Since there was no official record of her existence and Chief Harrison insisted on handling the case himself because it was his jurisdiction, the sheriff was not going to pursue it.

"He told me there were two reasons for this. Given that Foster and Truehardt had the door of their closet yanked off the hinges about their relationship they left Clinton, most likely for good. That leaves only McNeil left to press an investigation, and rumor has it that he's afraid for his life because of his knowledge of the Mintz-Hobbs affair.

"He then told me that he was an honest officer of the law and even though the three murdered men were scum and they probably deserved what they got, their fate should have been decided by the courts. He made it very clear to me that he didn't believe in vigilantism most of the time, but he was going to put his file on the case in his safe, and I should call Baby and tell her that as long as she never came back to Clinton, it would stay there.

"I called Baby and relayed his message.

"One week later the sheriff resigned and became the administrator of the Clinton County Shelter for Abused Women and Children.

"A short time after those events transpired, I received a letter from Baby saying that she was selling all but one of her father's remaining paintings. It seems that Rembrandt had stashed several of his finest works at the Clinton Fine Arts Centre for safe keeping several years ago. They were all but forgotten, except by Baby. She had learned of their existence in one of the letters from her father. The proceeds from the sale were being donated to that same Clinton County shelter."

"I'd say end of story, Kristen, but somehow, I think there'l be one more chapter being played out in California. But it's over for me. It's finally over and you know what else? So are the nightmares."

"You know, Dirk," Kristen said. "I think it's time to check out tan lines."

"Sounds like a plan to me.

"Check!"

Acknowledgments

Many people both family and friends provided encouragement to me while writing this book. At the top of the list is first and foremost my lovely and ever-patient best friend and wife, Pat.

Others who deserve a special acknowledgement are:

Dr. V, more commonly known as Veronica Shimp, DC of MD Anderson in Orlando, Florida, who gave us life and hope.

Jack DiMaggio, a very talented and knowledgeable artist in his own right for his input and continual inspiration to keep going.

Amy Rockwood, my first critic, my editor, and now my friend.

Pam Feldman, an avid reader of crime/mystery novels including this one. She was also my first reading sacrificial lamb and didn't burn the first draft.

Tom Beilein, former Niagara County sheriff and one of the most upstanding men and law enforcement officers I have ever had the privilege to know and work with.

Frank Stuart, a retired detective with the NYPD.

Susan Darnell, another friend who gave me a kick in the butt to finally start this journey.

George VC Muscato. Attorney-at-Law; George and I go way back as friends. He is probably the most formidable and judicious attorney I have ever had the pleasure to work with. And there have unfortunately been a few, none of whom could tip the scales of justice quite like George.

John M. Rosenberg, of Prudden and Kandt Funeral Home.

Kathleen Gantz, a former news writer for my then local newspaper who tried to convince me my future was not in news writing but perhaps in fiction.

Harry Cordell of Arden's Fine Jewelers, an experienced jeweler in the Villages, Florida, for his expertise in diamonds and diamond simulants.

The Gemological Institute of America (GIA) webpage.

And of course, in no particular order: James Patterson, David Baldacci, Sue Grafton, Robert Parker, Patricia Cornwell, Jeffery Deaver, John Grisham, Janet Evanovich, and Fern Michaels (The Sisterhood Series), who are some of my favorite authors and from whose literary spirit I drew.

Many thanks to all.

JC

Edwards Brothers Malloy
Thorofare, NJ USA
July 12, 2012